OFF-STREET PARKING

Bill James

severn House

This first world edition published 2008
in Great Britain and in 2009 in the USA by
SEVERN HOUSE PUBLISHERS LTD of
9–15 High Street, Sutton, Surrey, England, SM1 1DF.
Trade paperback edition published
in Great Britain and the USA 2009 by
SEVERN HOUSE PUBLISHERS LTD

British Library Cataloguing in Publication Data

James, Bill, 1929-
  Off-street parking
  1. Women detectives - Great Britain - Fiction 2. Murder -
  Investigation - Great Britain - Fiction 3. Detective and
  mystery stories
  I. Title
  823.9'14[F]

  ISBN-13: 978-0-7278-6691-2   (cased)
  ISBN-13: 978-1-84751-105-8   (trade paper)

Off- Street Parking is developed from Bill James' short story *'Emergency Services'*
which appears in the collection *The Sixth Man and other stories*
(Severn House, 2006).

All Severn House titles are printed on acid-free paper.

Typeset by Palimpsest Book Production Ltd.,
Grangemouth, Stirlingshire, Scotland.
Printed and bound in Great Britain by
MPG Books Ltd., Bodmin, Cornwall.

Please return/renew this item by the last date shown
on this label, or on your self-service receipt.

To renew this item, visit **www.librarieswest.org.uk**
or contact your library.

Your Borrower number and PIN are required.

4 1 0070687 0

ONE

'd like to put you right on something. OK?

Anyway, here goes: most people have the wrong idea about police informants – or grasses, snouts, touts, narks, pigeons, stoolies, finks – whatever you'd like to call them. None of the names sound flattering or wholesome. The general idea is that informers are skulking, scuttling, furtive little creeps who get an occasional dab in the hand for what they blurt, then lie low until they've got another morsel of insight to offer, for another sweetener – a small-scale, catch-as-catch-can, very secretive, very solo, sealed-off life. Well, it's not like that, or not often, anyway. Mostly, grassing is a weapon, a weapon in a war. And if you come across a dead grass – I mean a killed, murdered grass – you move gingerly, because you could be messing with dark, considerable, savage forces.

I have just come across what I take to be a dead grass – I mean a killed, murdered grass. Notice: I'm moving gingerly. 'Grass' – weird term. Rhyming slang? Grasshopper – copper? Or there's that old song, 'Why do you whisper, green grass?' Grasses whisper. But I should think grasses were called grasses before the song. They've made a verb from it now: to grass someone up. Although the language has gone haywire, we know what it means: to betray the someone.

The first thing you'll ask is, how do I know he's a grass? It is a *he*, though grasses come in all sexes. You'll say, if the usual notions about grasses are so wrong and they don't fit a pattern, why do I sound so certain, unless, of course, he has been grassing to me and I know him from close, face-to-face conversations, which is what conversations between an officer and his/her informants have to be. No, he hasn't and no, I don't, though I'd admit I'm trying to build up a covey of grasses for personal use. Which detective doesn't? Only detectives who won't get anywhere. Information: our careers are built on it. Where's *it* to come from? Not the Internet or *Whitaker's Almanack*. From tipsters, grasses, snouts, touts . . .

Me, I'd like to think I'll get somewhere. Oh, stuff that – the uncertainty. Me, I'll get somewhere. It used to be very tough for a woman to move up in the police. Now, it's only tough. I'm determined and sure I can manage this. Yes, there are moments when I doubt it – moments when some aspects of a case seem too brick-wall impenetrable, too complicated. Or too brick-wall impenetrable and too complicated for *me*. Perhaps then I'll want to dodge out and pass the problems to someone more experienced, or even, let's admit it, cleverer and with more flair. But this bit of dither will usually pass. I'm pretty buoyant and sure of my abilities. Not big-headed sure, just sure sure. I get fairly good personal assessments, and I don't think it is conceited to say I earn them. Or perhaps it *is* conceited. *So* sorry, but I'll say it, all the same. There's not much you get in the police without earning it. Mind you, these days some poisonous, unpromotable male colleagues refer in their crass, canteen fashion to my assessments as *arse*-essments, meaning the superior officer who gives them is tit-and-bum biased. But, in fact, some of my best assessments come from women superiors, though, admittedly, that might not be a totally convincing line. 'Call me Grenville,' one woman chief inspector told me. However, as to this late grass now being our topic, I am sure he's never been one of my troupe. I do not recognize him, and I am certain I would not recognize him, even if his features were in their original shape.

So, back to where we started. How do I know he is, was, a grass? It's not smell, instinct or telepathy. I've been in the police for nearly four years and a detective for two, but so far must admit I have failed to develop magical insights. I do definitely believe in magical insights. I'm certain I will start getting them soon. But this kind of magic can't come from nowhere. It needs years of service experience behind it, and at present I am obviously a bit short of that. Perhaps the magic isn't really magic at all, just experience brilliantly applied. I don't know. For now, though, all I've got to go on is observation, logic, deduction – those dull-sounding detective qualities they try to sell so fervently in training. You don't hear anything about magic there, of course: instructors would say, 'Let Sherlock Holmes and Miss Marple do all the sublime stuff.'

So, when I apply my banal observation, logic and deduction

to this dead grass I would say he is a grass because of the *way* he's dead. To which you might reply, 'Because of the way he's dead? What does that mean? Surely, he's dead from injuries and a switched-off heartbeat and blood circulation, as might be true of many violent deaths.' True, unarguably true. But to kill an informant is not just a revenge thing, although villains do get very unforgiving about grasses, as you'll probably understand. Nobody can be happy at betrayal. Yet, on its own, vengeance is a stupid, non-professional unBritish impulse. A Sicilian thing. The point about killing a grass is that, clearly, it should end one particular source of whispered treachery – his/hers. But there's a wider need, and here we come to the crux. This single death should also have clarion-type overtones. It means to be a vivid and irresistible warning. A warning to whom? A warning to anyone else who might consider turning informant, or is one, or has been one. The death needs to be not just a closure but a vivid, very memorable lesson. It requires some spotlight. The death has to be much talked about – so as to stop people talking, if you can follow that. Details such as gouging, face-carving, bone breakages, possible burning must get known about at least city-wide, even county- and nationwide, then reverentially enshrined in subsequent chit-chat – again, ironically, to discourage subsequent chit-chat, chit-chat directed from any future grass to his/her detective.

He was in a car, crouched forward, his face on the steering wheel, arms hanging down, fully relaxed, so that, if you didn't know as a certainty he was dead, you might *assume* and *fear* he was dead, but also wonder whether he might only be sleeping the sleep of the vastly coked or liquored, or knocked out by a stroke or heart attack, though still alive. Navy off-the-peg suit with 2006-style lapels, the peg it was off up among the higher priced peg division in, say, Marks and Spencer or even Austin Reed. Gold signet ring on the right little finger. Lumpy wristlet watch of genuine base metal, with minor dials as well as the main one, probably showing barometric pressure and the time in Addis Ababa. Black slip-ons, leather not plastic. I'm observing, you see. It's what I meant by saying this kind of death has to be a lesson. Or think of it as like a biblical parable, only the message is not about a Good Samaritan or the Prodigal Son, but the solemn and immediate need of existing or would-be grasses to reconsider and keep their fucking gob shut while their fucking gob is still intact and at the correct place in the topography of their face. The death must get publicity, gaudy, detailed, frightening publicity. It's an advertising campaign. This execution has to be on view, the way hangings, drawings, quarterings used to be in Britain, an entertaining and terrifying deterrent.

There should be witnesses to the discovery of a grass's corpse and then gossip, rumour to make it even tastier and more scary than it actually is. The corpse has to be, so to speak, eloquent, just as the grass might have been whisperingly eloquent when still a grass and pre corpsedom. This is what is known as 'on the grapevine' – not as theatrically and openly relayed as, say, the weather bulletins on television, but effective, just the same. As British Telecom say, It's good to talk. You can get dread into people that way. We – the police – might hold back from revealing the worst details about a murder, and that would be true of any kind of murder, not just the killing of a grass. But the grapevine will take no censorship. The grapevine likes to get attention and provoke cries of shock and worry, and you don't prompt these by editing out the rough bits. The rough bits could be regarded as the choicest bits, choicest in the sense of most influential.

Only very few grasses live rich. I say this despite a certain authentic quality in the reach-me-down suit here and, perhaps, the slip-ons. Of course, there may be some money in grassing, especially at the Supergrass level. But it is not usually a big career with a respectable salary, share options and capital gains like the chairman of Sainsbury's. In any case, few grasses are grasses absolutely full-time. They mostly have chickenfeed jobs in some crooked organization or other and the grassing comes when it's necessary to hurt an enemy and/or get rid of a rival. These are quite frequent and urgent necessities, though. The firms are slaughterously competitive or competitively slaughterous. Even rich grasses don't always live it up – I mean, with big properties and wild cars and Acapulco holidays, because this might get folk asking where the cash comes from. Dicey, that. Flashiness is not a grass quality. Good off-the-peg Marks or Austin Reed. Savile Row custom-made: an idiotic flaunt. More than one Savile Row custom-made: suicide.

This lad was dead in his ten-year-old car on the little slab of driveway that fronted the thirties' semi he shared with his wife/partner on this tidy-looking, open-plan private estate. Sweet suburbia. I'm in favour. I like the 'sub' part. 'Urbia' more often known as inner city, has lost nearly all its urbanity, you'll agree, especially if you live there. I'd say the burbs in general have less dog mess on the pavements and not so much rap blare from open windows. This estate's open plan which means no hedges between house and street, so if you've got a sleeping man or dead man in a car on the drive neighbours are liable to see him. It's a show, folks, even early in the morning. It's a topic, something for the jungle drums and/or grapevine. As good as neon.

And there are those thinkers about social trends and temperatures who would regard this sight as a symbol. Or what they might call 'a touchstone'. That's one of their words – touchstone. They mean that, as a symbol or touchstone, it speaks to us of matters beyond itself, itself being a dead, facially hacked man in a car on the drive. It *is* a dead, facially hacked man in a car on the drive, of course. But, for them, it is more than this: typical of a much bigger, wider condition. That's what symbols and touchstones *are* – typical of a bigger, wider condition. What is this dead, facially hacked man in a car on the drive typical of, then? Of a communal malaise. This is another term that's around, 'communal malaise'. Many people would argue that such a death, on such an ordinary, reasonably pleasant, private, housing estate, signifies in a strikingly major way. This, they'd point out, is a man in quite passable clothes and at the wheel of presumably his own vehicle – old though it might be. They would maintain that such an instance of brutality and violence says plenty – typifies, symbolizes – yes, says plenty about a grave crumbling of order, a moral falling off, throughout Britain, not just on this drive. And perhaps throughout the western world.

Possibly, their analysis is not total bullshit. I hear the phrase 'communal malaise' so often I occasionally think it might possibly mean something. But for me, having to take today's job attitude, he is just a dead, facially hacked man in a car, parked on a semi-detached's drive. I don't say that makes it minor, compared with a symbol or touchstone. This is a bad event, no question. But the badness is here, in the car, on the drive, actual, real, describable in notebook form, not out there acting up as something national, international, universal, cosmic. So, let's have more basic, actual/factual detail.

(1) The locks of the bonny piece of four-wheel history had been plugged with Super glue.

(2) When the partner/wife came out first thing and saw him there she called his name, thinking him to be asleep/drunk/substanced.

(3) She was angry with him, but kept her voice down so as not to draw attention from the other houses. 'What'll the neighbours?' as Dylan Thomas says in *Under Milk Wood*.

(4) He didn't respond, and she tried to open the passenger door, to get clòser with the tongue lashing. She couldn't shift the door. She went around and tried the others. All immovable.

(5) He still hadn't replied or budged, naturally, and panic started. She'd begun to realize that this could be more than her man having passed out pissed or high or a combination. More and worse.

(6) She ran to the house on their immediate left for help. Bugger what the neighbours might say now. Things had moved on.

(7) Mr Arthur Grain and his wife, both sixty-six, he a retired newsagent, were having breakfast. He abandoned this at once and came and did some prodding with a screwdriver, trying to free a route for the key.

(8) Others living near observed the crisis and gathered – those with time before getting off to work.

(9) Another neighbour, David Elwyn Jamieson, forty-one, self-employed design consultant, must have heard about cutting the Gordian knot and brought a hammer. They gave up on the doors and smashed the passenger window, away from the body, wanting some distance between the glass and the man inside so that he would not be injured by flying pieces, if he could have been injured.

(10) Several folk had been trying to get some response from him by shouting, calling his name. It was Claude: rather starchy and old fashioned for, as it turned out, a drug dealing grass, or ex-grass. They called louder when he did not shift or answer. People will always try to believe the least awful explanation for circumstance like these and, of course, they could not see properly at that stage what had happened to his face because he was pitched forward and lying on it in the driving seat.

(11) More households deduced something was wrong and attended in numbers or watched from their windows. The hammer on the glass gave the conclusive message to the street that things were deeply off colour in and around Claude Huddart's property.

Obviously, I was not present when all this early part happened. In fact, nobody had dialled 999 yet. They thought they could handle things themselves. I was given an account later by Mrs Alice Huddart – the common-law wife – and the Grains, David Elwyn Jamieson and several other neighbours, whose names and details I listed. As well as observation, logic and deduction, detection is about interviewing witnesses, especially if the witnesses were participants. Even when they had smashed the window and could reach the handle inside, the lock still refused to move, because of the glue. David Elwyn Jamieson put the hammer down and, as it was described to me, reached across through where the passenger window had been, gripped Claude with two hands on the shoulders and drew him gently back in his seat from the steering wheel. At this stage some of the bystanders might still have believed he was only sick or blottoed by drink or drugs, and Jamieson said he handled him with all the gentleness he could. But they now had a full view of the face. There were some gasps, a little screaming. They all realized he must be dead. Many of them had guessed, anyway. This gave certainty.

Jamieson seems to have been a very decisive member of the street grouping, intelligently decisive. They could all have made their guesses about Huddart's state from the way his body was slumped. But Jamieson must have reasoned that the face would tell them much more, when made visible by easing Huddart away from the steering wheel to rest against the back of the seat. For instance, they'd be able to see whether his eyes indicated anything, whether closed in sleep, a coma, unconsciousness, or open and lifeless. And, of course, his face did tell them something. It told them much more than they would have expected – much more than any of them would have expected, even those who'd assumed him dead.

I've mentioned that the police would not normally describe in full the kind of injuries suffered in such a case, and I'll abide by that. But I can say that the post-mortem found seventeen wounds between the hairline and his chin, three caused by a fist or cosh-type weapon, the rest by a knife. Death resulted from two 9mm Walther gunshot wounds in the chest from very short distance, this damage also visible when the body was moved back from the wheel.

Mrs Grain had followed her husband to the car, carrying her mobile phone. Once she'd seen Huddart's face and the bullet holes she told the little crowd she would call the ambulance service and police. Although this must have seemed to most of them the obvious – inevitable – reaction to what they now knew, I gathered from several witnesses that Mrs Huddart objected. When I heard this, it seemed to signal something odd. I began to wonder about Claude. I had his full name by then and did not recognize it as belonging to any of our famous local villains. But I thought of the death and mutilation as possible factors in a gang war. Elementary deduction; although I'd never actually dealt with anything similar, I'd heard of and read about such atrocities. Now and then the pathologists would even claim that the display mutilation had taken place after death, when the actual killing had occurred too fast. This would be true of the Claude Huddart post-mortem, though I couldn't know at the time his body was found, of course.

The fact that his name failed to register suggested a lad who would not be big enough to excite any major enmity among colleagues or commercial rivals, except by grassing. And then, to back up this speculation, there came the display aspect I've described. This was probably not part of a leadership battle within a firm, for instance, or hate between two gang chiefs. Possibly, I might be using the knowledge of hindsight a little here. Or more than a little. Did I really interpret things so clearly from the very first – clearly and, as it happened, imperfectly? Let's say, then, I had an eighty per cent opinion at once that this was a gang job, and a sixty-five per cent opinion at once that it was the brilliantly spectacular, minatory punishment of a grass. Alice Huddart's wish to stop the emergency phone call, or at least get it postponed, added points to each of those percentages. For the moment – the moment of my arrival at the Huddart house – I was willing to accept that she'd had an appalling shock: her man dead and defaced in his own car, in their own off-street parking space, not long after first light. I didn't altogether dismiss the idea that she might have had some prior knowledge of this, might even have had some part in it. I tried to shelve such suspicion, though, and take Mrs Huddart's reactions as genuinely as they seemed. That is:

(1) She would probably have been amazed, horrified, confused, her brain paralysed or strafed by panic, rational thought impossible.

(2) Instincts might still have worked, though. If Huddart was, in fact, involved with a gang, she might have absorbed via him a central philosophy of such outfits that all troubles, even the worst – maybe, *especially* the worst – are sorted out with no reference to the police/pigs.

(3) This could seem bizarre if Huddart had actually been a police/pigs informer, but Mrs Huddart might not be aware of this branch of his career. He possibly kept quiet about it out of shame and she would know only that he ran with a crooked firm. And so, her automatic attempt to stop Mrs Grain from phoning for official help. Although the Huddarts lived in suburbia, they didn't go for all the supposed suburban responses. Perhaps Mrs Huddart belonged to a culture that did not believe in official help, fearing official help could soon turn into dogged official nosiness and unforgiving official shitiness. Maybe the nearest she would wish to get

to the law was by being common-law. (But that's crude and unkind. After all, I suppose I'd rate as a common-law wife myself.)

(4) In any case, Alice Huddart might have had someone else she wanted to ring, before the medics and the rest were sent for. That is, if she knew more about the death than she let on. Perhaps she did ring someone else.

When I saw the group of obviously agitated people near the Huddart house I was driving through their avenue in an unmarked car to look at a dockside warehouse where there'd been a reported break-in overnight. I decided that could wait and drew in and flashed the warrant card about. They'd have wondered, otherwise: this was a youngish woman in a navy-blue business suit and white blouse, stepping out of an ordinary looking Ford Focus. I might have been just a curious passer-by who'd spotted the gathering and decided to stop on her way to the office. I *was* a curious passer-by who'd spotted the gathering and decided to stop, but a police passer-by.

A woman said, 'It doesn't look too good.'

'This isn't the kind of thing we expect in the Avenue,' another woman said. 'I was devastated.'

I could see into the car by then and thought of saying, 'Not as devastated as he is,' but didn't. Many people took their crisis vocabulary from bystander remarks made to TV news cameras. 'Devastated' figured often. Perhaps TV reporters handed out a list of suitable words to vox pop for their response to a disaster/crisis. In a minute I'd probably hear someone tell me, 'They kept themselves *to* themselves but seemed a very pleasant couple.'

'No, it doesn't look too good, at this juncture,' a man said. I found out later this was Mr Arthur Bertram Grain.

I introduced myself to the crowd: Detective Constable Sharon Mayfield. They made a corridor for me to get close to the car and I decided I'd agree with Grain's guess as to this juncture and possibly future junctures, also. It was, of course, the face and its injuries that took my attention first. I found myself counting them. That's what obeying frequent court calls as a witness does to you. Almost everything comes down to numbers. The number of wounds would, of course, say something about the degree of hatred and cruelty towards the victim, had they been inflicted while he was still alive, but this is not why they're so important in a court. Numbers can bring validity to a testimony, show care, actuality, precision, authority, data-based truth, method – as long as the numbers are correct, that is. I realized that most likely none of those wounds would have killed him though, nor even all of them together. I abandoned the counting as stupid. I'd reached nine.

There was something else about the face and physique that seemed to proclaim death. He sat behind the wheel, as if driving or about to drive. Yet the set of the body and the droop in the face – in what was left of the face – howled the message that this figure would never compose himself, arrange himself, to drive again, or do anything else again. I could not imagine his skewed left leg having the power to push down a clutch pedal ever, and he would need to in this old manual Citroën. I leaned in and held his wrist. He was cold. I found no pulse. This would be when I noticed the good, non-plastic, black slip-ons.

Grain said, 'Mr Claude Huddart, of this address. Here is Mrs Huddart.' He gave the 'Mrs' no slant or overtones.

'Is he dead?' she said.

'Who found him?' I said.

'I did,' Mrs Huddart said. 'Is he dead?'

'Has anyone called 999?' I said.

'My wife was going to,' Grain said. 'Mrs Huddart didn't want it – not immediately.'

'Perhaps she hoped he'd turn out to be all right,' Mrs Grain said.

'Yes,' Mrs Huddart said. 'That.'

'Did someone from one of the houses in the Avenue phone you, officer? You were here very quickly,' Grain said.

I didn't answer. Now and then silence can be useful. This is one of the first things you learn 'at Nelly's knee', as they call it in the service, meaning a kind of passed down, practical cop wisdom from old hands, part of the same canteen culture that produces male police crudity. The wisdom says that a bit of reticence, a notable absence of explanation, a portion of mystery, might encourage people to believe the police have more or less

mystical strengths, including telepathy, intuition, divine guidance, anticipation and clairvoyance. That will help keep punters
respectful and in check. *Some* of the punters, and only some.
There are other sections of the public who won't believe in
positive police attributes of any kind, and especially not divine
guidance. They will never show respect or willingly let themselves be kept in check. Those sections seem to be growing.
They have to be kept in check by other, more direct and obvious
methods, such as arrests, batons, stun-guns, courts and clink.
The public are a very mixed lot, and there are a lot of them.
They are also increasing, and they're getting a lot more mixed.

Somehow, though, this lot, this increasingly mixed lot, have
to be managed. So, it would have been tactically dim, and
unhelpful, to say total fluke brought me early to the Huddart
drive, and that I'd actually been on my way to somewhere else
but noticed the growing, agitated throng and decided to find what
was what. I've said already that I'd like to get in on the supposed
magic of top-flight detection. By ignoring the question about my
seemingly swift arrival, I could possibly give at least the appearance of magic, telepathy etc. That's the power of silence.

'Is he dead?' Mrs Huddart asked.

'I'm going to report the situation now,' I said. 'We need the
medics.'

'Are you sure about that?' Mrs Huddart said.

Did it sound like irony? Did grieving women do irony? But
maybe this was a species of grieving woman I'd never met previously. There'd be many species of grieving women I'd never met
previously. I called in to Control and said I'd stay on here.
Someone else could see to the warehouse. I went back and had
a more thorough look at the car, inside and out. The Super glue
must have been meant to help with the display factor. Whoever
had left the body there might have wanted to make sure it stayed
on view for a while after discovery. A natural impulse would
have been to remove Huddart from the car and get him somehow
into the house. Did Mrs Huddart look strong enough to have
lugged him that short distance herself if the Citroën had been
accessible? Maybe: people find astonishing reserves of energy
in a crisis. Or neighbours might have helped her. Was the Super
glue intended to deal with these possibilities and prolong the

exposure? I realized that this scenario assumed, didn't it, that Mrs Huddart wasn't a participant in the death? Or did it? If she *were* a participant, the display requirement would still exist, and the bunged-up locks gave her an excuse for leaving him there.

Broken glass from the window lay scattered on the passenger seat and some on the floor. Apart from this, I saw no evidence that violence of any sort had occurred inside the car. As everyone would expect for a ten-year-old model, the upholstery looked worn, but it had not been stained or ripped. Same for the roof lining. The other windows were intact. I recalled that scene from *The Godfather* where Michael Corleone's brother-in law is garrotted in the front seat of a car by Clemenza sitting behind, and his shoes burst through the windscreen as he struggles. Nothing like that here, nor like the blood bathed interior of another car, when someone gets accidentally shot by John Travolta in *Pulp Fiction*. Probably it's flippant to do this – think film – but the images gleamed in my memory and came back self-propelled as I examined the Citroën. This does happen to me now and then: a movie episode will edge its way into my head to match an actual situation. Some films get close to life, fiction but on the button. I reckon my head has a thousand good celluloid scenes in there, ready to stick themselves on to reality. It's not necessarily a plus in police work.

The Citroën would be taken away for proper forensic examination, and they might find something then. But the scan I gave with my head half through the smashed window told me nothing beyond what I'd seen already. I pulled back and straightened up. The car's bodywork was terrific for its age. It had obviously been looked after, polished often to keep the burgundy colouring aglow and fresh. I saw no dents, no evidence of repainting, no rust, tyre treads very legal. This car was a credit to the Avenue, ancient but not yet a banger. Mrs Huddart came and stood alongside me. Then, she also bent over and put her head through the hole and stared at him. She seemed determined to re-run how I'd looked at the inside just now. It was as if a queue had formed at some lying-in-state, and people took turns to nuzzle up towards Huddart via the window space and offer tributes and farewells. In the jumble of feelings hitting her perhaps she'd suffered jealousy. This was *her* man. Her dead man, and possibly dead by

her hand or assent, but still hers. She had to show it, and show
it in the only way feasible now. Did she find herself compelled
to equal this intrusive stranger's nearness to her dead husband
– this intrusive cop's nearness to him – during that little peek
of mine? Jealousy of a sort. Possessiveness of a sort. I could
sympathize. Alternatively – and there had to be this harsh
alternative – if she were implicated in the carving and death,
she might want to check what I could have seen when looking
and, suppose there'd been anything sensitive, give-away,
awkward, on view, she'd have time to cook a cover tale.

See? It's a right damn tricky one, dealing with somebody
whose grief is possibly overwhelming and utterly jonnock, but
who also has to be treated as a suspect, and the grief as phoney,
put on, acted out, a mask. The parents of that child missing from
a Portuguese holiday apartment, Madeleine McCann, would know
what it's like to be regarded in such a turn-and-turn-about style.
I didn't want to give Mrs Huddart additional agony, but, copwise,
I did want to question her, and question her *now*, before my big
rank bosses arrived to take over and shut me out. I had a place
at the start of a major investigation here, and – think career,
Mayfield! – I must fight against getting dropped from it. This
might seem an egomaniacal, heartless thought in the presence
of the awful death. But, police do deal with deaths and other
forms of human pain and tragedy. *How* we deal with them is
what marks us out as talented or average. I was turned down for
an accelerated promotion course. So, I had to progress by other
methods – thoroughness, push and, yes, a little steeliness now
and then.

The main way to fight for advancement in this game is to
know more than anybody else on the police side. Interrogating
Mrs Huddart at once, apparently so soon after the find, might
produce exceptional material: she'd possibly be still unsettled,
vulnerable and – perhaps – more liable to speak off her guard.
Is there any tried method to judge the genuineness and quality
of grief? What do you watch – the eyes, the hands, the mouth,
the brow for sweat or its absence? None of the training manuals
I've seen help on this. I ought to go gently, but if I went too
gently I'd lose the advantage of early arrival. There must be
nothing loud or hectoring: the crowd around the car had grown

a little in the last few minutes and parts or all of my conversation with Mrs Huddart would be overheard by some of them.

She said, 'I want him out of there.'

'The fire brigade rescue people will be here in a couple of minutes.'

'He could still be alive.'

'Well, yes.'

'So we should do something.' She had pulled back from the window and now started picking at jutting bits of glass still fixed in the bottom of the frame, as though clearing a way for herself to climb in. But after a minute she stopped and turned from the car. 'No, it's useless, isn't it? You wouldn't say so, but it is, isn't it?'

'Tell me about finding him,' I said.

She stayed silent for at least a minute. 'You think I'm part of it, don't you?'

'Part of what?'

'Yes, you do.'

'You came from the house to the car and saw him inside, is that right?' I said.

'Don't you? I'm a suspect.'

'What time? Had you heard anything from out here before that – during the night, for instance?'

Another silence. Then she said, 'You think he couldn't have got here unless I knew about it.'

'If we could fix the times.'

'Would I be so stupid?'

'Stupid how?'

'Would I be stupid enough to . . . well . . . Use your sliver of brain, will you? Would I be stupid enough to have him dumped outside our own house?'

'The discovery – when?' I said.

She glanced back at Huddart. 'Mouth-to-mouth,' she said. 'I could get in and try mouth-to-mouth.'

'The medics and so on are coming. Had you heard anything from the driveway earlier – during the night, for instance?'

She moved back to the car and again began pulling out the glass shards. She seemed half traumatized. Of course, that might be natural enough after such a find, if it was a find. And she'd probably be upset just by having to talk to the police. She did not weep, but her mind seemed to stagger and drift. She would slip into those long pauses and, when I repeated a question, would stare at me not only as if she had never heard it before, but as if she had never seen me before. 'I wondered if you'd heard anything from out here during the night,' I said. 'Do you sleep at the front of the house?'

'I was going to work. Claude had gone away on business and left the car for me to use.'

'Work where?' I said.

'He went by train.'

'Went where?'

'He wasn't due back until this evening.'

'So, he'd been away how long? A couple of days?'

'I do mornings three times a week in a service station. Seven thirty a.m. to noon.'

'Business? What kind of business is he in?' I made sure I said 'is' not 'was'. If she had some hope let her keep it for now. That was a basic kindness. But she went traumatized again for a while. Perhaps she did not know what kind of business. Yes, perhaps. She might have wanted to stay ignorant. Yes, she might. Maybe she considered the question uppity and irrelevant: he was obviously dead, wasn't he, and not much else mattered, did it? Did it?

'I came out at around nine o'clock last night to the car to collect some shopping I'd left in the boot.'

'And it was all right then?'

'What does that mean, for fuck's sake?'

'Well, was—'

She kept her voice low, but it rasped. 'You're asking, are you, was Claude in there dead and his face half gone? You think I'd notice him spread over the steering wheel but just lift the shopping, lock up the car and go back inside to watch TV? You dickhead, lady.'

'Did you lock up the car?' I said. If her account was true, Claude had been brought to the vehicle, presumably already dead and defaced, some time between last evening around nine o'clock and when she came out to it this morning. Incidentally, this is what I meant about grasses rarely being creatures of wealth.

It doesn't say much for Claude that his wife had to take a part-time job in a petrol station.

We hadn't moved far from the broken car window. She did not intend to leave Claude and neither did I. Different reasons, and difficult to be sure about hers. Loyalty? Affection? Love? Or maybe caution, in case his body told a tale somehow of what had happened and how? My motives? Simple: the evidence must be preserved more or less as it had been. He was sitting back instead of forward but that and the smashed window would be the only changes. The crowd on the drive had grown. People wanted to stare. I couldn't stop this, but I'd prevent them from interfering any further with the car. I told Mrs Huddart that she ought to go into the house and sit down, with one of the women neighbours to look after her, but she wouldn't. That I could more or less understand. I don't think I went too hard at the interview, though I did feel once or twice during those pauses that she might pass out. She was thin-faced, pale with large grey-green eyes, and would probably not have looked strong even before all this, busty but frail. She made me think of an Out Patients' waiting room.

She bent down again and once more pushed her head in through the broken window. It was as though even now she had not completely realized what had been done to Claude and meant to carry out another terrible inventory. Or, perhaps once the first shock had faded she felt able to bear getting near to him again, able to bear looking at him repeatedly from really close. There wouldn't be many more chances. I wanted to be reasonable.

They teach us to consider body language and I struggled to find something in hers. Again, difficult. She was crouched over, restricted in movement by the frame of the window. I had to study her from outside the car looking back across the bonnet and through the windscreen. She remained totally motionless, rigid, still no tears as far as I could tell, staring at Claude Huddart, thinking God knew what. I could not discover it, neither in her body nor her face. She did not reach out to touch him. Perhaps they had never been very physical with each other.

Oh, God, perhaps, perhaps, perhaps. Perhaps all sorts. I began to feel maybe I couldn't handle anything as dark and involved as this after all. Were warehouse break-ins at about my right current level? I needed some major experience, a lot of major experience, to back me in the matter of Claude Huddart. Some poltroon part of me suddenly felt glad to know a full call-out team would turn up very soon. I'd hand it all over then.

But how come I could collapse like this? Yes, how bloody come? Once or twice the same sort of break-up had happened to me before. Or more than once or twice. A couple of minutes ago I'd been determined to get my share of this case, and possibly beyond that. By fluke and/or inspired judgement I was first here. I'd longed to hang on to the advantage and exploit it. This had been 'my' case. Of course, behind such cockiness I'd realized it couldn't truly be my case. Constables with four years' experience in the police and two as a detective didn't – couldn't – manage something of this size. They'd be lucky to get much of a look in from the edge. But I'd worked full out to kid myself I could be big in this investigation. And now? The hellish uncertainties had begun to pull me down – and kick me once I *was* down. Should I mourn with Mrs Huddart or try to nail her as an accomplice and maybe worse in Claude Huddart's death? I watched her linger around the car, apparently unwilling or unable to leave him. I watched her seemingly convince herself that he must be alive and that she should help him. I watched that hope disintegrate and a renewed spasm of despair grip her. Real despair and sorrow? To me, they looked real, but I'd never before this attempted to distinguish genuine and manufactured sadness. Never had to. Oh, I'd often needed to guess at whether someone was lying to me. Commonplace – and different from trying to gauge the authenticity or not of sorrow. Could I dispute Mrs Huddart's argument that if she'd been involved she'd hardly consent to have his body left outside her front room?

The scale of these conundrums dazed me. Suddenly, I found I wanted out. Get someone else to seek the answers. Perhaps without noticing it during my four years I'd grown convinced and shaped by police reverence for rank – major crimes needed major officers to deal with them. Although it nauseated me to think I might unconsciously have come to accept that, I might have, all the same.

A platoon of top major and middling officers, led by Stuart Rendale, head of CID, arrived now with the fire brigade rescue unit. I had to turn away from Mrs Huddart and summarize for Rendale what I'd seen and heard. Then I went to the outskirts of the crowd. Would this be my only and final contact with the Huddart case? I kept my report short, with no mention of my feeling that the dead man must be a grass. Where was the evidence: only guesswork and make-believe? Rendale and the officers with him had probably seen a hundred murdered bodies in their time and heard a thousand witnesses give true, half true, half false, outright false, accounts of what had happened. They would do their own interpretations. I said only that Claude Huddart was Claude Huddart, and told how his partner had made the discovery and about the glue and the neighbours. The fire brigade began working on the driver's door of the Citroën.

'Good, Sharon,' Rendale said. 'But I don't understand how you got here so soon.'

'Luck. I was passing.'

'But sniffed out a crisis. That's not luck.' He was, or had been, the youngest detective superintendent in any British police force and would still be well under forty. No question he would make chief somewhere very soon. His was the kind of swift, non-stop advancement in the service I had in mind for myself. Or used to. Some of my confidence had slipped.

'Mrs Huddart, I'm sorry. We'll do all we can,' Rendale said. She had bent once more to the car window, as the firemen began levering. He crouched alongside her, his long, sensitive face near her shoulder. Rendale's considerateness and charm were famous – though apparently not enough to hold his marriage together, or so the buzz went. Even the major villains he so efficiently hounded would speak of him with something halfway to affection. He could wow juries. 'We all feel for you, believe me,' he told Alice Huddart.

She straightened. 'Oh, of fucking course I believe you,' she replied, her voice big enough and hard enough for me to hear although I'd moved far back now. The takeover of the case had begun. 'What else could I do but believe you? After all, you're the law, aren't you?'

Rendale nodded, not as answer to the question, but as though to forgive her the sarcasm. And as though to concede that what he'd said was a slice of stupid formality, because eventually he might have to interrogate her as a suspect and perhaps charge her.

A man near me at the rim of the crowd took a step closer. 'Name's Dince,' he said quietly. 'I want to talk, if that's all right.' He was around twenty-five, thin to very thin, newish jeans, oldish grey sweater, no coat, rubbish trainers, rough teeth, rough close haircut, fair, very calm, dull-eyed, slightly stooped, no athlete.

'Mr Rendale's in charge,' I said. 'Or there's Chief Inspector Phaeton.'

'Do you mind – I'd prefer not going to the summit – I mean, at this stage.'

'Well, I'm definitely not the summit,' I said. 'At this stage. You're a neighbour?'

'No. So, I'll be in touch,' he replied.

'How?'

'Yes, I'll be in touch. I just wanted to alert you – at this point in time.'

'Which point in time?'

'This one, on the drive.'

'I'm only here by fluke.'

'As the other officer said, I don't think I'd call it that.'

'What *would* you call it?'

'Obviously, I had to wait until you were by yourself.'

'Why?'

'Oh, yes.'

'If you try to contact me through the station, people there will want to know what it's about, and you'll be put on to Mr Rendale, or Edward Phaeton.'

'Fear not. I'll be in touch.'

His evasiveness angered me, but might this be a chance to recruit a grass? 'How are you involved in this?' I said.

'Involved?'

'Isn't that what you meant?'

'I regard it as an opportunity.'

'Regard what?'

'And, in those circumstances, it's important to act.'

'Which circumstances? Act how?'

'This could lead on,' he replied.

'Could it?'

'Believe me.'

Difficult. But I said, 'If it's important, I'll give you my home address.'

'I have it.'

'How? I'm not in the phone book.'

'I'll be in touch. Dince, Jeremy Naunton Dince. Got that? Remember it.' He eased through a group of spectators, walked behind Mrs Huddart and Stuart Rendale towards the street and away.

And more or less at once I went into another change of attitude and lifting of morale because of Jeremy Naunton Dince. This was a strange bit of one-to-oneness. He spoke as if it had been an arranged, schemed, confidential meeting. But he couldn't have known I'd be there. Hell, I didn't know that myself when I set out en route to a burgled warehouse. Odd vocabulary. 'Fear not.' Like the Bible? Plus corny politico-speech: 'at this stage', 'at this point in time'. You see, that's what I like about police work. Variety. No, it's stronger than that: changeability.

(1) You do operate within a very precisely organized system of duties, ranks and rules, and at times – as just now – I feel grateful for that. I can refer difficult things upwards to someone like Rendale. If you mean to progress and, as I've said, I do mean to progress, you can see very clearly the steps towards the summit, as Jeremy Naunton Dince called it, and you know exactly the kind of approved conformist behaviour that will see you right.

(2) On the other hand, if you can handle it, there may also be room for a little individual effort outside the regulations. I should have mentioned to Stuart Rendale, or Edward Phaeton, or some other superior, this man Dince and his apparent offer of information. I didn't, and not only because it was flimsy, and maybe not even as much as that. But Dince had said he wanted me, had somehow picked me out.

(3) Although there is the system's way of succeeding in the police, there can also be extra ways. That mysterious talk with Jeremy Naunton Dince had made me think favourably about these extra ways. Let's say I

aimed at a nice combination of all methods of success, the standard and the original. On its own, the system's way could be a bit slow. You had to jolly it up, if you had the talent and nerve. Sometimes I had. Sometimes today I had.

TWO

He walked away. Dince, Jeremy, Naunton, walked away? HE WALKED AWAY? If that was really his name.

No, for God's sake, I could not let it happen. He knew something, did he? Of course he knew something. How would he be here otherwise, spot on time for the finding of the body? Everything – he might know everything. But, then, he seemed to assume that *I* knew something, also, and possibly everything. Hadn't I turned up, too, spot on time for the finding of the body? He didn't believe that to be chance. Likewise, Rendale said he didn't accept I'd made it to the Huddart drive at or near the crucial moment by coincidence. But this was only Rendale's customary politeness/staff management: encourage subordinates with praise. Dince, though, hadn't been doing politeness. He thought we'd both been drawn there by special, independent information. Perhaps he wanted an exchange. He believed we both knew at least a fraction – if not everything – and that the two fractions put together might interlock brilliantly, conclusively.

He'd told me he was no neighbour. He had something he would not disclose to Stuart Rendale or Phaeton or any of the other main men, only to me, myself in person, at some non-declared date, perhaps because he believed I had something I could disclose to him as part of a bargain. Perhaps. Very perhaps. More bloody perhapses. I might be a fine choice – yes, of course, the best choice when on form – but how could he know it? And, in any case, I had let him hop off. Welcome and farewell in one whispered minute. Casual, damn casual. Furtive, damn furtive. But that was all right, wasn't it: good detective work would always have elements of the furtive? If you lived by, and on, secret information you had to expect the information to come secretly, someone sidling up to you uninvited and unannounced in a crowd and talking sotto, intimate and terse.

What were the prospects, then? He would be 'in touch'. So he said. I must sit and wait, must I? Not on. He would control things. This flouted all the rules on running an informant, and all the training. The detective had to be the leading partner. Allow the grass to reverse that and the cop could be in real shtook.

(1) The cost of information might soar.
(2) As part of his/her reward the grass would sometimes demand that the detective should ignore crimes he/she carried out.
(3) And he/she could also ask for reciprocal information – about, say, security measures at some burglarable site and the strength of police patrols in the area.
(4) When the detective had given in once to such pretty requests endless blackmail would probably follow.
(5) Or endless until the detective felt forced to get rid of the grass, 'get rid of' meaning get rid of.
(6) This could put the officer in danger of a murder charge;
(7) or in danger from a fight back by the grass, and the detective himself got rid of or maimed. A blackmailing grass would be ready and prepared for any attack by the detective. Grassing was a science not an art, meaning its likely procedures could be forecast and planned for.

Alternatively, Dince might decide against proceeding after all – might suddenly realize he had shown he knew too much and could be in trouble. Any crook would tell you he/she feared talking to the law machine because, even though the chat might be well-intentioned, it could be turned around and slanted by the police and employed to prosecute her/him. If Dince started to worry about that hazard, he'd jack in his wish to find out what I knew – was supposed to know. Probably he'd even come round to accepting that I'd been on the drive only because of efficient eyesight and inquisitiveness, not some confidential tip-off. He would disappear, resume his real name. Or pick up one of his other fifteen aliases. Dince? Who'd believe that was a true moniker?

Or – another *or* – perhaps matters between him and me were not as secret as they seemed. That conversation by the body, so brief and discreet, might have been noted, just the same. Possibly, he was not the only non-neighbour and non-emergency services member present on the drive. Suppose someone had observed that hurried, significant chat between us and later persuaded or forced him to decide against contacting me again, because what Dince knew was really so hot and dangerous, for himself and others. Possibly someone would silence Dince, Jeremy, Naunton altogether – as Huddart, Claude had been altogether silenced.

Had I started getting fanciful, frantic, pushed off balance by the sort of big-time horrifying violence which, until today, I'd only heard about, read about? Had naivety struck, four years into my police career? Fluke might have put me on to the Huddart drive at that early-bird moment, but fluke couldn't guide me now, in this bewildering aftermath. I needed old-sweat backup. Not available. Couldn't be. I had to behave as if Dince and I did have something private, undisclosed on the go. It must stay private, if it was.

Despite another of these morale wobbles then, I decided it would be stupid and feeble to let Dince drop out of sight, perhaps for ever. Dince was mine. Only mine. He wanted it like that. Hang on to him. Guard him. Suck him clean of whatever he had, if he had anything, especially if it incriminated him. Get truly naive and flagrantly impulsive – rush after him. And by getting naive and flagrantly impulsive I might eventually acquire some of that quality experience I needed – as solid substitute for the naivety and impulsiveness.

I didn't think I'd be missed. Rendale, Edward Phaeton and the other big people were busy with their heavy questions and examination of the car and garden and house. They had a ritual, knew how to focus, and the focus did not include me, except to supply Rendale with a sweet foreword. He'd probably regard my role here as finished. I had been stood down. Well, great. I did what Dince, Jeremy, Naunton had done and pushed my way out through the crowd of gawpers and unknowns and walked. He was a good stretch ahead by now. I hurried, but still only walking. He might have a car somewhere fairly close and once he jumped into that I could give up. True, if I were near enough to get the registration number he might be traceable, but tracing involved the headquarters computer and the headquarters computer staff. It would be an official, on-the-record inquiry and known about.

Dince could no longer be just mine. People might wish to discover – might reasonably wish to discover – why I had to find him. Dince would become general police property, which is what all grasses should be according to official rules. No individual officer 'owned' his/her informant. The contract bound the grass to the whole police organization, not to one of its detectives. Right. But I was not in the giving or sharing vein. Not at this stage, to use a Dince phrase.

. It wouldn't be like kosher tailing, by which I mean continuous observation without one's self being observed. Another science, and labour intensive. To follow someone secretly requires an enormous team, whether it's a vehicle operation or on foot. We were in a long, suburban street, with a few parked cars and an occasional environmental tree: no real cover at all, and the best gumshoe in the world would have had trouble staying unspotted. I have had the training but admit I'm not the best gumshoe in the world. Yet. It will come, I'm sure of that. You'd need half a dozen people to do secret surveillance in these conditions, each of them popping up at different places and relieving the previous operator. That way the target shouldn't notice the same face and physique behind.

In any case, I did not want to stay unnoticed. There is a brand of tailing where the follower *should* be seen by the quarry. The object is to make the prey scared, jumpy, oppressed – perhaps crack and do something irrational, like confess. Remember that creepy detective–prosecutor in *Crime and Punishment* describing this unnerving method to Raskolnikov, the murderer? Well, I required to be seen, but for a different purpose. I hoped Jeremy Dince would turn, recognize me, feel pleased at the urgency of my interest and wait; then agree to come to some reasonably confidential place – perhaps his car, perhaps a breakfast cafe, perhaps a park bench – and spill, supposing he had something worthwhile to spill. Spill *now*, *today*, not at a future, maybe never, date. This would be another episode in what he might see as our hidden alliance: an episode with some substance to it this time.

But *would* he spill when he found I had nothing to spill in return, nothing but what he'd been able to see for himself on the Huddart drive? I quite liked the notion of taking him back with me to Stuart Rendale and saying, while they still fiddled about with their by-the-book inquiries, 'I think you'll find interesting what Jeremy Naunton Dince has to tell us, sir.' I'd make it 'us' to emphasize that although I let Dince talk to him he was *my* exclusive find. I'd located him, developed him, solo, but as a fine team person I'd allow other officers to question him, the implication being that, as a fine and generous team person, I should be moved up in the team pretty smartly. Detective Superintendent Rendale's refined face would show scepticism as only a refined face can and so I'd tell him again, 'Here's your man, sir, Dince, Jeremy, Naunton, alias this that and the other.'

Dince did turn his head once and I gave a small wave, nothing to draw attention, except his. He must have seen it. I tried to make this a genial, relaxed wave, not a Nelsonian, semaphored order to heave to at once or be shot out of the water. Oh, certainly he saw it but kept going at the same pace or faster. Those downgrade trainers flashed like washed-out flags: more semaphore. Signalling what, though? 'Fuck off, Sharon Mayfield, stick to the arrangement?' Or, 'Follow me, Sharon Mayfield?' Had he realized while we stood near the Citroën that I would not be content with the fragments of conversation we'd just had, nor the promise of a future meeting, and was sure to come after him? The few words had been bait? I thought of yelling but guessed he would not stop for that, either. Perhaps, after all, he had said everything he meant to say for the day. He thought he had, perhaps. Or possibly all he had been instructed to say.

Yes, I realized now that, on the Huddart drive, he had looked to me like a subordinate, a messenger boy. Partly it was the clothes. They were not the gear of someone who had anything but dogsbody status in the kind of scene where he apparently worked. Fashion mattered there. I know some people dress down, as it's called, but I felt this outfit and the trainers were totally and sadly natural to him. Then, the dullness of his eyes and the stoop: they made him seem like someone who'd never make a go of anything alone. He needed to be led, to be dragooned. He seemed to have been made for those biblical words, 'Here am I, send me'.

Dince came to a junction and went left. As far as I could remember, it was Cinder Street, another long, residential stretch leading off the estate and eventually on to the main Tollgate Road. There'd still be minimal cover. But this had become irrelevant. He knew I was behind him, though that hadn't changed his behaviour, except he still might be walking slightly quicker. I felt sure that when I reached the junction and looked he would be gone. Probably this was where he had left his car. There'd be spaces. Many occupants of these houses had left for work. Some people felt more identifiable by their vehicle than by their face. Dince might be like that and would have jibbed at parking nearer to the Huddart house. Now, afraid of losing him, I started to run, transformed myself into a real manic sight – a galloping woman in heels and an office suit – but not a sight that Rendale and the others would spot, I hoped. They should be heads down, busying with Claude Huddart, and I'd be around the corner soon.

When I reached the junction, and stared up Cinder Street, Dince was still visible, and still walking. It looked as if he might have had a run himself, and faster than mine. The distance between us seemed much greater, but that might not be too troublesome. Perhaps he knew the area and realized that, no matter what the gap, I'd still be able to see him in this straight, long artery. I kept after him, walking again now. From this far, the stoop was not so obvious, but his fair hair and the trainers stood out as before. It had become like a kind of game, with its own silly rules. You did not run while the other could see. In any case, I felt tired and for the moment, walking amounted to the best I could manage. All the time, I waited for him to approach one of the parked cars, open it and get clear. Another part of the game: now you see me, now you don't. I'd have been unable to make out the registration from so far back. The game would be over. Dince might vanish in a puff of exhaust smoke.

But it did not happen like that. Nothing like. Instead, a car moving down the road in the same direction as us seemed to slow alongside him and keep pace. It must have overtaken me, but a lot of cars had overtaken me, and I wouldn't have noticed it as an important part of this scene. It looked like one of the bigger Audis, dark green. I saw him glance at it, and then glance again as if to check something, but he didn't stop or make any move towards it. Other vehicles had to get around the Audi. Was he scared, pleased, mystified by this escort? Too far off to tell.

The head movements had been jerky. Panic? Perhaps, though, someone in the car had called out to him, and he'd responded. A conversation? The Audi accelerated slightly and I thought it would leave him now. Had it been simply an innocent exchange of greetings? I felt happier.

But then, not far ahead of Dince, a bus stop offered some car-free space. The Audi pulled into the kerb and waited. Now, I did think I could read his reactions: they were more obvious, and maybe I'd drawn a little closer to him. He seemed shocked or excited, perhaps he hesitated momentarily. It looked for a second as if he would turn around and try to retreat. Yes, yes, let it be like that. He'd come towards me and we'd meet. The Audi might add up to a complication for me as well as him, but I'd try to handle that when – if – it did. He glanced back again, as though to check I was still behind him. This time I stopped myself from waving. He might not want the link between us known, if a link existed. We'd spoken a few guarded phrases together and then gone through the same couple of streets a few hundred metres or more apart. Did that add up to a link? He walked on. Perhaps he would be ashamed to falter. Possibly he had more to him than I'd thought.

A couple of men left the car, nimble, committed men, one from the rear, one from the passenger seat, and stood facing him on the pavement. OK, the nimbleness was obvious. But where did that word 'committed' come from? What did it mean? Did it mean anything? All right, they looked as if they would confront him. Of course they did. Did that make them committed? Fancy wordage. Again, I thought they might possibly be talking, possibly threateningly, though there was nothing in their hands. They were white, one squat, wearing a light-coloured, single-breasted suit and a flat hat or beret, near middle age, say about forty; the other younger, in dark-blue shirt and trousers, no jacket, longish brown hair, twenty-five or six. I wanted to run again and could possibly have dredged up some breath for it, but didn't. It might not do him much good with those two if they saw me hurrying towards them. But, my God, do I look cop, even in a business suit? I kept walking, same pace, like someone on her way to work. Perhaps I was.

He paused when he reached the two men. It could be that

he *had* to pause. They stood alongside each other, more or less blocking the pavement. Almost certainly now they had a conversation. I was too far off to gauge its tone. It could have been an amiable encounter of friends in the street, with a bit of gossip swapping. They were very close to him, really friendly, or not friendly at all, real comradeship, or real menace. I heard no laughter. I could see the features of the older man slightly better now. He was pale-skinned, broad-nosed with a small greying imperial beard at the end of his chin. He looked unfriendly and, yes, committed – committed to getting Dince into the Audi with them. The younger man had shifted so that he stood to the left of Dince and facing away from me. In a couple of moments the three moved towards the Audi. I could see no force used and still no weapon. The older man opened the rear door and climbed in first while the other one stood with Dince. This was the way you would put a prisoner into the back seat, so there would be someone obstructing the far door, to stop him jumping out the other side. Then Dince entered the Audi and the younger man closed the door and took the passenger seat. I was still a long way off when the car moved away fast and I could not make out the registration. But definitely an Audi and definitely dark green. I'd had no glimpse of the driver.

It was half-term and some children aged about eleven and twelve were playing in and out of a couple of front gardens near where the car had waited. A girl and boy fenced intently, viciously, with long poles, perhaps yard brushes amputated especially for the tourney. The boy was thin and crew-cropped, wearing a red and white striped football shirt, black jogging trousers and plimsolls. The girl had shoulder length fair hair and a round, slightly plump and smiley face, smiley even while she warred with the boy. I felt sure I would get go-stuff-yourself replies from her to any questions. She maintained the kind of personal cheeriness that could only stay active by being unpleasant to others. She had on loose, khaki skateboard trousers and a white, crew-necked woollen sweater. Another boy watched the jousting. He turned and glanced at me for less than a second, then went back to spectating the fight, occasionally grunting as if to tell one or other of them to liven it up and smash the opposition harder, preferably about the head. He had on a long peaked navy cap and what looked like a handed down turquoise and ochre shell suit tucked into brown fashion boots. When I reached the spot I did one of my best chummy grins, very conscious of its total uselessness.

I spoke to the three of them. 'Did you see the men who got into the car just here?'

'Which?' the girl said.

'Which what?' I said.

'Which car?' she said.

'The green Audi,' I said. 'And a fourth man driving.'

'There *was* a green Audi,' she said.

'It had a driver,' crew cut said.

'This Audi parked illegally on the bus stop,' shell suit said.

'Unforgivable,' the girl said. The pole battle was suspended so she could concentrate on her insolence. 'Imagine if a bus had wanted to pull in there, so passengers might alight, or then again, board.'

'No bus did,' crew cut said.

'And nobody waited to board,' shell suit said.

'But a possibility, surely,' the girl said. 'Some old gent with a walking stick – he'd have had to get off the bus in the middle of the road, owing to the Audi.'

'Which old gent?' crew cut said.

'If,' she replied.

'Did you hear them say anything, I wonder?' I asked.

'Who?' she said.

'The three men,' I said. 'Or the driver.'

'Oh, you wonder, do you?' the girl said.

'That's what she said, she wonders re them saying anything,' shell suit said.

'The tone,' I said.

'In which regard?' the girl said.

'Did they sound like . . . well, like enemies?' I said. 'Say, arguing, or one of them protesting.'

'Protesting about what?' the girl said.

'Or possibly it was all friendly,' I replied.

'Do you mean protesting about the car being on the bus stop?' she said.

'I wondered if you'd heard them say anything – where they were going, anything like that,' I said.

'She wonders whether we heard where they were going, anything like that,' crew cut said.

'And whether the fair-haired one said anything at all.' I'd stick at it.

'The fair-haired one. She's interested in the fair-haired one,' shell suit said. 'He's the star?'

'Would you go after them?' shell suit asked.

'Who are you then, the police?' the girl said. She pronounced it 'polees', stringing out the double 'e' sound like an attack. It *was* an attack, but I and the police would survive. She did not look at me and now resumed her fencing with the crew-cut lad, though not at full pace while she talked. It was just a token to tell me they didn't intend changing their game because I'd come along spouting queries. 'We don't hear nothing, we don't see nothing, never,' she said. 'We don't go in for tone.'

'It's rude to listen in to other people's talk,' shell suit said.

'A man might be in bad trouble,' I said.

'Which?' crew cut asked.

'I'd guess the fair-haired one,' the girl said. 'She's got a crush on him.'

'How can you go after them without a car?' crew cut queried.

'Did he say anything?' I asked.

'What do you think, Jason, did he say anything?' the girl asked the shell suit.

'If he's in bad trouble get him out of it,' crew cut said.

'You might be able to help,' I said.

'We don't go in for that,' the girl said.

'What?' I said.

'Help,' she said. 'Or tone.'

'We don't hear nothing, we don't see nothing, never,' the shell suit replied. He didn't bother with another glance my way.

I felt a fierce, awkward kind of responsibility for Dince. It was mad, really. He had come to talk to me on the Huddart drive, his choice. He had walked away, his choice. Yet I could not escape the idea that I had brought this on him, whatever it was. Fingered him. He had wished to speak to me and only me, and that made this sense of guilt very particular, very personal. Did these people in the Audi know Dince had just come from the Huddart house and what had happened there?

And then the indifference of these children, if you could call it only indifference: more like drilled-in bolshiness, little troops of the omertà brigade. This attitude of theirs seemed somehow to throw the responsibility for Dince even harder on me. Somehow? So, how? Well, it was as though these kids displayed that notorious, growing public wish to look away, when to look might bring danger and pain. These were absurd, inflated thoughts, weren't they? I couldn't make the answers from a handful of children symbolize the blind-eye to lawlessness by a whole adult world, could I? Yes, I could, because those kids' reactions did what symbols were supposed to do: catch in glaring miniature the widespread and general. But, of course, there might have been no lawlessness. Dince could be getting a lift from a few kindly chums, one professorial looking on account of the little beard and beret.

I would have liked to believe it but could not. I looked for a taxi. It was the wrong time of day and probably the wrong kind of street. Police did have the power to commandeer a private vehicle, but I doubted this was as big an emergency as that. It might be no emergency at all. I might look foolish. Eventually, I spotted a cab about to move off after putting a family down and waved. 'Into Tollgate Road and look out for a dark-green Audi,' I said.

'What? What sort of job is this? You police or something?'

'A dark-green Audi.'

'I don't want nothing difficult. I mean, with damage. This car's nearly new. There's difficult people around here.'

'Which people?'

'You police?'

'So?'

'You'll know the names.'

'Will I?'

'I'm thinking of Philip Otton, or the one they call Gleeful, or Ian Linter. I try not to get involved, not at my age. These are barons, Linter really big. If there's police goings-on around this way it's usually about Otton or Gleeful or Linter. Or their people. Is this about one of them? I don't want no bother with any of them.' The taxi man would have been about sixty, bald, fat, blotched.

'Just find the Audi, then you can quit. Anyway, we're probably much too late, unless there's a jam.'

There was no jam and no sight of the Audi in Tollgate Road or during a trawl of the side streets. 'There,' I said. 'Not a scratch to the vehicle. Give me your name and I'll recommend an O.B.E. for public spiritedness.' I told him to drive me back to the Tollgate Road junction and walked to the Huddart house from there. I'd have to give some tale if anyone asked where I'd been. Dince was still mine, only mine, even if I could not find him and might never see him again.

THREE

'They'll fit me up for it, won't they, won't they?' Alice Huddart said. It came out as part whisper, part hiss, almost a squeal of pain, and yet almost too, a flat, hopeless recognition, as if she would have expected nothing else, the repeated 'won't they?' touched by despair. They were questions but, by doubling them up, she was hoping for double certainty, not double doubt. And then 'fit me up for it'. The more formal, usual word would be 'frame', when it looked as if the police had concocted someone's guilt. But 'fit me up for it' contained a frightening sense of carefulness and precision and skilled, contrived malevolence. She preferred this phrasing. Perhaps she had heard a lot of villain lingo in her time. And she'd know that homely domestic tag: 'it fits you to a t', signifying, 'It's perfect and just for you, for you only'.

I said, 'Fit you up? I don't understand.' God, I had to say *something*, even something so half-witted and farcically false.

'You understand. You're part of it, I expect.'

'Of what?'

'Oh, damn clever – cop clever,' she replied. 'Dump him on our doorstep. Get you *accidentally* there for the discovery.'

'Nobody else got me there *accidentally*. I got myself there *accidentally*.'

'Well, you'll stick to the script. You have to stick to the script. Both of them in on it?'

'Which both?'

'Or maybe only one.'

'Who?' I asked. She'd shaken me at the start of this talk, and it grew worse. 'Clever? What's clever?'

'And he, or they, have picked a good one in you. Such an actress! You can play Stratford next.'

'I'm involved by fluke – if I'm involved at all now.'

'We're discussing your bosses, aren't we, or possibly only one of your bosses – Rendale, Chief Inspector Phaeton? You

can guess the questions they hammer away at.' She made a
decent shot at Phaeton's take-me-as-I-am Midlands accent:
'"But surely you must have heard something if the body was
put there during the night, Mrs Huddart? You sleep at the front
of the house, don't you? This would not be an easy operation.
Probably another vehicle to bring the body. Oh, certainly. So,
doors closing. Or perhaps they drove the Citroën away, put him
into it, then brought the vehicle back to your drive. You slept
through all that?"'

Questions I would have liked to ask, too – would *have* to ask,
if I had charge of this case, which I definitely didn't. 'Those are
just obvious, routine queries,' I said. 'They might come over as
. . . as, well . . . aggressive, but no. Standard procedure. Any
officer would ask them.'

'You?'

'I don't get to ask questions in an investigation of this
importance.'

'Phaeton has a way of saying the word.'

'Which?'

'"Body". He's magnificent at getting the absolute lifelessness
into it.'

'I don't know what you're saying. They have to build the
picture, that's all. They're following the pattern of a murder
inquiry.'

'"The body". That "the". Turns it into a thing. Not "his
body" or "Claude's body" or just "Claude". And what's the
suggestion? Obvious: I transformed Claude into "the body",
or, at least, helped.'

'No, that wouldn't be what was meant at all.'

'"At least two men to carry and arrange him in the Citroën,
if they did it here. No loaded footsteps on the drive, Mrs
Huddart?"' Again an imitation of Phaeton, but now with the snarl
and sting and disbelief stronger. I could imagine Phaeton's tall,
heavy shape leaning forward as he put the harsh question, dark
hair hanging down over his forehead.

'They have to try to visualize the sequence. It's a basic
technique of detective work.'

'"Loaded footsteps" – like removal men with a settee – as I
said, a thing,' Alice Huddart replied. 'He means because they

were carrying Claude. No, he's not delicate, that Phaeton. He talks like . . . he talks to me as though he was in a villain's house and I'm a villain's woman. He's just hard, crude.' She closed her eyes for something longer than a blink, perhaps re-running in her mind what she'd just said and imagining what I'd make of it. 'All right, perhaps it is or was a villain's house, and perhaps I am or was a villain's woman.' She stared at my face now to see if she could read my thoughts.

I hoped she couldn't. But maybe you *are* or were a villain's woman, Alice. Naturally, I didn't say it. Delicacy. Humaneness. Avoidance of the obvious. Would you know the formula 'fit me up' if you *weren't* a villain's woman, Alice? True, though, there *were* all those TV crime stories about flaky police to learn from. In any case, I didn't need to speak such slurs. Someone else would handle her interrogation, not a lowly DC.

'Once or twice I thought he was actually going to frisk me for a knife or gun,' she said. 'That kind of hostility.'

Do you know knives and guns, Mrs Huddart? Would he have found one or the other? However, once more it was a thought only, not words.

She put those wide, grey-green eyes on me again, full of sadness and fight. 'So, yes, you knew this was their scheme, didn't you – get Alice Huddart for it? You've hatched it between all of you? You're at a nothing rank, so they can pressure you, co-opt you. Where two or three police are gathered together, there is dirty work in the midst of them.' She tried a self-mocking, painful smile. 'God, see what I'm doing? I'm talking to you as if you're trustworthy and on my side. I'm an outright lunatic.'

So, she had wit and an education, this lady – could adapt a New Testament text on the hoof. Or had she heard Claude say something similar, perhaps heard it often from him. 'I've been away from the house,' I said. 'I couldn't know what they were going to ask, except it would be to pattern.'

Accurate enough: when I arrived back here in the gloriously undamaged taxi that failed to find Dince, Superintendent Rendale and Edward Phaeton had been outside, near the Citroën, watching a police photographer do all his angles. And they were still in the garden now. An ambulance stood in the road waiting to take Claude for his post-mortem. I would have stayed near the two

senior officers, in case they had something for me to do, and in
the hope they would think I'd been around the house and garden
all the time. But Alice Huddart had suddenly and very briefly
appeared at the sitting-room window and beckoned me inside.
She used the same kind of small, anxious, intimate wave I had
given Jeremy Naunton Dince in the street, meant for one person
only. But whereas Dince ignored it, I had responded and after
a minute or two joined her in the small, pleasant sitting room.

'You were away from the house?' Alice Huddart asked. 'How
come?' She'd made tea. The cups and saucers were delicate
china, white decorated with yellow flowers. It might be a villain's
house, but she wanted guests to see she could offer refinement
and quality.

'I had some inquiries to take care of,' I said.

'To do with what? To do with me? They sent you somewhere?'

'Where would they send me?'

'To do with myself?'

'Some inquiries,' I replied, readily.

'But I saw you on the drive very early, before any of the
others. Any of the other police. We spoke. You introduced
yourself. I heard that. You were told to get here early, were you?
Of course, they knew what you'd find. It takes the spotlight off
them, or him.'

'Which spotlight?'

'The investigation spotlight.'

'Gets it off whom?'

'Them, or him. It's clever.'

'What's clever?'

'You have to play along. I see that. Did *you* know what you'd
find?'

'I arrived by accident.'

'Oh, sure. And then you left for a while? Why? What
inquiries?'

'Yes, that's it, some inquiries elsewhere.'

'How could that be?'

'Yes, elsewhere,' I said, as readily as before.

She gave up on that one. 'Am I a heavy sleeper? He asks this
– am I a heavy sleeper? It's Rendale talking now.' She did not
attempt a version of his softer accent. 'It means, could *anyone*

sleep as heavily as that? It means, what are you asking us to believe, Alice? They're both at it. This is arranged. You – you're part of the team. You'd know. You've all got yourselves to look after. You look around for a way out and decide Claude Huddart will do. Decide *I* will do.'

'What's that mean, Mrs Huddart?'

'You know. They'd know.'

'No, I don't understand.'

'Maybe.' Her voice crackled with doubt or derision, or both, or both plus a fine range of other hate reactions. She'd decided to quit being a lunatic and to treat me as nothing but police, not as a possibly sympathetic woman working for a couple of toughie men. I did sympathize, but with a few obvious and massive uncertainties. I could feel her editing what she wanted to say, in case I was part of some pre-planned police deal and would pass it on and up. And, in fact, that's what a foot soldier detective would normally do with any worthwhile information he/she came by in a major case – pass it on and up for the senior people to evaluate and act on, or not. Alice Huddart knew the system. Her man had himself probably fed this system with offerings intended to go on and up to the high command. But what Alice Huddart might not realize is that occasionally a detective, such as this one, Sharon Mayfield, would prefer to keep something potentially special known to her, and her only, for future personal investigation.

'I think Claude could have been put there quietly enough, so as not to disturb you,' I said.

'Oh, thanks, thank you very much.' Sarcasm, yes, but behind the edge of it I thought there might be a fragment of frail, hopeful gratitude. 'You believe I wasn't out there, helping. Great! So tell them that, will you?'

'It's only my view. My views don't count for much.'

'But tell them.'

'All right.

'Or would it mean trouble for you?'

'Why trouble? I'm entitled to say what I—'

'If they've got a scenario they won't like you bringing snags. They won't *let* you bring snags.'

'What scenario?'

'As to how it happened. Or as to how they want people to *think* it happened.'

'And how would they want people to *think* it happened?'

'With my cooperation – or more than that.' She stopped and winced. 'My God, they might do a mock-up of things. A couple of your people arrive in a car and carry an imitation body from it to the Citroën on the drive, and they measure the noise level in my bedroom to establish whether anyone could have slept through it. Or they measure the noise level to prove that nobody could have slept through it. That would be awful, so awful.'

'Why?'

'Making a dummy of Claude. Lugging it from car to car. Police like these reconstructions, don't they?'

'Sometimes they help.'

'I loved him, you know,' she replied.

'Certainly. You've said.'

'Really loved him. Not just shacked-up and the wall-to-wall carpets and genuine china and all that. Loved. He could be a bit of a towering pipsqueak, yes, and for ever getting nowhere, waiting for the big chance that was never going to come, because he wasn't built to get big chances. He knew it. Claude had a lot of first-class humility. I told him once we should look at his stars in the paper and he said he didn't think he had any. He said, "I've got a birthday, but no stars, just one of those black holes." Yes, when you'd been Claude Huddart all your life you got used to insignificance. But he was mine. He could be warm and kind. He could even be fun. I wanted him. He could look good. Dignified. He could.'

They'd got the car doors open but hadn't yet removed the body. She glanced out of the window towards the Citroën and Claude's mutilated face, as though nobody would believe now that he could have ever looked good, or be fun. 'So, how could I wish him dead?'

'I'm sure Mr Rendale and Mr Phaeton won't—'

'I don't think they'd say I, myself, killed him, me, individually. Just they'll make me part of some conspiracy. But how could I? How, when I loved him? What woman gets her man carved, even a man like Claude?'

It was as near as I had seen her come to weeping, and still not *very* near – more as though she thought she *ought* to weep, a well-meant token, to match the circumstances and the memory of his sad starlessness. Her attitude to Claude badly confused me. It would confuse anyone, I reckoned. She loved him, but called him 'a towering pipsqueak'. And: 'What woman gets her man carved, even a man like Claude?' This seemed a bewildering mix of affection and contempt. Perhaps she'd say, 'Not contempt, accuracy.' I'd never met anyone of Alice Huddart's make before. I floundered.

'They'll suppose it's some sex thing – me two-timing him – me and someone, getting rid of Claude because he was in the way. Is that why they sent you off from the house?'

'You've lost me again.'

'To look for some sex angle.'

'Where would I go to look for some sex angle?'

'I don't know where, because there isn't one. But those two might think they knew something.'

'Knew what?'

'There's a film – *The Postman Always Rings Twice*. Murder the husband. It suits them to see it like that. Or to *say* they see it like that.'

'Why?'

'It lands the blame elsewhere, doesn't it?'

'Which blame?'

'But did they cut up the husband's face in *The Postman Always Rings Twice*, for God's sake?'

'They'll want the truth, that's all, Mrs Huddart.'

She gasped, as if the simplicity of this had winded her, simplicity in all its meanings, especially simple-mindedness, terrible, hopeful, hopeless greenness. 'Oh, absolutely,' she said.

'I'm sure of it.'

'Yes, and I'm really afraid you might be.' She seemed about to say something else, something blunt, not oblique and ironical, something dismissive. But she reconsidered. She'd be wondering once more how much of this conversation I'd relay to Phaeton and Rendale. To her I must sound like a committed disciple of the bossmen. And disciples reported in full back to their masters. She looked for another way to get to me. 'And you, Sharon,' she said, 'do you have a love interest? Married? Partnered?'

'Along those lines.' I kept it terse, vague, ambiguous, to block her.

'Ah, I'm the one to be asked questions, aren't I? Not you.' She had it about right. We were seated opposite each other, myself on a handsome black, leather, fat-armed chesterfield, perhaps Victorian or Edwardian and re-covered, and Mrs Huddart in a small armchair, also black, and possibly also old and nicely done up. Who had the taste, Claude or Alice? Hunched forward, she gazed or stared hard at me most of the time, obviously trying to get a give-away from my eyes, searching for signs of clever, treacherous policery, team-thinking, and betrayal. I had the idea she swung about in her opinions of me. At times, despite her suspicions, she might want to feel she and I had some sort of alliance because we were women, and because we had spoken together before Rendale and the others arrived. Possibly, she possessed no friends among the neighbours and sightseers who had gathered and, instead, fixed on me at her time of suffering. This made it twice today I had been picked out for particular contact: Jeremy Naunton Dince, or whatever his real name might be, and Alice Huddart. Maybe I should feel lucky, even honoured.

Instead, her attitude troubled me. I still felt sympathy but I was here as the police, and would have to do police things. I'd dropped into a situation where I must be detective first, then woman. I did not want Alice Huddart to rely on me and later complain I'd deceived her. There could be no female bonding. I owed her nothing. She must not count on me. She wore what I took to be her work clothes: grey, tailored trousers and a dark red cotton blouse, red, button earrings, perhaps garnets, black, half heel shoes; an outfit to proclaim competence. She had an unlit cigarette in her fingers and played with this skilfully like a magician, making it somersault back and forth across her hand. Dexterity, wittiness, the Bible, self-control – I got paid to observe, and I observed.

'You said Claude had been on a business trip. What business was he in?'

'They've asked me already.'

'*I* haven't.'

'You consider yourself independent of them?'

'I like to ask my own questions.'

'Yes, you do, don't you?'

'What business?' I said.

'Various. Oh, yes, various business activities.'

'Freelance?'

'An entrepreneur.'

'Buying and selling?' I said.

'That sort of thing.'

'Buying and selling what?'

'Various. One thing and the other. As it came.' She spoke wearily, as if she thought I would know Claude's commercial specialities from police gossip and asked only as a formality, or to annoy and humiliate her. 'Very various. So various he didn't really mention much about what he was doing this day or that. If they see something at a good price they think they can sell on they'll buy it – regardless of what it is. That's how the true entrepreneur operates. It's opportunistic, chancy, but sometimes profitable.'

Not enough for you to get a new car, though? I thought this – didn't say it. The car had become a tomb, the subject sensitive. Suppose I *had* asked I would have meant, did he stick to an old car to avoid conspicuous spending? If so, what did he want to hide – a grassing sideline, or something similar? Too hurtful now. Instead of focusing on the car, I asked, 'All the entrepreneuring – above board?'

'What did you say?' I heard that mixture of whisper and snarl again, and the words spoken very slowly.

My attempt at tact obviously hadn't worked. 'Legit?' I said.

'You don't care, do you?' Alice Huddart replied. 'Same style as Phaeton? I'm in a distressed state, you know. Your questions are getting oppressive. I could complain.'

'Sorry. Really, I am. But legit?'

'Right. I see your point. Who would I complain to? Phaeton. Or the other one. What use? You're all together. Of course legit. Would I have stayed with him if not?'

'Would you?'

She stopped playing acrobatics with the cigarette and lit it. A performance. She wouldn't be able to get an audience for this very often now that smoking in pubs and restaurants had been banned. She lifted the cigarette very slowly to her mouth and applied the lighter with a sweep of her right arm, then held it to the tobacco longer than was needed, like torching Joan of Arc, and making sure the pyre flames had good hold. Martyrdom. The drama, the ciggie art, made me wonder whether she knew Bette Davis' films, as well as *The Postman Always Rings Twice*. I felt pretty certain I'd seen old movies where Bette did significant moody lip and finger work with a cigarette.

Alice Huddart did not speak for a while. I had the crazy impression she wanted a cloud of smoke in front of her face because she was embarrassed by her next words. 'You're skilled,' she said eventually. 'I can't make out how much you know. Skilled at deadpan. Perhaps after all you're too low rank to be let in on much by your chums.'

'That does sound like me,' I said.

She took another long gaze at my face, another search for signs. I think she did not much care for what she saw. Or couldn't read properly what she saw. She gave a tiny shrug, drew mightily on the cigarette again, but didn't speak.

No, Alice Huddart was not my responsibility now, but I couldn't stop the queries coming, just the same. I reckoned I must be a natural detective. I couldn't switch off. 'Did Claude do some part-time work?' I said.

'Me, *I* do part-time. You're getting things mixed.'

'People in Claude's type of career often have a sideline.'

'Which type of career?' she said.

'The entrepreneur career you mentioned.'

'He did have several business outlets.'

'As an informant,' I replied.

'Yes, I know what you meant,' she said.

'How?'

'How what?'

'How did you know what I meant?'

'Yes, I knew.'

'Because you expected me to ask?'

'Why would I expect you to ask?' she replied.

'If you suspected or knew he *was* one. Or had been one. Did Mr Rendale or Chief Inspector Phaeton ask you about that? Sometimes a detective may have an informant he doesn't disclose to his/her superiors. It's against rules, but happens. Rendale and Phaeton might wonder if Claude did some whispering.'

'They asked about everything.'

'Informing would possibly put Claude in peril.'

'Yes, I heard they get peril, as you call it.'

'Oh, where?'

'Where what?'

'Where did you hear it?'

She smiled. 'No magic. No insider knowledge. I read the papers, don't I? Northern Ireland. Informants got killed there, didn't they? I don't know about carved.'

'And nearer home.'

'I expect so,' she said. 'It's a loathsome trade, isn't it?'

'Is it?'

'I suppose you people depend on grassing. But you know it's disgusting, just the same.'

'You're always telling me what I know.'

'I've told you I don't know what you know,' she said. 'It bothers me.'

'I'm looking at the chesterfield and the other things in this room. Beautiful,' I replied.

'Yes, I saw you looking. Making a mental inventory. You're asking where the money came from, are you?'

'Oh, you've got the part-time job, and then we have Claude's business efforts.'

'Right,' she said.

'Various.'

'Right. Yes, you are like Phaeton. As if I'm not entitled to a comfortable home.'

'So now and then Claude did show a profit, even if the big break wouldn't come?'

'Once in a while.'

'Which of the business activities was most successful?'

'Not any special one,' she replied.

'Various, I expect.'

'Right.'

'But speaking generally? Which . . . which ballpark?'

'I loathe jargon.'

'Did you help with the accounts? Anything like that? There *are* accounts, various accounts, are there?'

'Now here come your chieftains,' she replied. 'Get dutiful.'

Stuart Rendale and Phaeton entered the sitting room. 'Ah, you have some company, Alice,' Rendale said. 'I'm glad. Sharon can be very supportive.'

I watched the three of them, trying not to make it apparent that I watched them. I wanted to see how they behaved to one another. She'd said I could do deadpan, and I hoped she was right. There should be a degree in deadpannery. It would be more use to me in the police than Eng. Lit. A couple of Alice Huddart's remarks stayed word-perfect in my memory, or, at least, I thought word-perfect. 'It takes the spotlight off them, or him,' she'd said. And, 'It lands the blame elsewhere, doesn't it?' I'd tried to work out at the time what she meant, but possibly not hard enough, not doggedly enough. 'It takes the spotlight off them' had been about my early arrival on the Citroën death scene. She believed that was schemed. I'd asked her to say whom this took the investigative spotlight off. Answer: 'Them, or him. It's clever.' 'Them, or him.' I assumed 'them' meant Rendale and Phaeton together or one of them acting alone. I still assumed it meant Rendale and Phaeton together or one of them acting alone. If so, where did it take us? It took us to this: she thought Rendale and/or Phaeton were involved somehow in Claude's death and that I'd been instructed to get there soon after the discovery, so that they/he – whichever he it might be – could be told about the body in the Citroën as if they/he didn't already know of it. They/he would get no spotlight. This would have some fairly filthy implications about me, of course. It suggested, as she'd said, that I was in on the operation. *'We/I would like you to get over to the Huddart house at sparrow fart, Sharon, and come upon, as if by fluke, the annihilation and mutilation of Claude. OK? Give us a bell via Control when you've had a shufti. We/I will roll up looking startled and sorrowful.'*

Then: 'It lands the blame elsewhere, doesn't it?' Which blame? For Chaude's death, plainly. And what lands the blame elsewhere? What lands the blame elsewhere in her version would be the idea pursued by Rendale and/or Phaeton that the motive for Claude's death was sex – compare *The Postman Always Rings*

Twice. 'Elsewhere' she'd argue, equalled Alice and a so far unnamed lover. That left the obvious question: if elsewhere was not where the blame should go, where should it go? And the answer to this, in her view of things, ought to be Rendale and/or Phaeton.

So, yes, I watched the three of them. How would they treat one another – and, incidentally, how would they treat me, especially how would Alice treat me? Her script, as she might term it, had one very serious and very basic and very clear weakness. Clear to me, that is. And it would have been clear to Rendale and Phaeton also, if they'd known her suspicions. I really had arrived on the Huddart drive at that time by luck. Neither Rendale nor Phaeton had sent me, and not Rendale and Phaeton together, either. This start-point error in her narrative made me very sceptical about all her other theorizing. She might have had an appalling shock today. Perhaps I shouldn't expect her to analyse events accurately, coolly.

But, still, I watched. She'd said that Phaeton had already turned combative during a question session – Rendale, also, in his own smoother style. Neither of them repeated this now. They'd clearly decided to act considerate and respect the 'innocent until proved guilty' theme, although, according to Alice they thought her implicated in Claude's death. No, that wasn't the right way to put it: according to Alice they/he would make it *look* as if she were implicated in Claude's death, because this would conceal their/his own implication in Claude's death. Either way, the 'innocent until proved guilty' rule didn't really make much sense here – except that *I* might believe in it: DC Sharon Mayfield couldn't prove a speck against any of them.

'We must thank you, Alice, for your help at a very stressful time,' Rendale said.

'Absolutely,' Phaeton said.

She looked towards both men for two or three seconds each and gave a nod which could have meant anything, and was probably intended to mean anything – anything translatable as 'Fuck off'. After all, she would probably be thinking that one or other of these two, or both together, plus DC Sharon Mayfield, had created this very stressful time for her, so Rendale could stuff his thanks. She would also probably be thinking that one or other of these two, or both together, plus DC Sharon Mayfield, should be made to suffer for what had happened, but might not have much idea of how to bring this about. Perhaps she'd feel overwhelmed by the clutter of police bodies in this small room.

Alice stood up. 'Are you taking Claude now? I'd like to travel with him to . . . to wherever.'

Phaeton said, 'Oh, I'm not sure we—'

'Of course,' Rendale said. 'I'll have a car bring you back.'

FOUR

Dince, Jeremy Naunton – he's on my plate, isn't he? I owe him. I owe him, I owe him. It's a painful idea, damn painful, and it hangs around. Explanation: by keeping quiet about Dince – by making him 'mine', my secret contact – I became the only police officer who knew of him and what happened to him. That is, obviously, I knew what had happened to him *up to a point*, and only up to a point, a crucial, frightening point: the moment when those two accompanied him into the Audi. 'Accompanied' was a pleasantly neutral word, even chummy. Others less pleasant, less neutral, less chummy might apply: 'directed' him into the Audi; 'cajoled' him; even 'forced' him, perhaps. Those mickey-taking kids could have handed me guidance on that, but wouldn't.

The uncertainty gave me huge, long-lasting worries. Where did Dince go next? Where did they take him? Where was he now? In what condition? If I'd spoken about him to Phaeton and Stuart Rendale a full police search could have started to uncover these things – these things that might have followed the Audi kerbside urgent invitation to a ride. *Would* it have started, though? Why should they have ordered that kind of expensive, major trawl? After all, what I would have told them didn't sound much, did it? *A man came up to me on the Huddart drive and said he'd be in contact later. He claimed to have my address. I followed him on foot and he met two men from an Audi in Cinder Street. All three left in the car.* Certainty went no further than this, even if my nervy imagination did. So, they'd be riveted, would they? Rendale, in his polite fashion, might say, 'Really?' and turn to something else. Phaeton, blunter, might ask, 'So, what? You've managed a pick-up?'

In any case, because I'd stupidly, selfishly, made Dince 'mine, only mine' there'd definitely be no thorough, systematic trawl. If I wanted him found I must find him myself. How? I'd begun poorly. My questions to the children took me nowhere. Should

I have worked on them harder, given them a glimpse of that steeliness I thought I had? Steel? More like marshmallow. Was I sprinting to another collapse of morale? I'd thought I could mix team outlook with a slice of me-me-me individualism. This seemed out-and-out idiocy now. Had I just learned that police operations needed all-round, combined action, not solo stuff, not an *attempt* – an arrogant and clumsy attempt – at solo stuff? A private eye might do it all privately, like Marlowe in the *Big Sleep*. Not a police detective. But, God, Dince into the big sleep? Had I failed to stop him dropping off – dropping off the map?

I unearthed no data about him. He didn't have a record, or not under that name. The computer cross-referenced aliases and no Dince appeared among those, either. I fed in the fair hair, skinny body, age and absent dentistry and asked the machine to cough similars. Gamely, it produced a galaxy but none called Dince. At random and in despair I summoned a few pictures to the screen to match the names the computer *had* given, in case he was secretly a.k.a. Jones or Wainwright. These photographs couldn't help. I now knew a lot of male blond crooks in their twenties existed, who didn't eat enough, possibly because of poor teeth. The phone book and Directory Inquiries? Nothing listed. I'd realized that even to try was farcical, but I did. He seemed to have piled up some facts about myself, and I longed to reciprocate. Reasonable?

Anxiety hounded me. Possibly, I'd witnessed the criminal capture of a man, and God knew what the capture would lead to. It had not led to anything yet. No, no, I didn't mean that, couldn't say that. It had not led to anything discoverable yet, not on our ground. I went through all the latest incident summaries at headquarters looking for reports which might show Dince had been found somewhere. None. The age difference between those two from the Audi made me uneasy, one twenties, the other possibly forties. It seemed too big a gap for them to be pals of Dince. The Audi pair's styles didn't harmonize either – the older with an imperial beard, maybe a beret, and in a suit, the other long-haired and shirt-sleeved. But age and style wouldn't matter if they were simply parts of someone's workforce, colleagues, not friends. And their work? Getting Dince into the Audi as first move. Subsequently? Subsequently seemed well out of reach for me, so far. Out of reach for keeps?

When I say I searched for reports of Dince 'found', I mean found dead and perhaps disfigured, naturally. Naturally! Panic? Perhaps. But in my mind, unforgettably, I had the image of Claude Huddart spread over the wheel of the Citroën, and Claude Huddart's slashed face even more unforgettably. Maybe such abuse was the normal currency of this case. And, by talking to me the way he did, and promising more, had Dince made himself part of the case, and liable to draw on that grim currency? But, no, he had already been part of it. Otherwise, how did he know whatever it was he claimed to know, and how did he happen to be in that crowd around Claude Huddart and the Citroën? Did we have a situation where getting into cars could be fatal, notably Citroëns and Audis?

Clearly, the point about Jeremy Dince was not just that he might have landed in big danger: *Please, Jeremy, join us in the motor, do.* As well, he possibly knew something about how Claude Huddart came to be in the Citroën. I'd tried to write down accurately my conversation with Dince on the Huddart drive, so I could analyse it word by word. When I say I wrote it down, I don't mean in my notebook, of course. That would have made the conversation official. It hardly amounted to a conversation at all, and definitely not an official one. I'd noticed at the time the oddity of some of the phrasing and the biblical echoes – which, incidentally, Mrs Huddart could also produce.

But then the rest of Dince's words: 'I wanted to alert you,' for instance. This sounded like someone authoritative, purposeful, assured, in overall charge of the alarm siren, despite what he looked like. And kindly – as if he felt compelled to offer help. Then: 'I'd prefer not going to the summit – I mean, at this stage.' Another biblical echo – or anti-biblical echo? He didn't fancy looking like Moses, going to the summit of Sinai to bring down the commandments. Dince had had a nicely shaped plan. He saw nuances – the ways rank might affect response. He'd *prefer* – meaning he'd carefully thought all round the issue and even-tually decided on the low-level approach: the me approach, *at this stage,* which craftily left room for adjustment later, if neces-sary. So, where did this confidence and subtlety come from? I

had no information on that. On many matters I had no information. Most matters. This ought to be corrected. The other
major piece of information I lacked, of course, is how he knew
I'd be there, approachable in my low-level, non-summit role, on
the Huddart drive.

Dince had to be located. I was the one who had to locate him.
Of course. I'd already settled that. Nobody else knew about him.
Or nobody I was aware of, which, admittedly, could be different.
For a while I played around with the names he had given –
Dince, Jeremy, Naunton – in case they were a jumble of letters
which, reordered, would give his true identity: an anagram. People
did this sometimes when picking an alias, as though scared of
completely disowning their usual self. I can sympathize with a
fear of wipe-out. The self is all we really have, isn't it? Look
after it. Vary it, disguise it, but don't ever let it go. Or is that
utter, melodramatic wind? At any rate, I had no luck with Dince,
Jeremy, Naunton's letters rejigged. Jay Crondite Mennune did
not seem a goer.

Still very scared for him, I decided to take a drift around a
few of the city's drug-dealing bars and clubs. My thinking
went like this: I hoped, despite everything, that the car pick-
up had been nothing at all but a bit of comradeship, and that
by now Dince would be back to home territory, perhaps with
his couple of associates or more, despite the age and style
variations. These associates? The Audi pair plus, possibly, the
driver, unseen by me. And I assumed such places would be
Dince's scene because of his looks and clothes and, above all,
because of how Alice had spoken of Claude Huddart's career
– which seemed to connect in some way with Jeremy Naunton
Dince's.

Alice Huddart had referred briskly to 'business', as Claude's
occupation, but could not, would not, specify which branch of
business. That sort of coverall word often coded drug dealing –
not a code meant to fool anybody, just a sometimes jokey way
of dodging the crude, criminal job description, 'pusher'. Whether
big scale trading or disco trading or street corner trading – all
of it involved pushing, and was referred to by those doing it, or
connected with those doing it, as 'business'. They pinched the
respectable term from *The Godfather*: 'it's not personal, it's

business', a gangster would say to justify the latest garrotting. 'Business' – a very multi-purpose term:

(1) It might signify that all business was basically money-grabbing, exploitive, shady, ruthless, so why exclude the drugs division?

(2) Perhaps all crooks yearned somewhere deep down in themselves to become respectable and law-abiding, and therefore picked an honourable description for their illegal commerce.

(3) Did use of the word indicate self-mockery? It pretended to give acceptable status to a sector of flagrant villainy, but nobody actually did accept that status – because the villainy was so flagrant.

The other word favoured by Mrs Huddart – 'various', as in 'various business activities' – also served as a cosy, evasive, stick-on label for that kind of forbidden commerce. 'Various' meant its opposite, not various at all: drugs, drugs and drugs, though, in fact, the drugs could be various: weed, coke, crack, E., H. Alice Huddart would assume I knew what these standard terms signified – 'business' and 'various'.

Suppose Claude Huddart had been operating in this area. Suppose, also, Dince, Jeremy, Naunton had a link to him – a link strong enough to draw Dince to the Citroën and Claude's lying-in-state, his sprawling in a state on the Huddart drive. If Dince were involved with him like that, it seemed a logical guess he played in the same game, too. The Drug Squad might know Dince even though he had no convictions, but I didn't want to share things with them, at least not yet. Those 'barons' the taxi man had worriedly referred to – Sociable Ian Eric Linter, George (Gleeful) Mittle, Philip Otton: did Huddart have a business arrangement with one or more of them? Did Jeremy Dince? Very hazardous ground. I didn't need to be in Drugs to realize that much. These people looked after their 'businesses', and looked after them in various extreme ways that could terrify not just ageing taxi drivers.

Dince had claimed in his matter-of-fact manner that he knew how to find me, how to 'be in touch'. I felt rattled by this.

He obviously hadn't meant only that he'd discovered which nick I worked from. I'd actually offered him my home address, so any future meeting could be confidential. No need, he'd said – he already had it. If this were true, it showed he'd researched me *before* the unscheduled encounter on the Huddart drive, didn't it? Why? How? Well, perhaps the 'how' would not be difficult. He could have followed me home from work one day. I wouldn't have been watching for a tail, and he'd possibly got the address unobserved. But *why* did he want it? I'd been targeted, had I, earlier than Claude Huddart's death? What for? I had no answer, and nobody to ask, except myself – uselessly – or, naturally, Jeremy Naunton Dince. Another urgent reason to get to him, if he remained gettable to.

I drew myself a diagrammatic map featuring the four best known pusher pubs and clubs and tried to work out a visiting programme, depending on which I thought the most likely for Huddart and his companions to frequent; supposing that's what they were, and not avenging, competitive, warlike enemies. I'd scheme my prowl to culminate in this one and spend most of my time there. Perhaps I'd do quick stops at the others on the way. That brought risk: warning calls would go out from any one of them to the next if someone arrived on the premises who might be a touring plain clothes officer. Although these clubs fought one another for business, they'd generally unite against the police.

The drawing provided a crude way to picture the city, but roughly accurate, with the topmost point in the Gaston district. Near that topmost point on the right side of the figure, I drew a small square to represent the Pole Star club. About halfway down on the left and close to each other in the dockland area I placed two more squares for the Mikado Club and the Nag's Nostrils pub. Midway along the triangle's base I inserted another pub, the Clement, which stood on the borders of the Uphill and Montmerency estates. I put an M in the Pole Star square to signify that Gleeful George Mittle's dealers predominated there. For the Mikado and the Clement I put an L, standing for Linter. The Nag's Nostrils got Otton's O. Anyone seriously into the city's nightlife knew about this division of forces.

All these places allowed for blind-eyed drug selling but

appealed to different types of punters. It was a class thing, social class. Obviously, coke sniffed is the same up a prole or a bourgeois beak. The venues where people buy and use can be in very different categories, though. I'd been to three of the haunts, either working – that is, raids, mainly – or for fun, usually in a group. The two pubs attracted a wealthier, older, more decorous clientele than the clubs, and the dealing took place more or less discreetly. They both had wood panelling and polished brass fittings around the bars – that kind of wholesome, worthy, traditional English alehouse ambience. The Pole Star club? Pretty basic. A single story, shed-like building, its windows protected with heavy wire mesh, where the commerce went on with minimum secrecy: the crowd younger – average age not much above twenty-three – and noisier. The music noisy, too, and active until four a.m. I'd been there a few times way back as a party girl, but later in two big raids, part of uniformed support for the Drug Squad. Of course, once you'd done a raid it became dodgy to return one night as a paying customer. You had to hope the management would change – because of, for instance, jail – and that club regulars then and now were too knocked off to remember faces.

The Mikado. This one I thought might be a natural for Dince. Luckily, I'd never been there before in any capacity. As I heard it, the Mik attracted an unusually wide spectrum of patrons – across the board as to age, type of job, background, disposable cash. In a way, it defied my attempt to divide the dens by class. I'd make the Mikado my focus, with a short spell in the other three. That trio at the Audi – the trio I'd seen and had some tiny knowledge of – represented quite an age range and maybe a social range, too. Take the guy in the suit: I thought of imperial beards and berets as signs of bohemian and/or intellectual qualities. I'd guess on the basis of our chat – admittedly brief – Dince notably lacked these. On even less evidence, I'd guess the other, youngish man didn't match his chum. The cross-current Mik might suit them.

My objectives. Three:

(1) To comfort myself and kill off self-blame by discovering that Dince remained, in fact, OK and out with mates,

not lined up for, or already starring in, a Claude-
Huddart-type death scene somewhere.

(2) To encounter Dince before he could appear at the flat
and encounter me. This I recognized as markedly
illogical, since I had offered him my address. But I'd
felt I had control of arrangements then. Not now.

(3) To find out what Dince knew, or thought he knew, or
claimed to know about the Claude Huddart atrocity.

I couldn't be certain of an order of importance between (2) and
(3), but (1) was definitely (1). Pathetic, really. I'm a cop, not
the Salvation Army Missing Persons division.

No luck at the first three. So, I signed in and paid three
pounds for temporary membership at the Mik and waited. This
would be my own money, and likewise the taxi fares: the search
private, expenses non-reclaimable. So far, no Dince at the Mik
either, and no imperial beard or male brown hair, worn long.
I drifted about, looking, but not too obviously, I hoped. All
the time, I had to be aware that I might be identified as a
possible cop as soon as I entered the Mik, or either of the
other trading posts. Subliminal alarm bells would clang.
Anyone they didn't know, under sixty and not on sticks, they
would regard as a possible cop. Although I'd never been to
the Mik previously, some people are very quick to spot a plain
clothes officer. Not many women come to a club alone. The
management would guess police or tart and when they saw I
tried no pick-ups they'd ditch the short list and settle for detective. I noticed nobody tried to sell me stuff. They'd probably
fear an *agent prov* Drug Squad pounce. If somebody *did* try
to sell me stuff, I'd have to buy, as part of the charade. More
non-reclaimable expenses, and a waste: it was years since I'd
taken drugs myself.

Phone alerts might have gone out from the Clement, my first
stop on the circuit, to all other probable calling points, and anyone
who felt at all dubious would disappear. Might Dince feel
dubious? If the Clement gave a description of me and he somehow
heard it, Dince could possibly guess my mission – i.e., him, J.N.
Dince – and not wish his companions or anyone else to know
he had talked to the police. So, vamoose. I drank a bit, extricated

myself twice from some fairly nice, unslavering but determined chat-ups and kept an eye. Nobody fitted.

I realized, of course, that I might not be too safe in these special pleasure nests and the surrounding dockland streets and lanes. The fact I was a woman wouldn't make the hardest of drug gang folk any kinder: they'd accepted equality of the sexes years before official legislation, and slaughtered impartially. It would have been mad to start asking customers or staff if they knew someone called Jeremy Naunton Dince, and not just because this was probably an a.k.a. Although some clubs believed wholeheartedly in mucho blasto from their music systems, they believed likewise in total silence if anyone grew intrusive with questions. For me, this must be an eye job only and so far not a successful one.

I began to feel useless. It was eleven p.m., early for a club like the Mik, and I might need to wait for hours. For ever. The speculation that brought me here rested on hopelessly frail thinking, much influenced by the fact that the Mik seemed the best for me because I'd never been here previously. I began to wonder about some other, more direct way to find Dince. It struck me that the only real tie-up I had with him came via Claude and Alice Huddart. Dince had been at their house and seemed to know Claude, or at least *about* Claude. I'd been there by luck only, but I doubted that he was. Possibly he knew Alice, too. Perhaps she would point me towards him. I'd get a cab up to where she lived and, if lights still showed, I'd call in. If not, I would visit tomorrow. She might be friendly, seeing me alone: girl to girl again. I'd be able to come back to the Mik later. I had overnight membership.

As I prepared to leave, a very cheerful grandfather-type grappled with me, evidently keen I should stay and help make his night a time to remember and cherish, against his looming Eventide Home future. He wore an excellent flame-coloured toupee, with leather, dude-ranch trousers, holstered belt and long-tasselled waistcoat. He had snorted, swallowed or mainlined something energizing which furled his lips back like minor breakers on a beach, and probably reduced his charm: I didn't know, because I'd never seen his lips unfurled. At any rate, his charm registered low. I gave him an elbow in the chest, definitely not hard enough to break even old ribs. From kindness I spoke quickly and intimately to him of a rain check as he staggered a couple of steps towards spilled drink pools, his false hair brilliantly secure. He regained stability and dragooned the lips into a kindly smile. 'I'll see you again soon, babe,' he said, the accent sort of Princeton cowboy.

'Will you, pardner?'

'Oh, bet on it.'

'Enjoy the rest of the rodeo.'

'Oh, yeah, I'll meet up with you again very soon.'

The daft assurance bothered me. Probably, it had been produced by a formidable blend of booze, skunk and Lone Ranger dreams, but it also sounded as if he had some definite, reliable scheme that would bring us together again. Did I know him? Surely, I'd remember someone who looked like that. But perhaps he had a bulging wardrobe of different costumes.

There was nothing on the Huddart drive now. Their Citroën would have been taken in for close examination once the body was removed. But I mustn't think of it like that – 'the body'. As Alice Huddart had said, it made Claude sound like an article. Make it: 'once Claude was removed'. I passed in the taxi. Two ground-floor rooms still showed lights behind the curtains and the stairs and landing light also seemed to be on, reaching weakly through an open door into one of the bedrooms. Apparently, Alice Huddart had not gone to bed yet, perhaps could not face it – the inactivity and quiet and the plentiful, lonely time in bed to think about what had happened. That might be true, even if she'd helped bring about what had happened.

I left the taxi a hundred yards further on and began to walk back, rehearsing what I would say. Maybe she had seen and recognized Dince among the crowd around the Citroën that morning and would be able to describe his role in things, perhaps even honestly. Above all, I wanted her to tell me where he lived, so I could go there and check he was intact, then talk to him. Or, rather, listen to him. But I had to realize there could be reasons she wouldn't *want* me to find him. She might brick-wall, lie or play dumb. I had the idea she'd be gifted at playing dumb. Talking to me and to Rendale and Phaeton she seemed to have given only what she wanted to give. She'd tried to strangle my inquisitiveness with those meaningless, fuck-off words about Claude's commercial life, 'business' and 'various'.

I was about a couple of houses away and slowing my pace a little when I saw a sudden extra bar of light shine out from downstairs on to the front garden and guessed that the Huddart front door had been opened. I needed a hedge or two then, but this was an unpartitioned estate with landscaping ambitions, and not designed to give stalkers cover. At once I stepped into a neighbouring front garden and lay face down on the lawn like a soldier under fire: damp, though nothing fatal, and I detected no dog mess actually under me or near my nostrils. So, what was I supposed to be – a visitor or a snoop? I'd actually come here hoping to make a call on Alice Huddart. Why didn't I do it, then? I'd got my roles jumbled again. The segment of extra light, the open door, had shocked and confused me. I came to think I could be shocked and confused too easily.

If I held my head up a few inches I could watch the driveway from the Huddart front door to the street. Nobody appeared on it, though, going to or from the house. A small porch shielded the actual door from my sight, and possibly Alice Huddart had come into the hallway, about to leave. For where, so late? Or was she expecting someone? It would be late for that, too. And then I wondered, My God, was she expecting *me*? Had she read yours truly so well when we spoke that she could sense where my impulses and aims would lead? The open door flashed a signal, a welcome? Crazy. But the notion chilled me for a second, more than the wet grass. I've always loathed the idea that anyone could look into me, guess at my moves, anticipate me. That was like being a prisoner. It meant you'd lost some selfhood. Did Alice, as well as that ancient boulevardier in the Mik, know some scenario where I figured, but which I stayed ignorant of?

Or the explanation could be simpler, more banal, couldn't it? Much simpler. Had she seen the taxi cruise past? Not much traffic moved about the estate at this hour and the sound could have made her curious. She might be on the alert for *any* sounds tonight. The house had become a fulcrum of some sort, some monstrous sort. Had she watched me quit the taxi and creep back towards the house on foot? Did she know I lay stretched out here, peeping? That light on the stairs: she might have been in one of the dark front bedrooms watching. If you wanted to do some surveillance, the first lesson said, stay in shadow. I did not see or hear anything more and the hall light still reached out, edging its thin, yellow beam halfway along the driveway.

I remained still for another couple of minutes and then switched tactics. Carefully I picked myself up and stepped very slowly out from the front garden and back on to the pavement. I calculated that from there I should be able to look around the side of the porch and see the open door. If she spotted me it would be no disaster. She might know I waited nearby, anyway. And, even if not, I had come to call on her, hadn't I, and so here I was? All right, it would ensure I lost any chance of seeing where she might go, or who might call on her, but I'd begun to question whether she meant to leave the house, and question whether anyone might visit – anyone else, that is.

After a couple of steps, I paused. Now, I had a straight view to the door. As I'd thought, it stood ajar and I could make out Alice Huddart in the hallway behind, apparently gazing ahead, not in my direction. She had on a dressing gown, blue and long. She would not be going out. I crouched a little and gazed myself. Mrs Huddart's head and features were not completely clear to me because the light came from behind her, but I saw suddenly that she had begun to weep; weep, though, without any sound, without any movement in her face, except where the tears rolled. Her body, too, stayed utterly still. I realized then that she was staring not down the illuminated stretch of driveway but towards the shadowed spot where the Citroën had been, with Claude aboard – Claude's body. Sorrow could sometimes take a while to strike fully. Perhaps only at this moment had she begun to feel the loss, alone in the house: there seemed to be no children.

More likely she regarded crying – *her* crying, anyway – as a private expression only, certainly not to be given in to when the pigs were encamped on the property, staring, nosing, hatching their black theories. For a moment I felt ashamed now to be staring, nosing, hatching my black theories. That's what detectives did, though. Had she really loved Claude, then, and missed him unbearably now, longed for him, even though he had been that ramshackle dreamer and towering pipsqueak, in her words?

Perhaps Alice's love was big enough to embrace pipsqueaks and transform one of them into a prized, desired partner. Love could do such things, I knew. Hadn't we studied a poem called *Love's Alchemy* at school or university? Love could transform character-dross. That was the message. Maybe we all possessed pipsqueak, dreamer qualities and worse, and perhaps we searched for someone who would note these qualities and see them as assets – see them, maybe, as modesty and optimism and imaginativeness.

I decided I could not barge in on Alice tonight with questions and disclosures and false mateyness. No, not even for the sake of Dince's safety. Who said I could do much about that, anyway? I dreaded now that she would discover me, a spy to her furtive mourning, or whatever it was, and I pulled back as gingerly as when I'd advanced from my place on the lawn. I returned there and folded down on to it again, head low. This slab of grass had become a career aid. For possibly two or three seconds then, while flat and breathing only the wholesome smell of domesticated soil, I silently wept, also. It must be reaction to the surprise and sadness in seeing her apparently break after the control she had shown earlier: control and fight. But I soon put a stop to my sloppy sobbing.

I did more. I gradually came back to my cynical thinking, my cop thinking: had she seen me, knew I watched, and decided to put on a performance? She thought Rendale and/or Phaeton suspected she must be involved in the death, for sexual motives: that version of *The Postman Always Rings Twice* she'd gone on about. Did she intend her show of affection and grief now for Claude to counter that? I felt half disgusted with myself for the harsh interpretation of her doorstep tears. Half. I could not get rid of it. I stayed prone for about another five minutes. Then, the light on her path began to shrink as the door slowly, perhaps hesitantly, closed, as if she did not want to end that contact with the spot on the drive. I heard the catch engage and soon after a bolt was pushed across. I could stand now. I walked into the next street and mobiled for a taxi. I'd go home. I didn't feel up to the Mikado. Had my old chum in the wig assumed I'd return? Was that what he meant about our next, predestined rendezvous? He'd have to learn that his Wild West intuition could come a cropper once in a while. I directed the taxi past the Huddart house. It looked dark downstairs but a bedroom light had been switched on and curtains were drawn. I hoped she had been able to unload a fraction of her agony in the clandestine vigil – or whatever it was – and that she would sleep.

At home, I eventually slept myself – not by myself, though it might just as well have been that. I am living and loving these days and nights with the only lad I would want to be living and loving with these days and nights, but whose patience with the requirements of my job can run out now and then. Now, I suppose it is understandable. But I did not want to understand it. Why the hell should I? He had come off shift at eleven o'clock and was watching American baseball on television, waiting for me to return. And now I'd returned. So, Luke, get grateful. Or maybe not. Before bed I told him about my little profitless expedition around the clubs, pubs and other bright centres. He asked who'd ordered that and I said it was something I'd thought up myself – always the best kind of detective assignment. He frowned. Although Luke is a cop, too, and knows how an investigation can suck one into all sorts of different settings at all sorts of times, it doesn't mean he has to like everything I do. He *detests* some of the things I do. It was one of the reasons – the main one – why I didn't want Dince calling unscheduled at the flat. Scheduled might have been just about OK with Luke as I'd have charge of the arrangement then. Not if Dince simply showed up when he felt like it. Luke would object to being at his disposal. I saw Luke did not think much of my going alone and unnecessarily into those spots tonight. It was the kind of risk he might take himself. Luke didn't live by the book. Just the same, he preferred it if *I* did things by the book. Of course, his caring meant well, and could be a right holy, patronizing, fucking drag.

I'd brushed myself down pretty thoroughly after that sojourn on the Huddart neighbours' lawn, but some stains and dampish patches showed on my jacket and tights and I saw him give me a long, all-over look. In fact, I started to tell him about the late trip up to the Huddart house, would have given him the whole lawn saga, but he turned away, said he was going to bed. I could not be bothered sticking with it as a topic, and trying to get him intrigued. I might have sounded dull after the baseball. If he did

not want to listen, OK. Sometimes Luke could be damn moody
and sullen. So, I'd been out around the town. So, I looked a bit
messed about. What the hell did he think I'd been doing?
Whatever it was – that phrase was busy tonight – whatever it
was, well, whatever it was he could go on thinking it, or not
thinking it but sleeping on it.

When I went into the bedroom he was blotto, real or pretend.
I undressed and joined him, no body contact, though: that sad,
comical procedure where two near-naked people between the
same sheets are at a greater distance than if they passed on opposite sides of the street and with all their gear on. You'll know
the bit about needing one's space, or, actually *not* needing it,
and really needing something else, but having to act as if space
and space only is what one must have for now. There had been
other occasions like this. They passed. Relationships are uneven
and complex. Mrs Huddart had loved someone she saw at times
as a pipsqueak. And still loved him. By morning Luke would
probably have come round to admitting – admitting again – that
in my sort of work, done in my sort of way, there could be
unusual episodes. Sometimes, I thought it might be a mistake
for two cops to live together. Or, rather, I thought it might be a
mistake for a uniformed cop like Luke and a detective cop like
me to live together. When I say 'like me' I mean a detective
liable to act irrationally and/or stupidly now and then, not just
detectives as species. Occasionally, I thought that when it came
to Luke and me there could be more differences than overlaps.
But these differences did usually evaporate, and quickly. I guessed
that by breakfast things would be fine again. Perhaps before
breakfast. Some of our best sex was morning sex. Shifts dictated
adjustments.

It did not happen this morning, though. At just after seven
a.m. Luke answered a call on the bedside phone, then pushed
the receiver at me. It was done in the surly style of last night. I
was three-quarters out for the count but took it. 'Mayfield,' I
said.

'Who answered?'

'Who's speaking?' I replied, if that was a reply. Of course,
I'd recognized the voice immediately, despite my doziness. I
expected it.

'Was that the boyfriend? I know about him. Luke, is it? Also fuzz. Twenty-six, two years' more service than you, one point nine metres tall, eighty-two kilograms.'

'Is this Jeremy Naunton Dince?' I asked.

'Approximately. But I'd rather not have my name blurted like that when there's someone else close and listening. Very close. And an officer.'

'*Is* that your name?

'It'll do.'

'If it's not, why worry when it gets blurted?'

'All three names – like someone reading a charge sheet.'

'Do you know about them?'

'What?'

'Charge sheets. You told me the three names yourself.'

'Look, forget it, will you?'

'What?'

'I'm ringing to tell you to forget it.'

'What?'

'Ditch the personal efforts on this thing.'

'Which thing?'

'Don't play thick. The whole Huddart thing.'

'You were going to talk to me.'

'I *am* talking to you. Ditch it.'

'That isn't what you were going to say.'

'Isn't it?'

'You know it isn't.'

'I'm saying it now.'

'Are you all right?' I asked.

'All right?'

'Safe.'

'Of course.'

'Are you being . . .? You're being told to say this? I saw you when those two—'

'I know you saw me. Naturally I know you saw me.'

'Where are they? They're listening? On extensions? Should I say that? Well, I've said it. Have you, Jeremy Naunton Dince, been . . . are you hurt?'

'Just leave it, right? Let you masters deal with it their way. Better for your prospects, anyway.'

'Which prospects?'

'Generally. Life. Promotion. Generally. You didn't get on the accelerated promotion course for graduates because of pushiness at the interviews, as I understand it. Slim it down. And then poking around all those places last night. It's not – it's not convenient.'

'Who says?' I thought I caught for a second the sound of breathing that might not be his. 'Is there someone on an extension? Or alongside? It's a phone box call, is it?'

'So, ditch it?' he said. 'Please. Now, please?' He sounded abject, terrified, suddenly no longer cocky and know-all.

'Who said I'd missed the accelerated prom course because of pushiness? How do you know that?' But he'd put the phone down. I did 1471, of course and, of course, no trace. There might be other ways of tracking it, but only official ways, and I still wanted to dodge those.

Luke would be furious to know somebody could research my career so thoroughly that he'd discovered I went for the accelerated promotion course and flunked. I didn't much like it myself. Failed for pushiness? They didn't tell you why you'd been rejected, but I'd always assumed it was because I hadn't been pushy *enough*. Those days, I'd still been into diffidence. I've worked on correcting that since, and feel I'm improving. 'One of my contacts,' I told Luke, as if I had a million. 'I asked him to call me here if he had anything special. They're more at ease not going through the nick's switchboard. These people always fear they're being bugged. He's someone who could have been very useful. I worry about him. Nannyish? I'm not sure. In these circumstances I do believe anyone would be worried about him. You'll ask, which circumstances?' I paused, in case Luke did. He didn't. 'He's got some insights,' I said. 'Or he tells me he's got some, behaves as if he has some. And that could be as dangerous as *really* having them. I'm finding it almost impossible to evaluate him. You'll say, If he's got something to tell you and you've spoken before, plus this call today, why doesn't he say it? Sorry, I can't answer that one. As yet.'

But Luke was asleep again, or again pretending to be. Yes, his attitude remained understandable, perhaps – someone disrupting our lie-in and our privacy and our chance to make up

for the war stances of last night. But I still did not want to understand. 'He could be in a damn tough situation, Luke,' I said. 'I
mean, tough. Did you hear I got pulled into that body-in-the-car
case? I thought this contact might have told me the dead man
had been a tout. And, if so, it could have given some pointers
to who'd want to silence him – see what I mean? Who could
his grassing cause trouble to? That's why I say pointers. And
I'd have had them to myself. This would be something, wouldn't
it?' I was gabbling a bit, zigzagging about on wordage, longing
for a response, longing for Luke to share my excitement.

He slept on, or seemed to. So stuff him. Or, in point of fact,
not.

FIVE

I did not recognize him straight off. It was the strangeness of his clothes. No, for God's sake – not the strangeness – the *non*-strangeness. Partly, too, because of the different setting – a police station! And partly, again, because the huge bouquet of roses he held obscured the lower half of his face. He was magnificently dressed now in a traditional double breasted navy-to-black suit with a heavy chalk pinstripe. This outfit could have been built at any time in the last hundred years. It would always and never be in fashion. Secured with massive black, horn buttons, the jacket hinted that by wrapping itself so splendidly around the wearer it would confer on him some of its own gorgeous, muted, freakish timelessness. This suit spoke for Britain, and in a fine, fruity accent. This suit brilliantly testified to enduring values and repeated victories over moth.

His shirt was unbeatably white, the collar dashingly wide-cut, and his blue, silver and amber tie looked like real Bond Street silk and about seventy-five pounds' worth, or possibly three for the price of two, bringing it down to almost a giveaway. The suit could be a stockbroker's chosen gear or brewery chairman's or juke box manufacturer's. He wore a navy-to-black trilby very straight and didn't take it off even when I approached and, with a swirl of his arms, signifying comic gallantry of some past, very worthwhile epoch, he handed me the bouquet. The fact that he kept his hat on should have helped me identify him, but I was slow.

'Oh, don't, don't tell me you have a down on roses, dear lady,' he said. 'I know some women do. Roses they see as hackneyed, trite.'

Did I have a big frown on, concentrating?

'Are you familiar with that sharp little Dorothy Parker poem, *One Perfect Rose*?' he said. He lowered the bouquet to give the rendering a clear field. His accent went New York educated,

and softened womanishly. '"A single flow'r he sent me, since
we met." But the solitary perfect rose was all he sent her, and
she'd have preferred a limo,' he paraphrased. 'Then, again,'
he continued, 'some see roses as wreath-like, funereal.'

'They're lovely,' I said. 'But—'

'But I shouldn't? Oh, indeed, I *should*. My behaviour last
night – outrageous. Indeed, near abusive.' But he sounded half
proud of it.

Then I knew. The trilby fixed in place allowed the wig a better
chance of looking less like a wig. His complexion should have
given me the signal: that writ-like pallor and dryness lit up
here and there by jam-packed clusters of vermilion broken veins.
We were talking in the foyer at headquarters. Cornelius Wilkes
running reception, watched and smirked, almost giggling. He had
rung up and left a message on the answer phone to say a gentleman
'with generous floral tribute' wanted to see Detective Constable
Sharon Mayfield, and could I come down as soon as I was free?
The tape gave the time and forty minutes had gone before I heard it.

'He's over in the waiting room and refuses to leave the
generous floral tribute, but says he has to deliver it in person
to the lady, meaning you, Sharon. The gentleman provides no
name but looks loaded, not very young, and well fed on all
kinds of commodities.'

I had been tied up in a meeting on the Huddart case chaired
by Stuart Rendale. I listened to the tape, then went to the waiting
room.

Now, I said, 'Well, this is remarkable, I'll admit. At the Mikado
you promised you'd—'

'Find you?'

'That we'd meet again soon. And, now, here—'

'Oh, that was the night's intake blah-blahing. I tend to get
oracular. But I needn't tell you. It's harmless.'

'Impressive.'

'Total fantasizing on my part. However, one can do a little
amateur detective work one's self, you know.' He smiled. His
lips looked normal at the moment, not pulled back as they had
been when he appeared as the junkie, piss-artist, uptown cowboy
last night. And, yes, laid out in that ordinary, mouth-framing,
lippy way of lips they did strike me as less ghastly.

'And my name,' I said. 'You have that.'

'Quite.'

'I'm getting used to people whose names I don't know knowing mine.'

'That's the trouble with celebrity.' His voice was big, gushingly affable, hugely upper-crust, at least as hugely upper-crust as the suit. His voice had not been like this at the club: more nasal and US Atlantic coast, though different again for the line of poetry – feminized but tinny and with an edge. He must adjust it to whatever outfit he had on or whatever the occasion. Perhaps this amounted to a costume now, the suit and gorgeous tie. It tallied with today's role. Possibly he kept the venerable suit and so on for police station visits. What was his natural gear like, and his real tone?

As a matter of fact, he lowered his voice suddenly and became purposeful, confidential. The change astonished me. For these couple of seconds he ceased to be the rather goofy, beautifully mannered tailor's triumph with three dozen roses, and became formidable. His face tightened up and his jawline hardened. His eyes stayed matey and vivid, but looked commanding, too. You could see how he might have earned or bullied or tricked his way into a suit like that, as well as the expensive bronco clobber and a stay-on-in-hurricanes toupee. Who paid him, though, and for what?

'I expect you've been talking about Claude Huddart,' he said.

'When?'

'While I waited here.'

'I'm sorry I was so long.'

'It *was* Huddart? A case conference, I believe it would be called.'

'A routine meeting.'

'Right. But you're involved in the Huddart matter?'

'Are you concerned with that in some way?'

'I like to keep up to speed on such things.'

The modern moment of slang – 'up to speed' – seemed strange coming from this venerable suit. 'Such things as which?' I said.

'Yes. I feel it as . . . well, almost as a duty.'

'A duty to whom?'

'To oneself, but a social duty, also.'

'In what sense a social duty?'

'Well, a social sense.'

'You knew him?'

'Could we get out of this building briefly?' he replied. It was almost down to a whisper. 'Probably best.' Then, at once, he reverted to his loud friendliness for Cornelius to hear: 'Deserved all I got last night, certainly. No injuries – not physical at least. To my dignity, yes, such as it was and is. Oh, yes, indeed. But wasn't I asking for it? My, I could have faced arrest, you being who you are, a veritable officer.'

'There's a coffee shop across the street,' I said quietly. 'I'll come over in five minutes, when I've put the flowers in a vase.' Then I switched on some volume and good nature, too. 'I think everyone was a bit . . . a bit relaxed last night.'

'Kind of you to be so understanding. Grand of you to accept my apologies.' He held out his right hand, still in a superior leather glove, and shook mine. Again his voice sank, but managed full, snarling rancour all the same on the piled up sounds: 'Just junk the fucking rubbish bunch of rubbish roses if you like. Put them in the shredder? It's a rough way with Mother Nature but Mother Nature has worse done to her. Think of elephant slaughter for tusk ivory and raids on rare birds' nests.'

'I do, I do.'

'The roses were my cover. That's what you call it in the police game, cover?' He turned and walked out of the building. For that age he seemed good on his pins, though he'd staggered for a moment when I handed him off in the Mik. But, then, he'd been well juiced and/or skunked there.

'Where did you find him, Sharon?' Cornelius asked. 'Golden Oldies night? And does Luke know you have such a dapper, generous chum? That fiery hair under the hat – a rug? Or shouldn't I ask?'

'No, perhaps you shouldn't.' I took the flowers up to the Ladies and stood them in a washbasin. Actually, I loathe all cut flowers, not just roses. They look so damn pleased with themselves and idiotically serene, the petals smug, and snugly layered, like knowing this was just how they had to be and feeling OK with it. Then I went down the emergency stairs and left the building at the side, avoiding Reception.

In the coffee shop we sat with espressos at a table away from the window. He spoke quietly again. He still had the boardroom accent, but the words came in spurts, as if he felt baffled by the topics and nervous, a few of his sentences verbless, like sporadic, feeble jabs at sense. 'To speak true, Sharon, no trouble at all in tracing you or in finding your name. They were handed to me.'

'I don't think I like this.' No.

'Information about you very available.'

'From?' I could do verbless myself.

'So, perhaps after all I was right to sense and blurt we'd re-encounter. Fated. I didn't know the details of how it would happen, the method, that's all. As a matter of fact, I didn't feel altogether comfortable about . . . No, not comfortable at all. Why I'm here.'

'Comfortable about what?'

'Too easy.

'What?'

'Getting the facts on you. Yes, uncomfortable.'

'But you *wanted* the facts – to make your prediction work.'

'Uncomfortable. Yes, why I'm here. The roses – no part of it. Not in the least. Obviously.'

'I appreciate the gesture, anyway.'

He pursed the lips a couple of times. This signalled hesitation. He seemed unsure about whether to say the next bit. 'People came looking for you at the club last night, just after you'd left.' He did another pursing. 'Look, I recognize this is tricky territory. I do the buffoon act, but I see at least some of what's what.'

'What *is* what?'

'Right.'

'When you say tricky, tricky how?'

'My impression was you came to the Mik looking for someone, or more than one, and then someone, or more than one, show up at the club looking for *you*,' he said. 'This was bound to intrigue me. The sort of circularity. Plus, I learn you have been scouring other places, too.'

'Who from?'

'Who from what?'

'Whom did you learn it from, suppose it's correct?'

'Patently, I have to ask myself, am I barging into something I don't comprehend?'

Well, yes, you might be. But I didn't comprehend it, either. I left both thoughts unsaid. 'How many people?'

'In which respect?'

'How many people supposedly looking for me?'

'How many would you expect?'

'Why would I expect any at all?'

'I don't know. That's what I meant about barging into something I don't comprehend.' But he stuck his old, multi-tinted face a further six inches towards me, still all tightened up and brave to indicate he would barge in anyway.

'How many?'

'For instance, as starters, I don't understand what you were doing in the Mikado. Only one sort of woman goes to a club on her own – not your sort. But, some kind of police operation? You had a rendezvous with these people?'

'Which?'

'The people who came looking for you. You'd grown tired of waiting? Or some other priority? If you're on that Huddart matter there'll be lots of aspects for you to get to handle. *Is* it the Huddart matter?'

'Go over it for me, will you? Tell me how it happened, stage by stage.'

'That's how you're trained, isn't it?'

'Which?'

'Stage by stage. The sequence.'

'How do you know about the training?'

'Or possibly there'd been some phoning,' he replied. 'A customer in the Mik sees you, perhaps recognizes you, and makes calls to people he knows will be interested. Or she. They arrive.'

'Which customer in the Mik?'

'Or the manageress.'

'You?'

'You're very distinctive. It would be easy to give a description of you.'

'So, they arrive. Three? Four?'

'Ah, I thought so.'

'What?'

'You're ahead of me. That's unnerving, a bit. It's possible I'm telling you things you already know.'

'So it *is* three or four?'

'Three.'

Damn. Of course, I wanted it to be four. Badly wanted it to be four: Dince, the two who'd intercepted him near the Audi, and their driver. The full crew. So, who was missing? Dince? Oh, God. 'Right, they arrive. Together? You can describe them – give me their descriptions?'

'They're looking for someone. It's obvious – staring about. As ever, the club lighting is low, the place is crowded. A search will need time. They split up, take a section of the Mik each.'

'The club is busy, people arriving all the time, but it sounds as if you watched these three from the start. Why? You recognized them? One or two of them? All?'

'They seemed intent, not just there for a night out.'

'That was enough to grab you?'

'On a mission of some sort,' he replied.

'You're sure you didn't recognize one or more of them?'

'Somehow, I definitely felt they'd been summoned.'

'Somehow, definitely? Is that gibberish?'

'It happened somehow – I can't account for it – but I definitely did feel it.'

'One of them thin, fair-haired, mid twenties, awful teeth?'

'I didn't see teeth.'

'But the rest of it?'

'Yes, more or less like that.'

'How do you mean, more or less?'

'Yes, more or less.'

'It's important. I really need to have one of them properly identified. The others – also important, but secondary.'

'Important, why?' he said.

'And one older – forties? A bit of beard?'

'They're not rough – not shoving people out of the way so they can do their trawl. But . . . intent. Yes, a mission. Somehow,

this became plain. Somehow definitely. And then I think one of
them must have talked to Ursula behind the bar, asked about
you. They'd do a description. As I said, easy enough. And she
would probably mention our little moment of flagrant, spectacular contact. Yes, let's put it thuswise, shall we – me getting
absurdly, antiquely familiar, you retaliating with the bionic
elbow.'

'Did you hear this?'

'What?'

'The conversation with Ursula?'

'It must have happened.'

'So, you didn't hear it? See it?

'I'm not hard to find, because of the fancy gear and so on,'
he replied. 'After the chat with Ursula, a pair of them approach
me – the beard and another one.'

'Which?'

'They ask where the lady cop had gone – their phrase, "the
lady cop" – and wanted to know had I been acquainted with
Detective Constable Sharon Mayfield for very long? They meant,
had I known her long enough for a grope to be treated by her
as reasonably all right, playful, even though she'd pushed me
off, playfully pushed me off. They were civil enough, but I had
the impression . . . the impression they were serious. Very. I could
act a bit confused, of course. It's a way to dodge out of things,
defuse things. The buffoon. But I wasn't so far gone I failed to
register what went on. Never am I that far gone, however it might
look.'

'I'm sure.'

'So, you'll say, if I'm not farthest gone, only far gone, why
would I make an unforgivable sortie at your body, me being my
age? Was it a sane thing to do, or just a dopey lunge from a
crumbling drunk?'

'Funny things happen in clubs. Tits unsettle some.'

'Well, yes. And at the Mikado, and in fact, at all the spots in
the happy triangle, as it's called, one would be very foolish to
swamp one's brain altogether. These can be perilous realms.' He
chuckled. His face relaxed and he drew back again in his chair.
'Some of my family who found out about my little excursions
somehow, refer to them as "slumming". Somehow they found

out, and they definitely refer to them as "slumming". More "somehow definitely".'

'Where *are* your family, then?'

'I regard "slumming" as a harsh and snobbish term. And one meets plenty of professional folk, even above that, out looking for comfort and excitement at these venues. But, then, I suppose *they* could be said to be slumming, too. So, some truth in it, maybe. Whether there is or isn't I don't let myself tumble too far. I tend to exaggerate, play a role as a merry old has-been in quaint clothes and on a super high. I'm usually on a high, but not a super high. Not helpless. This way, I remain safe – accepted and safe. As yet.' He took a small, self-congratulatory sip from his cup. 'I felt I owed you something, you see.'

'The roses. Really not necessary.'

'Roses and what one might call insights. These add up to more than the flowers.' He nodded a few times. Then his face grew agonized. 'I was obnoxious, typically obnoxious.'

'Not at all.' His grand politesse became infectious: I felt I should let this one-time cow-punch say what he had to say at his own pace. I would have loved to ask again now, straight out, and persistent, whether these people who'd quizzed him at the Mikado were strangers to him. I would have liked to ask him – perhaps straight out, perhaps with deviousness and disguise – who he truly was and what. Whom did he belong to? But I waited.

He said, 'Certain changes.'

'Yes?'

'Oh, indeed.'

'Changes of what sort?'

'Systemic.' The jargon came easily from him, as if he used it in normal chit-chat every day. People owning a suit like his probably *would* be familiar with such lumpy, ugly terms: because their clothes were beautiful it didn't follow their vocabulary would be. The word 'systemic' could be heard a lot lately, anyway. When the government made some super blunder they'd say in defence that the fault was not 'systemtic' only catastrophic.

'Which system?' I said.

'You know of Claude Huddart's death? Of course you do. A meeting about it while I waited with the roses.'

'Everybody has heard of it. Big media coverage, as is to be expected.'

'And you know about the disgusting shiv work on his features? But, again, of course you do! Aren't you a detective?'

'How do *you* know about it?' I said.

'The media, as you say. How could one *not* know?'

'And only from the media?'

'How else?'

'Have the media said anything about the carving of his face?'

'Oh, they haven't?'

'I don't think we'd tell them something like that,' I said. 'Or not at once.'

'Oh, I wonder how I would know of it, then?' He did another lip purse while he explored this mystery. It didn't seem to worry him too much that he'd shown special knowledge. 'But wouldn't there have been a crowd of neighbours around the car?'

'Were there?'

'People observe, don't they? Something like that – the disfigurement – they can't miss it. This is someone in a car and, as I gather, stuck in the car for a long while. All those windows – car windows, house windows. There'll be gossip about. People will mention the mutilation. It adds impact to the tale.'

'Where would you pick up the gossip?'

'A general buzz.'

'There is?'

'It's such a shocking case.'

Evidently, he didn't intend getting specific. I left the topic. We both turned to our coffees. After a while I said, 'Which changes are you talking about?'

'Systemic.'

'Fundamental, then?'

'You know about them?'

'These changes are tied up with what happened to Huddart?'

'You *are* on that then?' he replied.

'Everyone wants to help on a case like this.'

'Which part of it are you concerned with?'

'The top people will run the Huddart inquiry,' I said. 'Mr Rendale and Mr Phaeton.'

'When I say changes, I mean business changes.'

'Do you mean business as in . . .?'

'The special powdery meaning of business, yes.'

'So, systemic changes in the way the drugs trade here operates?'

'These systems are quite complex and sophisticated.'

'How do you know about them?' This was a bit head-on. I'd been going to let him get to things at his special pace, if he ever did. I'd become restless.

He said, 'I'm interested, you see, when things like this are in prospect. I have to consider how such changes might . . . Well, they could have some bearing on me personally.'

'In case you can't get your stuff regularly?' I said.

He frowned, evidently finding the words distressingly crude. My courtesy had begun to fade a bit. Espresso did not smooth out impatience the way alcohol could. I didn't want to sit here too long in a cafe with this relic, talking so earnestly. People might think we were lovers. God!

'Yes, Huddart was probably caught up in it, somehow,' he said. 'I feel sure of that.'

'In the systemic changes? This has not been in the media, either,' I said.

'No, no, certainly not.'

I did not bother to wait for any explanation, or none, this time. 'You said Huddart was probably caught up in these changes. Do you mean you're not as sure of it as you said?'

'I hear things. I'm supposed to be rich and late-life roystering and harmless. That above all – harmless. So I do get told things. I can take these random bits, plus what I see, and then try to spot a pattern, you know.'

'Yes, I imagine you'd be grand at that.'

'People will talk to me sometimes and not worry too much about what they say because they think I won't understand it properly, anyway, and will have forgotten it by tomorrow.'

'What kind of pattern?' I replied.

'Plus there's a wife, isn't there? A Mrs Huddart. Alice?'

'A partner, I believe.'

'Which might lead one to further smart guesswork.'

'About what?'

'Oh, the usual sort of thing. She's attractive, I expect, is she? Not too old? Legs and so on?'

'Do you mean like *The Postman Always Rings Twice*?'

'Ah, literature,' he replied with a jolly grin. He had really looked after his teeth. 'One adores books.'

'The Dorothy Parker reference proved it.'

'Some might feel queasy about going where Claude had been. That's a taste matter, though.'

'You're looking for a sex motive in the Huddart death, are you?' I said.

'There are truths to be found.'

'And they made a film of *The Postman Always Rings Twice*. Actually two. Hollywood always rings the tills twice.'

'Everyone knows how the drugs game is run here, of course,' he said. 'I wouldn't presume to tell you.'

'Yes, go on, presume.'

'A structure. Certain central pillars. Most folk could name them.'

'*You* name them.'

'For example, Sociable Ian, influential massively at the Mikado, and at the Clement, I believe. A genuine baron.'

'Ian Eric Linter.'

'Correct. I said you were sure to know him.'

'Know *of* him. I've never met Linter. I'm not Drugs.'

'He's, obviously, the biggest and most settled firm of all. By Appointment to some extremely distinguished names and noses. Incidentally, I think those boys who came looking for you at the Mikado might have been Sociable's.'

'Why?'

'Why what? Do you mean why did they come looking for you? I could only speculate about—'

'No, why do you think they were from Linter's lot?' I asked.

'Possibly came over from the Clement. As I've said, I observe. I have these aged but still sensitive antennae, Sharon.' He glanced down towards his midriff, as though the antennae were actually anchored there and keen to start waving and registering. 'They might cause me peril one day.'

'You mean you're guessing that they came from Sociable?' I said. 'You guess regularly.' Possibly I sounded edgy again, professionally disrespectful of his magnificent old intuitions, sceptical that they were *only* intuitions. How could he intuit so much?

'Oh, you're police, and police wants facts, don't they?' he said. 'Facts are everything – as long as the facts suit you, that is.' He put a hand up to his mouth in supposed horror. 'No, I mustn't say that, mustn't tease and malign. But there can be more to a situation than facts, you know. More than ascertainable facts. More than the ascertainable facts at any particular moment. But all right, my dear – these men *might* have been from Sociable. And might not. Correct.' He called for more espressos. 'In a way I could wish this cafe were not quite so near police headquarters,' he said. 'Are we obvious?'

I hoped not, though probably for different reasons from his. 'But you walked into the building carrying a wagonload of roses. Didn't that make you obvious . . .?' I let the sentence hang, as though I would have liked in a friendly, reciprocal, coffee-house style, to add his name.

He stood at once, bowed slightly and said, 'Ronald Desmond Blenny.'

'Wouldn't all those roses make you obvious, Ronald?'

He sat down again. 'They might have been for the chief constable – because he's doing such a fine job.' The coffees came. He sipped again. 'And then, as well as Ian Linter, there are those lesser, though aspiring, teams led by the abnormally handsome Philip Otton – oh, do watch yourself there, Sharon – and George Mittle, respectively – or Gleeful, as George is amusingly known, Protector and Provost of the Pole Star.'

'You said changes.'

'Indeed. These are seismic, systemic changes at such an early point they have been spotted by very few.'

'But spotted by you, of course.'

'Probably not even spotted by your Drug Squad experts yet.

No, certainly not by your Drug Squad. Huddart might have known of the developments, though. Oh, would certainly have known of them, believe me. But your specialist colleagues? No.'

'Yet picked up by your wondrous antennae? Were you born with them or have they come through nurture?' I said. 'How does Ronald Desmond Blenny know so much – or guess so much?'

He crouched lower over the cup, almost a cringe, as though to admit he could be accused of bragging and might deserve my sarcasm, but also as if to say he stuck by his elderly, unique, perceptive insights, regardless. 'How would it be, Sharon, if Phil Otton and Gleeful decided they could no longer compete with Sociable Ian on their own, but that together they might be strong enough to finish him and take over his business?'

'An alliance?'

'Now you'll see why I say systemic – and seismic.'

'If it's true.'

'This is standard commercial practice, and even more usual in savage trades like pushing. Standard political practice, too.'

'Otton and Gleeful hate and distrust each other,' I said. 'I'm not in Drugs, but – as you might say – most folk know that much.'

Once more he gave a modest, marginal, apologetic, wholly confident, but now *seated* bow, the fine trilby still in place. He had not taken off his gloves, either, and went through some trouble gripping the handle of the small cup. 'Correct,' he said. 'But listen to a parable, Sharon – history: in 1941 most foreign affairs gurus would have said Churchill and Stalin hated and distrusted each other, wouldn't you agree? And then dear Adolf invades Russia and suddenly everything is changed. Winston and Joe are allies, comrades, warrior pals.'

'"My enemy's enemy—"'

'"Is my friend." Likewise, Philip Otton and Gleeful look at Sociable's operation and see he's so big that any time he wishes he could eat up either. Perhaps one of them's had a tip that this is just what Ian is about to do. He will annihilate Philip or Gleeful first, then swallow the pathetic, lonely survivor. Did I already hear of a turf spat at the Nostrils?'

'Did you?'

'Suddenly, Ian would be in that blissful state of monopoly trading which all dedicated businessmen crave, and Ian is extremely dedicated. If he wasn't called Sociable, that's how he'd be known – as Dedicated Ian. Otton and Gleeful might feel they have to strike now or suffer. Pre-emptive.' He swallowed his coffee, maybe to illustrate how Ian would dispose of Philip or George when one of them stood solitary. 'But I must go. It really is exposed here.' He sat on, all the same.

'They combine to live?' I said.

'Well done, Sharon.'

I felt like a school kid congratulated by the teacher for having understood the screamingly self-evident. 'And Huddart is, was . . .?'

'Did Huddart have some negotiating skills?'

'Buying and selling,' I replied.

'I knew you'd be on the case and well briefed, you see.'

'I don't feel well-briefed.'

'Huddart could have been enlisted as the fixer.'

'Arranging the treaty between Philip and Gleeful?' I wanted to ask whether it was only Blenny's antennae again which suggested this to him, or whether he had some real solid information and, if so, where it came from. Did he live and earn inside one of these firms, although so old? Why did he spill so much to me? He said it was as recompense for his half-baked boob-grab leching at the Mikado. Really? I kept silent, though; I had come to wonder whether Ronald's tips ought to be considered very earnestly, no matter how they reached him. After all, his antennae had told him I had some familiarity with the Huddart situation, so they might be generally accurate. It seemed pointless for me to go on denying that I knew parts of the case.

'Huddart the intermediary,' he said. 'The broker. That might be within his range, don't you think? I've never met him, but I gather he could have made a fair go-between – suitably smarmy and subtle.'

'Possibly.'

'Clearly, that kind of work might make him a target.'

So, Claude Huddart, not a grass, but a gifted schemer? 'You're saying Sociable killed him? Had him killed? And how does Alice, the common-law wife, fit into it, then?'

'There's always a place for sex. It might be an extra. But possibly not Linter. We have to consider it could be George – Gleeful George. Did he decide Huddart was selling one or other of them short in the scheme to divide up Sociable's empire? Alternatively, Otton. You've heard of shoot the messenger?' He stood up. 'One really loathes to be melo-dramatic, but may I suggest we do not leave together?'

I felt I had to get some proper police cynicism back into things, regardless. Everything he had told me might be deepest woolliest fantasy. I said, 'You think Ian could be lurking out there? Or Otton? Or Gleeful George?'

'Or we might be seen by someone significant in your building,' he replied.

I was stunned, as I had been when Alice Huddart said something like this. 'What? What do you mean, "significant"?'

'Significant.'

'For God's sake, who? Mr Rendale? Mr Phaeton? Who signi-ficant? Significant how? Because they're running the investigation? Or are you saying something more . . . more . . .?'

'Significant.'

'More dubious,' I said.

'I know you're going to, as it were, sit on these – saucy phrase, I'm sorry, don't fret, I shan't get libidinous again – I know you're going to sit on these little items I've presented you with and make use of them, if at all, strictly in your own interests. I have the feeling you are that sort of girl, you know. It's instinct again, I'm afraid – but reliable, I believe. You want to excel, and will go your own way about it. Grand. Do wait a little while after I've gone, will you? Lurk, to use your word.' He began to move off. His voice went up and banged around the coffee shop, reaching all the other customers and the staff. It turned him into a fluting, historic Hooray Henry again, instead of a possibly inspired underworld analyst and notable career adviser to detective constables. 'This has been delightful. Do give them all my very, very best when next you're in the Mikado and so on, Mavis, Tarquin and Felicity etcetera, oh, and not forgetting Beauregard, of course. But how could one!'

SIX

drove to the Huddart house. This call would be official, not a freelance, flippant, ego-fuelled, undisclosed jaunt. Orders. Tactics. Even, strategy. No need to stretch out face-down on someone's lawn breathing botany. A straight, doorstepping trip. As a matter of fact, my briefing came at Superintendent Rendale's conference, while Ronald Desmond Blenny, so nobly kitted, waited downstairs with the rubbish roses. Against expectations – mine – I'd been given a segment of the inquiry to handle. Rendale seemed really impressed by my early arrival on the discovery morning. He regarded it as luck, but as well-exploited luck. Chief Inspector Phaeton also offered some praise.

The assignment :

(1) Look at all possible sexual aspects of the Huddart case.

(2) Direct initial inquiries towards Alice Huddart.

(3) Try to establish whether she had cause to want her husband removed, this probably based on sexual involvement with someone else;

(4) but also determine the Huddarts' financial state, in case it led to domestic stress.

(5) Arrange to interview her, with repeats if appropriate.

(6) Discount the 'unlikelihood of location' theory, i.e., arguments that she would not be party to a crime which left Huddart dead on their own driveway, because it must make her a suspect. She and perhaps an accomplice, accomplices, might have calculated on, aimed for, this response and decided to utilize it. That is, a double-bluff.

(7) Seek evidence of any illicit sexual relationship (see 3) and interview the man/men allegedly concerned.

(8) These to include:

   (a) Proprietor of the petrol station where she worked
       part-time.
   (b) Any acquaintance and/or colleague of Claude.
   (c) Any neighbour.
 (9) Interview nearby householders for evidence of
     possible disharmony between Claude and Alice
     Huddart – rows, violence.
(10) Similarly, trace and interview relations of Claude and
     Alice Huddart for this type of evidence.
(11) Evaluate during close, one-to-one conversations the
     genuineness or not of her mourning.

Of course, at this conference I couldn't mention my midnight
glimpse of Alice apparently poleaxed by grief as she gazed from
the hallway of the house to where the Citroën coffin had lately
stood. Besides, for reasons I'd already run through in my head,
that incident might have opposite interpretations. I stayed silent
and made a note of my new duties. I liked lists. They suggested
a kind of tidiness and mastery over events. It excited me to have
landed an important fraction of a major case. Detective Chief
Inspector Phaeton told the conference that I had established 'a
nice warm relationship' with Alice Huddart. This should be helpful
now. He'd seen us chatting on the day Claude was discovered. I
had the feeling Phaeton would say whatever suited him, and this
suited him, for reasons I couldn't sort out yet. I've had nicer and
warmer relationships with a revolving door than the one with
Alice Huddart. Again, I did not argue, though. Phaeton seemed
impressed that she and I were talking on our own, actually in the
house when the main police party arrived. Well, yes, we talked,
but the talk hadn't really gone anywhere, had it? Well, yes, it *had*
gone somewhere. It had gone towards Alice Huddart's distrust of
the police, including Phaeton and Rendale. And me.

   'See if you detect anything more than an employer–employee
relationship with the petrol station guy, Sharon,' Edward Phaeton
said. 'Your female sensitivity will pick that up, I know. Mr
Rendale and I do wonder about Alice.'

   'She seems . . . well, she seems a trifle beyond Claude,'
Rendale said. 'A big trifle. Like it's a mistake she's with him.'

   'Yes, beyond,' Phaeton said.

I couldn't be sure what this meant. I supposed they would have noticed the fine, grey-green eyes and slender-to-frail, yet womanly, figure of Alice Huddart, and wondered whether the house and car and clothes and income and body and face that Claude could provide would be enough to hold her. This was even before what had happened to his body and face. I wondered about the reasoning. Wouldn't Alice simply have walked out on Claude and gone with someone else if she wanted an upgrade? Many women quit a relationship. So did men. I'd considered it myself occasionally. More than occasionally. Good God, was it necessary to have Claude killed and carved? Phaeton would probably reply that the carving could be a ploy to deceive us. It made this death look like the display slaughter of a grass. Really? Far-fetched? Too elaborate? I doubted whether Claude would turn out to have big riches or a double indemnity insurance policy. No sex-plus-money motive comparable with *The Postman Always Rings Twice*.

But I did as instructed. Detective constables did do what they'd been instructed to do by detective superintendents and detective chief inspectors, at least up to a point, if the detective constables wished to survive and make progress. That would include most detective constables. Again, me, for instance. I decided not to ring ahead to Alice Huddart to say I'd call at the house. Now and then it's best just to arrive, so the customer is unprepared. That's what 'doorstepping' meant. I wanted to get everything I could out of this trip.

I did suspect that Rendale or Edward Phaeton or both would go and look at what they now considered the more likely sides of this case themselves. They wanted the personal glory of a successful hunt. All senior officers everywhere wanted that. Still young for his rank, Rendale might be hoping, by a few brilliant triumphs, to ease his advance into the select realm of assistant chief, and above. He would look great in that fine, pale-blue uniform, his body lean and solid, his face resolute and intelligent. Edward Phaeton was second to Rendale, younger still and clearly on his way up, fast. Two ambitious, capable, contriving detectives. I tried to guess or intuit what they might already know, without, of course, telling anyone. Perhaps they'd heard some of the rumours given me by Blenny about the drug firms

– the potential shifts and battles – and would corner that part of the investigation themselves. A crime with a large 'business' dimension would interest them. They'd hope the seemingly isolated Huddart death might in fact offer a route to destruction of one or more of the local drug empires – Otton's and/or Gleeful's and/or Ian Linter's. A victory of this scale was bound to earn national media notice, Home Office notice: due recognition and probable advancement for Rendale and/or Phaeton.

Their priority now would be to discover the route from the Huddart drive to the firms. So much major detection worked like this: a seemingly one-off event leading to a complex range of crime. Systemic. The possible sex side of things might be merely an extra to this big objective. I had the impression I'd been allocated the least promising subcategories of the inquiry. But I did remember how Rendale and Phaeton had seemed to believe at the outset – yes, seemed – that this case was simply a love idyll, with fatal violence, and a sharp or pointed instrument.

I preened for a moment in front of the women's washroom mirror at headquarters and muttered, 'Meet the new romance and bank account expert, S. Mayfield, DC. but with glittering potential.' I did some work with the make-up to get my image right. I had to look as if:

(1). I was in touch with my own and the world's hormonal impulses, and (2). also appear brilliantly fiscal.

Lipstick not piled on, but not negligible, either. Similarly mascara. My eyes had to show worldliness, familiarity with the ways of love, familiarity with the delights and pains of money or its absence. That comment by Phaeton about 'feminine sensitivity' and my ability to pick up signs of sex on the go was mainly ironic, of course. But there could be something in it.

I must act grateful for this step up to the big time, even if only the edge of the big time: luck had managed it for me, only luck, but, as Rendale saw things, I'd capitalized skilfully on that luck. For now, though, I'd do what Blenny suggested, 'sit on' the bonus facts about Claude's life he'd recounted over coffee. Facts? Possibly. Or might they be only the clever-clever, speculative, crackpot ramblings of a pensioner with a combined habit and thirst? He had virtually provided this description of himself. When an opening showed, I might do something to test his guesses and theories, if that's what they were. Did Huddart's death flow from those 'systemic' changes Blenny spoke of? He'd hinted at a link but never explained how it operated, nor tried to explain. In any case, Phaeton and Rendale possibly had the same material from different sources, and maybe in more solid, reliable form. Ronald Desmond Blenny collected and conveyed scraps, hints, rumour. He dreamt of himself as a cowboy. Perhaps he dreamt of himself in all kinds of roles – test pilot, heavyweight boxing champion, channel swimmer. And did he also dream of himself as a know-all, inside observer of the substances racket, a voice from the crooked centre, slurred but on the ball?

A revisit to the Huddart house struck me as the obvious first move now. Before leaving, I reclaimed Blenny's perfect roses from their washbasin and distributed them. 'Flower arranging' in police slang meant a nice, soft office job, as against the street, and, suddenly, here I was, a flower arranger, but only for ten minutes and with not much flair. It became a matter of where I could find containers for the blooms, tricky in headquarters. A few of the girls had vases on their desks and I dished out some to each. I felt like a church warden brightening up the nave, some nave.

Of course, the girls asked where the roses came from; a detective gets offered all sorts of sweeteners but not usually anything as brash and corny and basically valueless as flowers. I told them I didn't know. And in a sense, I didn't. They might be a genuine act of contrition for Ronald's antique sexual grope. Improbable? Of course improbable: he had done next to nothing at the Mikado – certainly nothing to deserve a huge peace offering. Or, they could be part of a careful scheme to get to me and unload ideas on behalf of a boss: the roses as 'facilitators' – the way public relations firm might woo influential people with ice-breaker gifts. But Blenny must have sensed I found the flowers unpersuasive verging on obnoxious, so he'd tried to neutralize the error by telling me to mince them.

Besides, I had to ask which boss would want to influence someone as low-level unimportant as DC Sharon Mayfield – despite potential – with tales about Claude Huddart and organizational tumult in the firms? Gleeful? Sociable Ian? Philip Otton? Not too likely. And which boss would have a quaint bit of work like Ronald Blenny on his staff? *Seemingly* quaint, that is. I had seen him temporarily ditch that pose and become . . . become what? Tough? Incisive? Wise? Wily? Yes, all those. And, also yes, didn't he boast of exaggerating his silly harmlessness as a survivor's technique? For most of the time, Blenny behaved as if he had no boss at all – that lordly accent, his stupendous clothes, the loud poise, occasional glimpses of masterfulness. But lots of people with bosses acted like this, to compensate.

The main part of the bouquet I took down to our cafeteria and made a show near the serving hatch in a big earthenware jug borrowed from the kitchen. It looked reasonably OK. Perhaps the roses would temporarily take the edge off that hostile term 'canteen culture' so often used to describe police solidarity and its supposedly macho, stick-together, right-wing gospel. Well, maybe more than supposedly. As I drove to the Huddart house I still had a sickening, sycophantic flower smell on me, and I opened both front windows of the car for a disinfecting breeze. As Blenny had said, some people loathed roses because they saw them as funeral flowers. I didn't want to go into this house now ponging like a wreath, when wreaths were too exactly apropos here at present. Did that make sense?

I found Alice had another visitor. That shouldn't have surprised me. Naturally, people would call to comfort and support her – friends, neighbours, relatives. But for a few seconds I felt confused. And, for the same few seconds, my police mind – my utterly unadmirable, stoat-quality police mind – raced off to a rotten thought: when I secretly watched her weeping in her hallway and gazing down the drive, was she, in fact, not agonizing over Claude but regretting that the man I found her with now had not turned up? It struck me when I saw her companion today that Phaeton and Superintendent Rendale might have had things right after all: this could be her employer and whatever else, surprised in her home by my unscheduled call, perhaps exulting in the convenient removal of Claude. Possibly I'd misjudged Rendale and Phaeton and they were not shipping me off to a dud region of the case. Sex, sex, sex. Experience and Hollywood might have taught my superiors the power of murder's eternal juicy basics.

The man was around Alice Huddart's own age – say thirty two, or three – exceptionally good looking in a blond, bony, Nordic way, about six foot tall, slim-to-thin, expensively dressed in a beige, silk lightweight suit, and what could be a handmade shirt. It was richest blue, silver striped, and very nearly tolerable with beige. Some kind of motif in red and gold featured on the left breast of the shirt, perhaps a monogram. He had undoubted smartness, but a different kind from Blenny's. This lad really projected himself, would probably produce a high reading on the Irresistibility Scale. Not just probably; I felt it myself. He could excite. He met at least eighty-five percent of the usual requirements, the visible usual requirements. He stood behind her in the hallway of the house when Alice Huddart opened the door.

'Oh,' I said, 'should I come back later? Not urgent. I hadn't realized you'd have company.'

'And *I* hadn't realized I'd have two lots of company, him and you.'

'Oh, many will wish to condole with you, Alice,' he said. 'And to offer whatever help we can, inadequate as it must surely be, though.' He shook that long, elegant head eloquently, gently. I found it odd that he should have come to the door with her when I rang the bell. It was as though he must protect her or keep tabs on her and what she said. Either way, it seemed proprietorial. I could see now that the shirt letters were P.D.O., presumably his initials.

Alice Huddart said, 'This is Phil Otton, a business acquaintance of Claude. And, Philip, this is Detective Constable Sharon Mayfield, the first officer here yesterday by at least half an hour. I still don't know how she did it. And she's unlikely to tell us, isn't she? First thing they issue them with at training school: a gob zip.'

So, not her employer, but the handsome second string baron Ronald had warned of. He shook my hand with great gravity. His eyes went over me, but nothing offensive, just part of the welcome. Actually, I could have done with something a little warmer and more personalized from him. It was the kind of greeting that people did make in this sort of situation. That is, it certainly contained some solemnity and sorrow, but also a shared jubilation at being personally still alive despite the corpse context. We went into the sitting room.

'She claims fluke brought her here so promptly yesterday morning,' Alice Huddart said.

'Chance can work like that,' Otton said.

'Yes, fluke,' I said. 'I'd been sent to a warehouse break-in.'

'But a special kind of fluke, police fluke,' Alice said.

'I was driving towards Tollgate Road and saw the crowd,' I said.

'Shall I tell you what I mean by "police fluke"?' she said.

'Probably,' I replied.

'I mean no fluke at all,' Alice said. 'Something planned, set up, concocted and based on snoop information amassed for . . . oh, for God knows how long . . . and then referred to as good fortune only, because the police always want to hide where their sneaky inklings come from.'

'Which inklings?' I said.

'I should be asking that,' she said.

'Well, ask. But I won't be able to answer.'

'Because you've been told to keep it zipped?'

'Because I don't know.'

'They leave you in the dark, being just serf rank?'

'I *am* serf rank, but I can't say if they leave me in the dark.' This was, or, at least, might be, a grieving woman, so I tried to stay polite, fangs at rest, for now. Her aggression could be sorrow in another form. That often happens. I'd thought earlier she would perhaps refuse to let the police witness her distress. She'd fear we might try to cash in on such weakness – pressure, bully, manipulate, when her resistance was down. And, of course, that contained some truth. Hadn't I schemed along those lines myself? She didn't weep now, or seem near to weeping, but her face looked even paler than when I first met her, and the general appearance of frailty greater. She'd have her terrible stresses, whatever the realities here might be.

'If it was luck why are you still on the case?' she said. 'I'd have expected them to say, "Thank you and goodbye, Sharon".'

'So would I,' I said.

'But there might be an explanation,' she said. 'I think they believe you have a special, personal skill. That's why you arrived first.'

'What skill?' I said.

'Like mock sympathy. Manufactured empathy. You've been on a course to learn how to produce them?'

It was odd to hear her suggest the same flair as Phaeton did a little while ago. But at least she ought to know that sympathy or empathy, mock or real, hadn't helped me much with her.

'Anyone would have felt your grief,' I said.

'And then people watching this house,' Alice replied.

I turned and looked through the window both ways along the Avenue. 'Where?'

'At night.'

'Watching? Why? What would they hope to see?'

'Again, I should be asking that.'

'Again, I wouldn't be able to answer.'

'Someone – maybe more than one – around here. Perhaps flat in a neighbour's garden. More snooping. Tell me, would *you* like that kind of thing around *your* home?'

'Not us,' I said.

'I'm telling you,' she said.

'I'd have heard about it if we were running that kind of operation.'

'I'm telling you.'

And, yes, she *was* telling me. No need, Alice, dear. I wondered whether she shut the front door earlier than she'd intended because she sensed or spotted the snoop/snoops. A closed front door might have signalled to someone – say, Philip Otton – to postpone a visit last night. Perhaps I should have hung about and checked whether it reopened later and let the light out once more as a come-on, a welcome.

'Did you know Claude at all . . . Sharon – if I may?' Otton asked.

'Who knows what she knew, knows?' Alice Huddart said.

'No,' I said.

'Claude – so prized by all who did know him, so sweet-natured and genial,' he said. 'How, oh, how could this have happened?'

'We have a strong chance of finding out,' I said.

'Really?' Alice Huddart said. 'By spying on me from a neighbour's lawn? How is that supposed to help?'

'The department will use all its resources,' I said.

'Really?' she said.

'A major inquiry,' I said.

'And now?' Alice Huddart asked me. 'Now, you are here for what?'

'Oh, such terrible events take a great deal of effort on the part of the police, Alice. I imagine Sharon was not able to talk fully with you yesterday out of respect for your shock, trauma, indeed. Understandable. Absolutely. I believe that, in this regard, policing has progressed remarkably in recent years, would you not say, Sharon – an increased awareness of, and consideration for, people's feelings at a time of crisis? I'm definitely not implying that police were ever crude and inhumane in such circumstances, but there has been an obvious advance in the, as it were, *care* aspects.' His voice, semi-educated, mild, exciting, phoney as hell, unflustered.

'I wanted to check you are all right, Alice,' I said.

'There, you see?' Philip Otton said.

'So, we'll say I'm all right, shall we?' She was profile on to me and kept her head very still as she gazed at nothing much across the room. She wanted to show strength. But profile didn't do all that well for her. She looked hard and a little beaky. Her beauty came over best at face to face full on. 'So, what's all right? Would you really expect me to be all right? Am I a fucking zombie? "Your man's dead on the drive, Alice. How you feeling? All right?".'

'As Mr Otton said, we recognize a responsibility to you,' I said.

'Dig, dig,' she replied. 'And ultimately bury me.'

'It's grand to see you have friends who'll call by and offer support,' I said.

She relaxed her pose and turned towards Otton for a second, then switched to me. 'Look, you've heard of Philip, have you? Philip Dominic Otton. Police like all the names, don't they?' She waved a hand in his direction, as though he were some sort of sample, or adhesive relation.

'Heard of me! Why should she have heard of me, Alice?' He tutted mildly for a time and with what might be a sudden show of nerves smoothed down one smooth lapel of his gorgeous

jacket. His hand looked surprisingly lumpy and hard, like a road
worker's. It seemed wrong for the beige suit.

So, Philip Dominic Otton, were you, are you, fucking Alice?
I'd heard of him, naturally, and long before Ronald Blenny
mentioned the name, though I'd never seen him or a photograph.
People like Otton didn't let themselves get pictured by the media,
unless they were done in court, when they couldn't prevent an
entrance or exit shot. As far as I could remember, Philip Dominic
Otton had never gone to trial. Yes, we believed in using all the
first names, even three or four.

I did feel a kind of pity for Alice Huddart, though not entirely
along the lines described by Otton in his testimonial to the new
police. But, suppose they *were* lovers, might he have bulldozed
her into:

(1) participating in the murder itself and
(2) the driveway exposure as a way to make it appear
    punishment of a grass? Did she have regrets now? And
    then, of course, matters didn't stop at (1) and (2). There
    was:
(3) the mutilations. Could she conceivably have been brow-
    beaten into approving those, even if she'd agreed to
    have Claude taken out? Perhaps she *hadn't* approved
    and they came as an unexpected, deplored addition.

The notion made things harder for me. I had been trying to
work out – to sense, to divine, to intuit – whether these two
were a coupling couple. But by speculating on how they might
have differed on managing the death I turned them back into
separate, self-willed people, and found myself looking for
signs of this apartness, rather than their secret, fuck-based
unity.

'But perhaps your bag really is warehouses, Sharon,' Alice
Huddart said, 'so you might not have come across Philip. He's
not a warehouse kind of person.'

'What kind of person is he?' I said.

'Philip is Philip,' she said.

Her answer surprised me. I wouldn't have expected such
cryptic, showy silliness from Alice.

'"Philip is Philip!" Oh, I'll take that as kindly meant, so thank you very much,' Otton said with quite a worthwhile laugh. First-class, much-tended teeth, better even than Ronald's. 'I believe, Sharon, there *is* a tendency for the modern police officer to know a lot about a very narrow area. Life has grown so complex, that specialization becomes inevitable – as Alice hinted just now.'

'Oh, God, platitude time,' Alice said.

'Those days when a police officer could deal with poor behaviour by a clip around the ear are gone,' Otton replied.

'Even in those days a clip around the ear for murder wouldn't suit, would it?' Alice said.

'So many names one hears,' I said. 'Hard to remember all of them.'

'Phil lies lowish, even though he advertises himself on his shirts.'

'Alice jokes. It's so good to see her sense of humour is intact, despite everything. Very often Claude has spoken to me about it, said how it had helped him through many a crisis.'

But not this one.

'I expect you know what she wants to ask you, Philip,' Alice said.

'Do I?' He sounded amazed, but most likely wasn't. Fairish try. In this small, pleasant room, I'd taken a place on the chesterfield. The other two occupied armchairs, Otton with his legs stretched far out but still seeming quite tense. It suited him, made him seem like a young, worried hospital consultant or senior croupier.

'I said you and Claude met through business, Phil,' Alice Huddart said. 'I'm sure she'd like to know what *kind* of business.'

'Oh, that's an easy one,' Otton said. 'Various.'

'I mentioned various to Sharon when she asked me yesterday about Claude's career. I did say "various", didn't I, Sharon?'

'Buying and selling,' Otton said. 'Entrepreneuring, if you'll forgive the pompous term. I'd bump into Claude during all sorts of negotiations. Oh, yes. And he was always gentlemanly, even when we might be rivals in a possible deal. I feel intensely that this is how business *should* be conducted. Competition, certainly.

That is the essence of commerce. But competition which does no damage to the personal relations of those engaged temporarily in it. I see business as rather like a rugby match. For eighty minutes the players go at it ding-dong and ferociously, but then shake hands and join one another for a friendly drink in the clubhouse.'

'Yes, that queer oblong ball *is* like not just business but life,' Alice said. 'You never know which way the bounce will go.'

I listened, watched, sniffed for sex, as industriously as Rendale and Edward Phaeton could have wished. Not a simple job: if there *was* any sex, Alice and Philip knew I'd be looking for it, of course, and work at concealment. I assumed the vats of bullshit and deadweight cliché he tipped out for us were meant to help with this. There couldn't be anything less touched by romance. Also the unpredictable rugby ball. They sat about as far from each other as feasible in this small room. I did not notice any brief, loving glances. Their conversation could be seen as familiar – full of joshing and put-downs – but nothing closer, at times almost hostile. It might be a very chic performance, possibly even in the same class as Alice Huddart's weepie session on the doorstep last night. But was that pure, cruel cynicism in me? Today, she seemed almost jaunty, brassy, rather than tearful. High? Had Otton brought something helpful from stock? Or once more she might be determined to hide her pain and vulnerability from me, from any cop.

'I know Sharon feels thrilled and educated by your analyses of modern police philosophy, Phil, but it's all beside the point, isn't it? She thinks what she's been told to think.'

'That's harsh, Alice,' Otton said, 'I don't—'

'Her leaders want to believe I did it,' she said, 'or want to pretend to believe I did it, perhaps with a special, interested friend as accomplice, such as you or someone else.'

'Oh, Alice, really!' Otton said.

'Interested in the sense of hoping to gain from Claude's death,' she said. 'Gain what? Me. That would be worth it alone, wouldn't it, oh, yes, indeed? Also anything I bring – some insider knowledge, some money.'

'Please, Alice,' he said. 'You're stressed, but you must not talk like that.'

'It's true, isn't it, Sharon?'

'People who know you and have seen you and Claude together would regard the accusation as absurd,' he said.

'Tell him, Sharon,' she replied.

'And they'd also find it absurd – even supposing such an appalling act were possible – yes absurd, farcical, insane, to suggest Claude's body would be left on your own drive,' he said.

'A kind of sophisticated ploy. That's how they'd see it, wouldn't they, Sharon? And it's not just wouldn't *they?* Wouldn't *you?*'

'Did you engage Claude sometimes to do special business assignments, Mr Otton?' I replied.

He produced astonishment and frowned large-scale, as though totally baffled by the question. The frown did no serious damage to his looks. It suggested depth of personality. 'Assignments? What assignments? Claude wasn't an employee of mine, you know. He ran his own company. I couldn't send him on assignments, even if I'd had assignments for him to do.'

'Specific commissions, for a fee,' I said.

'Now, who have you been talking to?' Alice Huddart replied. 'This one's no pushover, Phil. She networks. People confide in her. She's been on that sympathy–empathy tuition weekend.'

'Specific commissions?' he asked, thin eyebrows high through puzzlement, or just high.

'I hear he had excellent negotiating skills,' I replied.

'From me, she hears it, Philip.'

'Certainly he did,' Otton said. 'I respected him as a competitor. I've already mentioned this.'

'Did you use him?' I asked.

'I have staff who handle that kind of thing,' he said.

'Which kind?' I said.

'The kind you're talking about,' he said.

'Which is that?' I said.

'Negotiations,' he said.

'Which kind of negotiations?' I said.

'I don't know. I'm rather lost. You mentioned negotiating skills. I'm sure Claude had them, but I don't see how they might have been of use to me,' he said.

'For a major project, really special, needing deep aptitudes,' I said.

'Which major project?' he said

'Something systemic,' I said.

'God!' Alice said.

'It's hard to think of such a task. What would you have in mind?' he said. 'Which system are we discussing?'

'Occasionally, I gather business heads will hand over preliminary stages of a complex, difficult transaction to someone skilled in such work, and whom they both trust. More or less trust. Banks, for instance, will handle early approaches in a takeover for corporate clients.'

'Takeover?' he said.

'As an example,' I said 'Ultimately, of course, the chiefs of the companies concerned must meet and agree on the main principles. But the detail will have been settled and cleared away already.'

'Possibly,' he said. 'I'm afraid I don't see the relevance of this to . . . to the death of Claude.'

But I thought it cleverer not to bring out more clearly Ronald Blenny's information about the merger moves, and Claude Huddart as the possible go-between and fixer. Supposed information: after all, it was *only* what Ronald said, possibly no more than one of his war-game scenarios. 'Just a general notion,' I said.

'Police have a lot of those, Phil,' Alice Huddart said. 'The process operates like this: they form a general notion based on nothing much and then they go out and twist and manufacture things to fit the general notion. You've had *your* say about police method, Phil, so now we'll have mine.'

'Do either of you know someone called Jeremy Naunton Dince?' I replied. 'Though possibly an alias.'

'How true!' she said.

'You do know him?' I asked.

'Jeremy Naunton flits about,' Otton said.

'Flits about where?' I asked.

'The business world,' he said. 'Capacity unclear. But, then, that goes for so many, doesn't it?'

'Does it?'

'He arrived here the morning Claude was found,' Alice Huddart said. 'Didn't you walk off after him, Sharon? I thought I saw you from an upstairs window starting a stalk. My mind was all over the place, as you'll understand, but I thought you actually seemed to run, though I could have it wrong – you were quite a distance by then. Something serious?'

'And do you know what's happened to him?' I said.

'In what sense?' she asked.

'Jeremy Naunton follows an in-and-out sort of career,' Otton said.

'In-and-out of where?' I asked.

'They're like that, some of them,' Otton said.

'Which some?' I said.

'I'd hate that kind of life myself,' Otton said.

'Which?' I said.

'Unchartable,' he said. 'They feed on crises. Opportunistic. Courier duties and so on.'

'What kind of crisis?' I said.

'Oh, yes, find a crisis and you'll most probably find Jeremy Naunton Dince, or someone similar,' he said. 'They won't necessarily have caused it. They just batten on it.'

'Similar in which way?' I said.

'This hovering around a crisis,' he said.

'But what connection did he have with Claude?' I said. What connection did Otton have with Claude, come to that? However, I was more likely to get an answer about Dince. Was I? 'Why would he be here?' I asked. 'Why would he have been here so soon after the discovery of Claude?'

'He spoke to you, I expect,' Alice replied.

'Claude knew all sorts, commanded the affection of all sorts,' Otton said. 'I feel it a boon to have met him. I'm sure Jeremy Naunton Dince, or whoever he is today, would share that response.'

'You don't know *where* he is today?' I said. 'Or *who* he is?'

'That's what I mean by "unchartable",' he said.

'Did he make some promise – when he spoke to you?' Alice Huddart asked. 'Has he failed to deliver?'

'That would be so like Jeremy,' Otton said.

'I don't understand how he should be on the drive at the time,' I said.

'Ditto, but about you,' she said.

'Would you know his friends, colleagues, Mr Otton?'

'Not sure he'd have any,' Otton said. 'He's on the move all the time. That's their chosen mode.'

'Whose?' I said.

'People in Dince's game,' he said.

'I'm still not clear what that is,' I said.

'That's how they want it,' Otton said.

'You mentioned couriering. But what else?' I said.

'Yes, that kind of thing,' he said.

'And would he courier for just one firm?' I asked.

'Whatever comes up. True casuals.'

'On the move between where and where?' I said.

'That's what I mean by "unchartable",' he said.

'For instance, a man of around forty with an imperial beard,' I said.

'It's quite possible,' Otton said.

'Have you run across someone like that with him?' I said.

'This would most likely be a short-term connection,' he said. 'If someone's useful to Dince, he'll spend as much time with him as is productive. Then he's gone. What I mean by "opportunistic". I don't say this in criticism. It is the nature of their work, that's all.'

'Productive in which way?' I said.

'A catch-as-catch-can quality about Dince,' he replied. 'And all the time he hopes that one day he'll catch the big one.'

'The big what?' I said.

'Deal.'

'What sort of deal?' I said.

'Any sort. That's what I mean by "unchartable" and "opportunistic".'

'Do you think he'd come close to something like that now?' I said. 'Possibly somehow linked to Claude.'

'Something like what?' he said.

'Big,' I said. 'Seismic.'

'My! Seismic as well as systemic!' Alice said.

'I don't monitor Dince's activities,' he said.

'But maybe a buzz around?'

'What did he say to you?' Alice Huddart asked.

'I wouldn't put much reliance on it,' Otton said.

'A couple of mysterious words and then he'd be off, I imagine,' Alice said. 'Bait. He'd be good with bait. But what's next? He's not so gifted at this.'

'That's Jeremy!' Otton said.

'What is?' I said.

'Follow-up always problematical,' he said.

'You sound as if you see him quite often,' I replied. 'You're very familiar with his methods.'

'Methods? That's not the word for how he works. It sounds too organized,' Otton said.

'Did you lose him, despite your little canter, Sharon?' Alice said. 'Had he disappeared when you turned the corner?'

'Typical,' Otton said.

'Jeremy can certainly be elusive,' Alice said. 'He was probably hidden away somewhere chuckling while he watched you try to find him. That sort of infantile jape. He'll grow up eventually – I mean, if he *does* get to grow up.'

'He has a mischievous side, yes. No great malice, though,' Otton said, 'unless necessary.'

'When he spoke to you here, would it be side-of-the-mouth stuff?' Alice said. 'Jeremy's strong on making arrangements.'

'He seemed to have something confidential.'

'"Seemed" would be right,' Otton said. 'Part of his salesman technique: convince the punters you know more than they do and are willing to share it for a fee. Share it little by little but for big by big fees.'

'And did you tell Chief Inspector Phaeton about Dince?'

'Mr Phaeton?' I said.

'He'd know Jeremy,' she replied.

'Edward Phaeton – very much in touch, I hear,' Otton said. 'Definitely not one of your desk-bound senior officers. He's out there, watching, mingling, noting. An admirable reminder of the kind of policing I spoke of previously.'

'Hear from where?' I asked. 'In touch with what, with whom?'

'You didn't tell Phaeton or Rendale?' she said. 'Well, it was your choice, certainly. You'd have a reason, I expect.'

'How would they know Dince?' I replied.

'I can understand your not wanting to bother them with

something so insubstantial as a talk with Jeremy,' Otton said. 'Or, perhaps to call it a talk is overstating. An exchange.'

'And yet it must have got to you, or you wouldn't be asking about him now. And you wouldn't have galloped after him,' she said.

'Did the man you mentioned – the one with the beard – did he come into this episode in some way when you were tailing Dince?' Otton asked.

'You *do* know him, do you?' I replied. 'So, is he friendly – to Dince, I mean?' I said.

'I should think Jeremy would be all right,' Alice Huddart said.

'All right in what sense?' I said.

'Yes. All right,' she said.

'Safe?' I said.

'He's survived worse than this,' she said.

'Oh, unquestionably,' Otton said.

'It's nice of you to fret about him, Sharon,' she said.'Perhaps Phil is right and the police *have* become more caring. But I don't imagine I'll get told much now, shut up here since . . . since the Citroën. I can't give you anything on Dince's situation today.'

'Dince is wary,' Otton said. 'He knows the scene. He'll be OK.'

'Which scene?' I said.

'That's how they talk – Phil, Dince, even Claude,' Alice Huddart said. '"The scene". It's shorthand.'

'For what?'

'When I said "unchartable" it might have sounded like a criticism, but in another respect it's a strength,' Otton said. 'He's not easy to surprise or intercept. He's never able to get complacent.'

But I might have seen him surprised and intercepted.

'Yes, I'm cut-off here at present. Some people are so horrified by . . . by the Citroën some people won't call,' Alice said. 'It would upset them too much.'

'Unforgivable, that mode of death,' Otton said. 'Barbaric.'

'People are afraid of grief, embarrassed by it, and leave one alone,' Mrs Huddart said. 'Except for Phil, of course, Phil on a duty call.'

'Oh, Alice, really . . .' he said.

'And you, Sharon. But you have rather particular laid-down objectives, haven't you?'

'I don't know whether we've been of much service to you,' Otton said.

'How can we be, when we know nothing?' Alice said.

'At least Sharon has learned how much we both prized Claude,' Otton said. 'How he was prized generally.'

'She heard you say it, but does she believe you?' Alice said.

I left them then. They both came to the front door to watch me go, like hubby and missus. 'Where now then?' Otton asked.

'Oh, she'll be off to see Terry Kale, my splendid employer,' Alice Huddart said, 'won't you, Sharon? Her chiefs want an all-round picture. It doesn't matter whether it's right or wrong, as long as it's all-round.'

Fair? Of course not. Her suggestion was we'd build a case against her regardless, and make it thorough and watertight regardless: regardless, that is, of the truth. She didn't deal in fairness. Aggression, resentment, spite – these she fancied more. Perhaps I could part sympathize. But I had to consider, too, that the aggression, resentment, spite might be a mask. She would attack. She would treat as an outrage and contemptible any suspicion of her we showed, even when the suspicion made obvious sense. *Especially* when the suspicion made obvious sense. She aimed to blow it away.

So, then, would I, in fact, go to see Terry Kale, her boss at the petrol station now? I had my orders, but would I? Sitting in the car near the Huddart house for a minute or two I listed what might be headed 'Factors arising from the meeting with Alice Huddart and Philip Otton' if this had been an official report. It wasn't and wouldn't be. These factors piled up – twenty-three of them. What they told me lay somewhere between nothing and next-to-nothing.

(1) I'd surprised her by my unannounced doorstepping.

(2) I'd discovered him there. A plus?

(3) He was on the kind of terms that apparently made it natural to visit her today while she mourned. Another plus?

(4) But I could not be certain what these terms amounted to.

(5) They were lovers? Possibly. Yes, possibly. I'd seen no unambiguous signs of this. They had seemed familiar with each other, but that could be friendship only.

(6) For instance, they might have grown to know each other via the Otton–Claude connection. But consider (8b) in my original list of points for investigation.

(7) If they *were* lovers this presumably made Kale irrelevant. Kale = employer, nothing more.

(8) Even if Alice and Otton were having an affair, it did not inevitably mean they conspired to kill Claude. God, of course not. The assumption could be preposterous and cruel.

(9) Perhaps Alice's tears last night had been genuine. Or not.

(10) Perhaps Otton's testimonials to him just now were also. Or not.

(11) And what had the business link with Otton consisted of? Was Ronald right and it had been close?

(12) Or should I take Otton's tale of only bumping into Claude now and then in business situations as the accurate one?

(13) And the business? No real mystery. I would check whether Philip Otton or Claude had actual convictions for drug trading. Even if not, people in the Drug Squad might be able to tell me a bit about Philip. Yes, *might*. They did not give out information very readily, that lot. Which detectives ever did, particularly to other detectives, technically colleagues, potential rivals? Drug Squad members were worse than most for secrecy, though. They had their networks to guard, systems where a lot of money moved, like tens of thousands and even hundreds of thousands. Who wanted outsiders poking into such delicate realms, failing to observe the subtleties? For the most established people in the squad, outsiders meant everybody not squad – and even some officers who *were* squad but not quite trusted: in the squad, but not quite in,

in the sense that those already in and fully in, kosher in, would not allow them fully and kosher in at this stage, though they might qualify to come in in due course, when they'd proved themselves reliable.

(14) I had never doubted the business to be drugs. This did not help in deciding who killed Claude, though.

(15) If there had been some business two-timing of Philip Otton by Claude, and then terrible retaliation by Otton, as Ronald had hinted, would Philip be up there now, ministering to Alice – accepting this is what he *was* doing?

(16) It had shocked me a little that when I left he stayed on. Didn't he care if it looked as though he had stepped in there with Alice immediately after her man's death? Perhaps this suggested the relationship was truly only one of caring friendship. Yes?

(17) And now, something troublesome. Did I want it to be like that – Philip and Alice good mates, not lovers – yes, did I want it to be like that for reasons not altogether connected to the case? Listen, detective, this detective told herself, does this detective detect a touch of ungovernable sexual interest from you in the beige-suited, Viking-like blob of dubiousness? Was it jealousy not shock that hit you when he remained with Alice instead of leaving at the same time as you?

(18) Are you hanging about now in case he comes out, and not because you wanted to do a bit of professional tracking, either?

(19) But could I seriously think warm thoughts about someone who probably ran a middling-to-sizeable drug firm and might have killed Claude Huddart, or arranged it?

(20) I'd been preoccupied watching for eye messages between those two. I tried to recall now whether there'd been any coming from him to me. After all, I'd be at least eight years younger than Alice Huddart, though mature with it, if that's what he went for.

(21) No other car was parked close to the Huddart house. Had he left his somewhere near but unnoticeable, the

way I did previously? If so, what did this say about the relationship? Furtive? Not merely pals? Shit.

(22) But perhaps he came by taxi. I should have asked. Yes, I should have asked for two reasons, one of them not proper or much to do with police work, and therefore stronger.

(23) And suppose he *had* come out and I'd managed to contrive a conversation. What would I say? *'I love the suit, Philip, and not a blood stain on it.'*

SEVEN

I t was almost one p.m. and I decided to go home and then
call on Kale, the garage owner, after his lunch break. I had
a reason for the delay, and a stupid, vain, compulsive one. It
dismayed me that Alice Huddart could foresee so damn correctly
what I'd be up to next. '*Oh, she'll be off to see Terry Kale, my
splendid employer. Her chiefs want an all-round picture. It doesn't
matter whether it's right or wrong, as long as it's all-round.*'

Were the tactics, the itinerary, so damn obvious? So pre-
programmed? So crude? She made me sound like a pinball: I
scoot around the board with no choice of destination, just
bouncing out of control from one call to the next because . . .
because that's how it had to be with me. So, boom, boom, in a
pathetic fightback I'd postpone the trip to Kale for an hour or
two. And this was supposed to prove my precious selfhood and
gave me the power to act as I wanted. Oh, hell, such footling,
shuffling wackiness.

Luke was working nights and would probably be out of bed
by now and around the flat. I felt I needed to see him, talk to
him, realign him on my sexual map after that session of happy
mental wanderlust inside and outside the Huddart house.
Shameful. Degraded. Luke had many irritating aspects, dud
aspects, but at least he did not flog drugs or kill.

God, though, it must be thrilling to be killed for.

*Stop that, you disgusting, libidinous cheapie. You're a police
officer – not to mention half of an established, loving, strong
relationship.*

I had another reason for going home and for wanting to see
Luke. He played soccer in one of the police sides. So did two
lads from the Drug Squad. Football esprit de corps seemed as
powerful, even more powerful, than squad loyalties. An unbreak-
able united brotherhood, the Round Ball Congregation,
worshipped their jolly God, soccer. I thought Luke and I could
lunch out at Bertie's, the squad's favoured pub, and its sort of

unofficial headquarters. We might run into the sporting buddies, perhaps guide them towards a little chat about Phil Otton and Claude and get some background. If a woman wanted to lever useful talk out of men it often paid to fake reverence for their little game. This talk wouldn't be up to Oxford high-table standard, but possibly informative all the same, if you had patience and the ability to cut in when a tiny pause in football discourse showed.

'Why Bertie's?' Luke said.

'You like it there. Camaraderie.' He stared at me for a while – probably guessed something might be up. But he did not say so. Mostly, Luke behaved with delightful consideration and politeness: he would never get high rank in the police. The Huddart case looked as if it should be on the plate of two separate, sealed-off, detective groups: the murder experts, naturally – what Americans call Homicide; but also the Drug Squad. Both groups would be terrified of getting left behind. And both groups would be careful about what they told the other, if anything. This was policing at its purist and most obstructive. I'd picked up an old John le Carré novel, called *The Looking Glass War*, at a second-hand book stall recently. It described internecine battles between departments of the security services. The police could be like that, and especially detectives.

We found only one of Luke's pals at Bertie's – Warren Dell, tubby, balding at twenty-eight, sometimes dreamy-looking behind heavy-rimmed spectacles, but, really, not so dreamy at all. We ate Lancashire hotpot and discussed defensive plans, soccer defensive plans, that is, and how to transform them instantly into sweeping counter-attack by getting the ball out to one of the wings, who'd be comparatively unmarked because all the enemy should be upfield trying to score. This clearly was a massive subject, and it would have been a deep tragedy to miss it, or any part of it. If we hadn't turned up today Warren might have sat there alone with his beer and lunch, while all those polished schemes remained unexpressed and only latent in his head; such appalling waste.

I'd been through enough of these discussions to absorb some lingo and basic ideas, so I would speak now and then on their topic before I tried to get mine going. The lads expected me to join in the soccer seminar. They would not have understood indifference. I knew about all sorts of balls – through-balls, cross-balls from the counter-attacking wing, back-pass balls, long-throw balls from touch, curve balls from a free kick. Then what about the fluctuating mathematics of team formation: 4,4,2 as against 4,4,1,1? I usually went for 4,4,2, because if you said '4,4,1,1' it sounded like '4,4,1, won', which meant victory but a player short. Almost any figures would do as long as they added up to 10, plus a goalkeeper.

When the pre- and post-match talk seemed exhausted I said, 'Guess what, Warren! By a brilliant chunk of good fortune I'm on the Claude Huddart case.' It was a bit blatant and frothy – could you have a brilliant chunk? – but twenty minutes had gone on sport gab and I needed to get clear of the mud and into sanity. I had worked a counter-attack.

'That right?' Warren said. 'A tough one, I hear.' Of course, he sounded guarded. He would have noted the brutally abrupt change of topic – brutally abrupt *attempt* at changing the holy topic. Luke would probably have noticed it, too, and might now feel he understood why I'd insisted on Bertie's. I watched Warren's secretive, schoolboy face, and tried to read whether the name was familiar to him. He'd have heard about the killing, of course, but I wanted to discover how far his previous knowledge of Claude went, his and the squad's. Luke watched me watching. Perhaps he disliked my sneaky attempt to lead a team mate into coughing something worthwhile, not just soccer schlock. Poor Luke.

I was expecting some fine, professional, keep-your-nose-out-Sharon blankness from Warren, but he tensed up, then leaned forward over the dishes and said quietly, 'What sort of stuff are you getting?'

'As you say, tough.'

'Yes, but—'

'Oh, definitely tough,' I replied. Sit on it, to quote Ronald Blenny.

'Tough how?'

'It goes in so many possible directions. A load of potential links.'

'Yes? And you've been given one to trace?'

'Something like that.'

'Which?'

'Which what?'

'Which direction?' he said. 'Which link?'

I had the startling idea then that Warren wanted as much out of me as I hoped for from him. He might even think Luke had brought me here to say what I knew – enlisting his girlfriend to help a dear footballing mate: how pals should be. This was that precious, match-of-the-day, Bertie's Bar bonding. I almost giggled. The whole idea of the meeting had been upended, had it, at least in Warren's head?

'Had you heard of Claude Huddart before?' I said. 'Run across him?'

'Who've you been talking to, Sharon?' he said.

'Early days,' I said. 'At this stage.'

'Oh, of course.'

'Was he pushing?' I said. 'In one of the firms? But, more important, possibly doing some boardroom manoeuvres?'

'Who?'

Who! That seemed like a sudden, involuntary shut-off in Warren, as if the normal opaqueness of the squad had taken over – the time lock on a safe closing itself. Mad. Pathetic. Who else had we been speaking about? But, treating it as a totally reason-able question, I said with lovely politeness, 'Actually, I had in mind Claude Huddart.'

'In a Citroën, wasn't it?' he replied.

'You know the car?' I said. 'Has it cropped up earlier?'

'Earlier than what?'

'Than now. I've got the reg, if it would help remind you.'

'Remind me of what?'

'If you've met with this Citroën before. Have you?'

'How do you mean, "met with"?' he asked.

'Yes, that's it, met with.'

'In a business sense?'

'Right,' I said.

'This was an old Citroën, I gather.'

'Yes. You know it?'

'Mostly, the cars we see in a business sense are new BMWs. That's the car of choice for successful dealers. Punters wouldn't trust the stuff to be good stuff if the pusher came in an old Citroën. A BMW and occasionally a Lexus are a kind of tin packaging for the product.'

'Claude might not have been a pusher.'

'Not in an old Citroën, that's a fact!'

'So, you wouldn't have ever come across this vehicle?' I said. 'In a business sense.'

'When you mention "boardroom manoeuvres", what do you have in mind, Sharon?' he replied.

You've never heard as much dazed puzzlement as Warren packed into his voice for this. He had to stop chewing for half a minute, to get it right. His tone control was in the Philip Otton class.

I said, 'You could probably answer that there are always board-room manoeuvres of one sort or another going on.'

'I could?'

'I'm sure.'

'Are there?'

'What?' I said.

'Boardroom manoeuvres always going on?'

'Routine, I imagine. Who's in, who's out?'

'Who is?' he said.

'Which?'

'In, or out.'

'I wondered if you'd had an inkling,' I replied.

'What kind of inkling?'

'Anything systemic.'

'Which boardrooms did you have in mind?' he said.

'Companies looking for dominance, even for monopoly.'

'Which?'

'Inter-firm deals – that sort of thing.'

'What kind of deals?' Warren replied.

'Reshaping. Mergers?'

'Systemic reshaping?' he said.

'You know of some?'

'You two, you answer questions with questions,' Luke said. He thought everything could be cut and dried, simple, like chasing vandals or fighting Hitler. In a way it was nice in him, undevious, four-square. Sometimes you had to get devious, though. Most times in my corner of things.

'These deals will often need a fixer, a middleman,' I said.

'In what sense?'

'To help bring people's interests together. A pathfinder. A marriage broker.'

'Which deals?' Warren said.

'The way City commercial banks will handle the preliminaries of a proposed bid, for instance,' I said. 'The heads of the companies concerned act personally only at the last, conclusive point.' Thank you Ronald Desmond Blenny and your undoubtedly close study of at least the *Financial Times,* and even the *Economist.*

'Which companies?'

'That's an example,' I replied.

'But of what?' he said.

'The role.'

'Whose?' he said.

'The "fixer" or "middleman" in our scene would be the equivalent of a City intermediary bank.'

'Which scene?'

'The business scene here.'

'Intermediary in which way?' he replied.

'Settling the detail. Obviously in the kind of context we're talking about now, it could be a dicey function. This is not, in fact, the City of London.'

'Right,' Luke said.

'Dicey how?' Warren said.

'He/she could be blamed for terms in an inter-firms agreement which didn't satisfy one or more of the participants. There'd be accusations of betrayal, of slanting the terms in favour of one or other.'

'Which one or other?'

'Say, merger conditions between two outfits.'

'Which two?'

'Difficult at this point.'

'And which "fixer" or "middleman" are we talking about?' he asked.

'They presumably recognize the risk – the caught-in-crossfire risk – but accept it for the sake of a lumpy percentage, and a possible future enhanced status as dealer.'

'Percentage? Enhanced status?' he replied.

'There might be an immediate notional, but measurable, gain when, say, two companies join and are then strong enough to see off another. The fixer or middleman would expect a share of that gain – his/her percentage: a kind of abattoir fee – or like bonuses in the City.'

'Lumpy,' Luke said.

'Very,' I said. 'And, afterwards, when the combined companies are working well, the fixer or middleman should qualify for a juicy segment of their operations – his/her enhanced status, as I've called it. After all, in a sense, he/she is creator of that newly formed company, the way Garibaldi helped bring Sicily and other states together and made Italy.'

'The Risorgimento,' Luke said. He would. He always wanted to stick names on things, get them defined. He found it hard to deal with anything you couldn't take a book out on from the library.

Warren said, 'Sharon, do you know a man called Dince, twenties, or possibly an alias, Charlton or Marshall-Cape?'

'Dince?' I said.

'Jeremy Naunton, when he's using Dince.'

'In what capacity?'

'Thin, fair-haired, ghastly teeth,' Warren replied.

'Was he connected with Claude?'

'These folk – they drop out of sight,' Warren said and touched his spectacles with one hand, as if trying for better focus on missing people. 'It's their style, their manner, but sometimes when they disappear it's because . . . well, because they've been removed.'

'In which sense?'

'Taken out.'

'By?'

'They're very near the edge all the time.'

'Which edge?'

'They take a wrong step and that's it,' Warren said.

'And you think this Dince could have been removed? Because he took a wrong step.'

'On the other hand, he might show up again at any time. I check for collatoral sightings, naturally.'

'Connected with Claude, how?' I said.

'That's why I wondered if you had anything on Dince,' he said.

'What do you mean, "that's why"? What's why?'

'As you said, Sharon, so many possible directions in this kind of inquiry.'

'But what's the significance of Dince?' I replied.

'These cases – there's no head-on method of coming at them, is there? Everything's roundabout, oblique. In a way that's their fascination. But, at times, this can become frustration, instead.'

'Dince and Huddart have both been noticed by the squad?' I asked.

'Noticed in which way?'

'Yes, noticed.'

'Obviously, we notice a lot of characters.'

'What exactly would make them noticeable?'

'The Citroën – on his own drive! That's . . . that's, well, unprecedented,' Warren replied.

And he most probably had it right. Before now there wouldn't have been any recorded case of a shot, hacked man dead over the steering wheel of a Super-glued old Citroën on his home's off-street parking spot. 'Yes, you could call it "unprecedented".'

Naturally, there is a point when refusal to tell a fellow detective anything at all, while pretending to take part in worthwhile dialogue, becomes silly and self-damaging. One of the great policing skills is to recognize, in a constructive, collegiate, unhangdog way, when this moment has arrived. It's not something taught at training schools, because, clearly, by suggesting situations would come when it might be all right to disclose material to a colleague, it implied there must be other, longer periods when to keep one's comrades in the dark was desirable and perhaps obligatory. That cannot be officially endorsed.

No, this secrecy aptitude has to be picked up on the job. I realized its power early by discovering how much I was shut out from by people like Warren. Inevitably, reciprocal hoarding soon became a habit. Institutionalized concealment. But nobody could hoard for ever. Now and then, disclosure has its benefits. Or, at least, *partial* disclosure: let's not overstate. Also now and then, you might get the idea that others actually already knew about what you might be hiding and simply played you along for their own dirty purposes.

'Possibly I did see someone who'd fit your description of Dince near the Citroën,' I said.

'Ah,' Warren replied. 'You were there very promptly. As I heard.'

'It just happened like that.'

'Ah,' Warren said, 'I expect so.'

'Sharon was actually on her way to look at a warehouse break-in,' Luke said. 'That's it, isn't it, Sharon? She noticed the gathering outside the Huddart house and went to investigate, as a good police officer would.'

'How I managed to get on to the case at all,' I said.

'Ah,' Warren said. 'And you also noticed Dince?'

'I noticed several people there, naturally, and spoke to some, including Claude's partner.'

'Did you speak to Dince, or him to you?' Warren said.

'The possible Dince.'

'Right.'

'Why would he be there?' I replied.

'I expect people have wondered how *you* could be there so soon,' he said.

'It was her route to the warehouse,' Luke said.

'Right,' Warren said.

'Who is he?' I said.

'Dince? He can be Dince or Charlton or Marshall-Cape, depending on mood.'

I said, 'Yes, but—'

'He might have been just passing, the way you were, Sharon,' Warren said. 'I don't mean on the way to the warehouse, but just passing.'

'He seemed to be on foot. Does Dince live up that way?'

'He moves about a lot.'

'Yes, I heard that,' I said.

'Where?'

'You already knew about him, did you,' I replied, 'you and the squad, before he surfaced on the drive?'

'Rendale and Phaeton are running this case personally, I understand. Edward Phaeton really hands-on.'

'You think that's strange? Why?'

'Plus Rendale himself. This is truly heavy.'

Warren mopped at some hotpot with a piece of bread. There'd be nothing more about Stuart Rendale or Edward Phaeton. 'Lately, I met a man called Ronald Desmond Blenny,' I said. 'Elderly.' I added that so Luke would not get tense and jealous.

'At the Mikado? What costume?'

'Can't sort him out.'

'Oh, yes, a user. Age shall not wither him, but crack or H might.'

'Are you sure that's all – a user?' I replied.

'How do you mean? Believe nothing he says, obviously. Full of shit. All kinds. But Dince,' he said. 'I'd really like to talk to that one. You could let me know, maybe, if . . . well, if it just happens that you bump into him again – not necessarily at a murder site. Anywhere.'

Humour. It's a tremendous gift some have, isn't it? The cheeky sod. How might I get someone to break his leg next fixture? Luke couldn't do it, even if he wanted to, because they were on the same side. Soccer did have certain rules and decorum and, on the whole, these barred crippling your own men. And Luke wouldn't want to do it, anyway.

'The way I see this, Warren – we have three important firms here. What if two of them agreed to get together and eliminate the other? Trade divided two ways instead of three, and profits lifted in proportion.'

'No, that's not the way *you* see it. That's how *Blenny* sees it,' Warren said. 'A Blenny for your thoughts. I can imagine the noisy, deluded, classy voice tutoring you.'

'Has he talked to you, then, along those lines?' I asked.

'Who's this Blenny?' Luke said.

'A would-be know-all. A fantasist,' Warren said. 'He gave you this analysis, did he, Sharon?'

Luke said, 'But Sharon wouldn't just accept what someone like that told her in a club.'

I saw Warren's attitude had begun to rile Luke. He'd always defend me. I felt more or less grateful. I had to. But Luke didn't understand how these detective jousts operated. 'Warren, there has to be a possibility Claude was doing something with or for

Phil Otton,' I said. 'Hasn't there? Or with Gleeful George Mittle
or even Ian Linter?'

'These names! Don't they come up all the time, though?' he
said.

'Do they?' I replied.

'Why do you lead with Otton?' Warren said.

Because I caught him at the Huddart house with Alice.

That didn't need to be said, though. 'The order is immaterial.
His name popped into my head first. Random.'

'Another thing that just happened, is it? Warren said.

How about getting both *his fucking legs broken?* 'When I say
"doing something" I mean handling the kind of preparatory
negotiations I spoke about earlier. Setting things up for the
principals.'

'Yes, I understood that,' Warren said.

'There's three firms. Suppose Claude was acting for two. The
other one might not be happy with that.'

'Which two?'

'I don't know yet.'

'Wouldn't Blenny make a guess for you?' Warren said.

'Or one of the two Claude might be acting for could turn
unpleasant, if they thought him best disposed towards the other,'
I said.

'And "unpleasant" means dead and mucked about with in the
Citroën?' Warren said.

Of course, I wanted to ask him direct if he and his friends in
Drugs thought someone from Otton's or George Mittle's or
Sociable Ian's lots had done Huddart. And especially I wanted
to ask direct whether he/they thought Otton. Naturally, Warren
would not have answered, or not answered in a way that could
be called an answer. In any case, I found I couldn't put the question: Otton was so lovely, so clean-looking in his unmarked beige
silk suit and clashing blue shirt, that I'd hate to slur him, at least
in public. I found it impossible to say anything to suggest Otton
could be in league with Alice – not because of the filthy deceit
and brutality this might mean, but because it would hurt to talk
as if the two were lovers. My observant, traitorous mind said
they possibly were. I jibbed at speaking the thought though, in
case this made it sound more likely: verbalizing would do that

sometimes. And I dreaded that Warren, at last fed up with the messing about, might confirm it with some roundabout, cryptic but intelligible comment. I did not want it confirmed, not a bit.

These reactions disgusted me. How could I have pitched myself into such rotten confusion? Answer: the usual way. Sex.

Warren stood up but didn't go at once. He seemed indecisive suddenly, hesitant. Then he crouched over towards me, as if wanting more privacy. The bar was crowded. I recognized some faces from around headquarters, probably Warren's colleagues in the squad. He must want to make sure they were cut off from what he said. 'Everyone has to think about the long-term,' he muttered. He looked even more like a schoolboy, whispering some subversive message to a mate in class.

'For sure,' I said.

'I don't apologize for saying this.'

'Why should you?'

'The pension will be all very fine, yes. Unequalled in the public sector. Oh, yes. But I can certainly understand anyone who makes extra provision for the future. That's only sensible.'

'"Go to the ant thou sluggard. Consider her ways." That's the worker ant, storing up all sorts.'

'Exactly.'

'Long-term,' I said.

'Or like Churchill said – important to have money when you're young, but vital when you're old.'

'Who do you mean?' I said. 'Can I guess?'

'Exactly.'

'Exactly who?'

'We see people like Otton in his damn suits and George Mittle and Sociable similarly, don't we? The BMWs and Lexuses. They seem to harvest what they want, no effort or hackery. I can understand the point of view that asks, Am I just supposed to watch these crooked sods pile it up regardless, flaunt it regardless? And these aren't worker ants.'

'Who does ask it?' I said.

'You're supposed to stop them doing that, aren't you – piling it up regardless?' Luke asked. 'Between you, you and Sharon. People in your sort of jobs. It's what you're for.'

'Oh, exactly,' Warren said.

'Who *do* you mean, Warren?' I asked.

'Don't tell me you haven't thought like this at times, Sharon, Luke. The future – it's there for all of us, isn't it?'

'I hope so,' I said. 'It's quite an item.'

'What?'

'The future. Many have remarked on this.'

'Is that right? Who?'

'Well, who wrote Proverbs?'

'Which proverbs?'

'The Old Testament: "Boast not thyself of tomorrow." That's the future – problematical. And, "Take therefore no thought for the morrow." Sermon on the Mount.'

'These are points of view, yes,' he said.

'Certainly.'

'But my own feeling is we have to think there *will* be a future, and cater for it in the present. Surely, anyone with a fragment of brain can see that.'

'Cater for it, how?'

He did move off now. 'Well, look out for Dince, would you, Sharon?' he said. 'Or the aliases. This has been so worthwhile, and I don't mean only about the football planning and Bible study.'

'Has it?' Luke asked, when Warren had gone.

'It's one of those meetings where what they don't say is what's worth listening to,' I said.

'And what didn't he say?'

'Almost everything,' I replied. 'I don't think I've ever heard so much not said in a conversation.'

'He says "exactly" quite a bit, but not exactly how to cater for the future,' Luke said.

'No, I did notice.' And he wouldn't tell me why the Drug Squad were interested in Dince. At least he seemed to think on balance Dince to be still alive, though. He had skirted my question about Blenny, tried to dismiss him as a junkie fool. He had mentioned Phaeton, and Stuart Rendale, and then refused to spell out why their personal concern for the case caught his notice, perhaps the squad's notice. What did that hush-hush, impassioned monologue about boosting one's already beautiful pension prospects mean, and his clear envy of the BMWs and Lexuses?

He had dodged when I asked about Claude, and would probably have dodged if I'd asked about Alice Huddart and Otton.

'Have we got time to go home?' Luke asked.

I knew he meant time to go to bed. 'I should say so.' It was important to remind myself where I belonged. Not just important: crucial. I had to get myself sorted.

As we were leaving Bertie's Luke said, 'I thought you did really well with him.'

'Thanks. How do you mean?'

'Telling him nothing. Lots of seemingly bright, interested talk, but non-stop stalling.'

'Thanks.' Luke had begun to learn. 'Obviously Warren didn't believe I'd appeared on the Huddart drive unplanned. He thinks he's dealing with a liar, so retaliates by talking vague and evasive. It's traditional.'

'How the hell do we ever catch anyone when people like you two spend all your time trying to fuck each other up?'

'But us – let's just fuck, shall we? I do like love in the afternoon.'

EIGHT

Of course, that was stupid and flip and empty – 'I do like love in the afternoon' – as if we needed special timetabling to get it on. An old Billy Wilder film called *Love In The Afternoon*, with Audrey Hepburn and Gary Cooper, occasionally made it to the movie channel, and possibly I parroted the words from there; not that I looked like Audrey Hepburn of the mid-1950s, and not that Luke looked as old as Gary Cooper then. As a matter of fact, I wanted to look like Jessica Lange in that remake of *The Postman Always Rings Twice* and, as starters, I did have a nice wide mouth. Unfortunately the resemblance stopped there, though. My praise for love in the afternoon was not really so much about love in the afternoon as about making an exceptional diversion to the flat – for some love in the afternoon. I'd intended to go straight out to see the petrol station owner after Bertie's. Sticking an utterly unscheduled bed trip in ahead of this, showed urgency, passion, surely: it's better to travel hopefully than to arrive, folk wisdom said. Maybe, but not better than to come. I wanted something that might seem irresistibly powerful, so I could blank out the idiotic, unconscionable lech blip I'd felt seeing Phil Otton. I'd even shelve a murder inquiry. I needed something fierce as antidote. 'You've got to shag the arse off me, Luke,' I said.

'How true.'

'Nothing half cock.'

'Rationing's over.'

I had to wonder whether I might be using him. Answer: somewhere between probably and yes, but in a good cause, surely. *Our* cause. It was constructive, or hoped to be.

Later on, driving out towards the petrol station where Alice Huddart had her part-time job, I wondered about two further topics:

(1) Did I smell of sex?

(2) Was the silver Volvo in my mirror tailing me?

About (1) I didn't care much. What did sex smell of, anyway? Cloves, apparently. Pleasant enough, I'd have thought, and delicate. About (2) I did care, a lot. I felt menaced. But perhaps the case had started to unsettle me and make me nervy – all that undisclosed information, alleged information, and raw rumour niggling deep inside. And then came the fact that I couldn't actually tell which *was* information, which alleged information and which raw rumour. They overlapped one another.

It was not far to the garage, not really a long enough ride to judge if another car deliberately stuck with mine, and yet I had the feeling it kept me in pretty well continuous sight. If so, this must be someone clever, someone who knew how to make sure at least one vehicle lay between us most of the time, as cover – at least one but not more than two, or following grew tricky. Would-be secret, urban gum shoeing by car is a very high skill. You have to cope not only with the victim vehicle, but all the other traffic, which doesn't know about your subtle mission, and wouldn't give a monkey's if it did – cutting in ahead of you, delaying you, blocking vision of the prey. Possibly the Volvo driver was surveillance-trained. How could that be? I did not know the car, and it stayed too far back for me to manage a good look at who drove. Another tailing knack.

But I thought, maybe – a big maybe – the middle-aged, beardy man from the pair who picked up Dince in the street. I felt unsure where this idea started, and tried to decide, as I drove. It might be only that Dince and those two dominated my mind still, and I rushed to identify one or other of them, even though the car had been changed from Audi to Volvo. I'd have preferred if it was Dince. Two reasons:

(1) I felt I knew him – sort of knew him – after that conver-
    sation on the Huddart drive. Nonsensical, of course:
    the conversation had been tiny, and without revelations,
    hardly a conversation at all, if a conversation meant

interchange. He did nearly all the talking, much of it
opaque.

(2) As ever, I longed to know he was all right. I feared
that from stupidity and slowness off the mark I might
have let him stroll into . . . stroll into an Audi with a
pair of unknowns. That is, definitely unknowns to me,
and perhaps to him. Or possibly *knowns* to him, but
not knowns that he would want to meet and share an
Audi ride with.

But now, grabbing momentary, distant, partial glimpses of the
Volvo driver, I had the impression of squatness, even bulk,
which couldn't be Dince, nor the younger of the Audi pair. If
it *were* the middle-aged man, he had no hat on today and there
seemed to be a lot of dark hair, some of it down over his forehead making identification difficult. The beard had been skimpy
and I wouldn't expect to spot it in these conditions. He appeared
to be alone. Where would he have learned police-style tagging
tricks?

And then the other big question: why would he or anyone
else want to follow me – that serf DC, as Alice Huddart put it,
with my dubious store of information, alleged information,
rumour, all mixed up together and none of it very reliable? But,
of course, only I knew the dismal extent and the frailty of this
information, alleged information and rumour. Others might
believe I had built a store of magnificent, genuine, exclusive
stuff. Perhaps that's how some people thought of me: not as a
serf, though definitely only a DC, but as a gifted and formidable cop, likely to have such a store of magnificent, genuine,
exclusive stuff, and *only* magnificent, genuine, exclusive stuff.
Suppose that Audi pair had seen Dince talking to me on the
Huddart drive, or suppose they had questioned him about where
he'd been and what he was doing, and he mentioned me. They
might think I could lead them to further fine discoveries. So,
stick the Volvo on her. It delighted me to imagine that's how
I'd be rated, how I appeared to them. This might not match a
resemblance to Jessica Lange, but it would mean I looked like
a capable detective. But I'd rather not have the Volvo at my
arse, thanks.

After a couple of miles, I decided I should maybe revise my guess at Volvo man's identity. The fear came back that I might be forcing a resemblance on to him only because I had it ready in my head. Many experiments have shown we tend to see what we expect to see. The notion hit me that he might be not the middle-aged man from the Cinder Street episode with Dince, but my colleague and superior, Detective Chief Inspector Edward Phaeton. I couldn't be sure where this suspicion came from, either. He had the same kind of physical solidity and a lot of dark hair. Phaeton was not middle-aged, of course, and too tall to be described as squat. But I had only an intermittent view and it's hard to estimate properly a seated driver's height. He might be able to take an unmarked Volvo from the headquarters' pool, and he'd know the tracking game. But why would Phaeton want to tail DC Mayfield? The same question remained. I think I would have expected him to be looking at some other, major aspect of the case, not haunting me in my hunt for the catastrophically sexual.

There is tailing and there is counter-tailing. They embody a kind of science, not quite eligible for the Nobel, but notable. It is a matter of systematically – scientifically – reducing possibilities until an almost inescapable conclusion is reached, as, say, with DNA. On a main, urban road, a car seemingly dogging yours might, in fact, simply be following this route because its destination for the moment, and possibly for many moments, happens to lie in the same direction as yours. The driver of such a vehicle will hardly be aware of you, let alone committed to pursuit. There could be many vehicles in this category behind and ahead. How, then, to test the situation and get a clearer idea of the second vehicle's motive and purpose? The answer is easy, and a central element in surveillance training. I can more or less recall the pages in the handbook now, that slightly comical, bullet-point speculation and thoroughness.

It is the main road, the main road as fact, which provides the chief problem: a lot of vehicles and a lot of vehicles going the same way for the present, nearly all of them of no consequence, but possibly one of real consequence, the tail. How, then, to isolate this relevant vehicle and identify it? Solution: remove the obscuring element – the main road. That is, get off it. Yes, leave the main road and take one not so main. Here, there should be less traffic. Now, mirror watch to see whether the supposed stalking car turns also. If it does, the possibility it is on your route only by innocent coincidence becomes smaller, and the probability that you have a bloodhound sniffing your exhaust greater. This is progress.

We are still not in an area of total certainty, though. The possibilities of chance must be reduced further, by turning off this side road into another, and then, supposing it necessary, another and even another. A whittling down process. If the second car is still hugging your rear at the end of these manoeuvres the likelihood becomes overwhelming that you do, in fact, have meaningful company. Then? Well, according to the manual, your reactions will depend on the nature of the case. Here begin the bullet points. They had to be learned more or less word-perfect:

(1) You can temporarily abandon the journey and return to base. This might apply if it is imperative to preserve the secrecy/security of the original destination. The second car will most probably have fastened on to you from your start location, so by going back there you will give away no information not already known.

(2) You can stop and see whether the second vehicle does too. If it does not, you may have proved (a) that, despite appearances, this was no tailing car and the similarity of route only an exceptional coincidence. Or (b) you may have successfully challenged the second driver and forced him/her in the interests of secrecy to avoid a confrontation. (c) It might be possible to identify or achieve a description of the driver as he/she passes. (d) This development is not necessarily final: the other car could wait ahead out of sight until you continue your journey and then resume slipstreaming. Watch for this possibility.

(3) If the aim is to expose the tailing, you may stop in such a position that the second vehicle cannot pass and

also has to stop. Points to consider: (a) this could impede other traffic, too, and cause potential danger. Accordingly, (b) it might be necessary to activate the inner-cabin blue lights to show this is a police interception.

(4) You may approach the driver of the second vehicle to identify him/her and seek an explanation of his/her behaviour. Points to consider: (a) Do you judge this procedure safe? That is, safe in a road traffic sense, but also (b) in an encounter sense, i.e., (c) is the location where you have stopped remote, with few people about? This is an obvious likelihood if, in the procedure for deciding the nature of the second vehicle, you have turned into increasingly minor roads. (d) Does this remoteness and absence of witnesses increase the risk to you? (e) Relevant to this consideration: have you discovered, as you near the second vehicle on foot, that its driver is not alone, and you are therefore out-numbered? (f) Also relevant to this consideration: have you reported in your location and intentions and asked for back-up?

(5) You may remain in your vehicle and wait to see what action the driver of the second car takes. Points to consider: (a) You could be at a disadvantage, seated as compared with someone standing if he/she walks from the other car. (b) It would be difficult to accelerate away [see (6) below] if the other driver is leaning in through your window space to talk.

(6) You may suddenly accelerate away, though at legal speed and, employing surprise, hope to lose the second vehicle by further uses of the minor roads, especially if you are familiar with the local geography. This could be a very practicable measure if you accelerated away while the other driver was walking to your car, and before he/she might be leaning into the window space of your car, see (4b) above. He/she would have to return to his/her own vehicle before being able to follow. This may provide useful time to get clear.

(7) You may, in any case, rejoin a major road and aim to lose the second vehicle in the increased flow.

(8) Other considerations apply if you believe the driver and/or personnel in the second car might be armed. This situation is dealt with later in the manual. DO NOT FAIL TO READ IT.

I turned off into a very minor street, then slowed to see if the Volvo came, too. Traffic here was negligible and when he showed I would have a good sight of it and the driver. It did not show. This might make my fairly photographic recall of the manual redundant, except for its implied message that, if the second car didn't come after me, it could signify there was no chase, merely a harmless, natural spell of shared main road, my suspicions brought on by pitiful nerves/panic. But I had to think that anyone trained, would know the ancient switch course ploy, and decline to fall for it. Edward Phaeton would certainly know it. Might mature-aged green Audi man know it? Probably anyone with a tiny amount of standard intelligence would spot this move and avoid the trap.

I went on, did three sides of a rectangle via other small streets and came back on to the main road without any further mirror sightings: or without any further mirror sightings during the detour. Four minutes later, though, I observed the Volvo again, still with a vehicle shielding it from me off-and-on, still doing nothing to get any nearer. Did this almost magical reappearance give the message that life could not be reduced to a well-meant table of points? As some thinker said, 'The essence of life is statistical improbability on a colossal scale.' Were there more things in motorized surveillance than were dreamt of in any training guide, Horatio? However, I did look for rational explanations of how the Volvo came to be back on track, on *my* track, and itemized them in my brain:

(1) Its driver knew about the manual and expected my return to the main road, so had lurked somewhere.

(2), He had guessed or intuited or foreseen my destination and realized I'd ultimately have to resume this route, unless I aborted. And there would be no obvious reason to abort if I believed I had lost the tail.

(3), They'd fixed a locating bug to my car, which would make all the dodging about useless.

(4), The Volvo *had* followed me around the minor roads, but somehow kept out of sight, and then rejoined the big traffic with me, but discreetly back.

I activated the handbook's paragraph (2) and suddenly pulled into the side and stopped. This was a principal highway, so I could not follow paragraph (3) and block it, but the car would have to pass, and I might get a decent look, including one at the registration. But the Volvo's driver seemed ready for this ruse, also. He pulled in and stopped, still a good way behind me. When the traffic thinned for a moment, the car U-turned fast and disappeared. Further expert driving? I could have turned myself, perhaps – done that classic tailing gambit and become the stalker instead of the stalked. I considered it, still longed to discover whatever I could about Dince, and especially where he might be and in what condition. That didn't stand up logically, though. Nothing suggested a connection between the Volvo and him, except my early identification of the driver as from the Audi – most likely wrong.

Probably, the only similarity between Dince and the Volvo was that I knew hardly anything about either. But, although I had very few reliable facts, I did feel certain Dince was not the driver. In any case, the traffic offered no break again for three or four minutes, to allow me a 180-degree turn before pursuit. By then the Volvo would probably be gone. Would certainly be gone, because the driver must sense I might come after him and he'd do a swift series of shake-off drills around back streets, as officially recommended (1) to (7) in the manual.

I went on towards the garage, still watching the mirror, but did not see the Volvo. That didn't necessarily signify anything: I hadn't seen it around the side streets, but it might have been there. Perhaps the point of the tracking had gone, though, once he realized he was spotted. I felt certain now it had been a tail, though not at all certain about the driver. I needed a nice, shapely breakdown of conditions. God, had tabulation got into my blood? I seemed hooked on numbered paragraphs:

(1) Someone wanted to know my investigative programme.

(2) He did not want me to know he wanted to know my investigative programme.

(3) But Phaeton already knew my investigative programme, didn't he? He and Rendale had ordered it.

(4) So, if it was someone else in the Volvo, he might hope to use for himself my list of possibles to be visited.

(5) Perhaps the Volvo had been with me when I went earlier to see Alice Huddart. Had I been properly keen eyed on that journey, or later?

(6) It could have followed Luke and me to Bertie's and then picked me up again outside the flat smelling of cloves. (But if they'd located/bugged my car, these plod stages became unnecessary.)

(7) The Volvo's attention was very worrying – and very promising, because;

(8) The Volvo might still lead somewhere if I could find it again. Possibly the driver would return to near the flat as a way of fixing on to me afresh – that's discounting a bug.

(9) Obviously, I had become important. Great. It was due.

(10) A different car might be substituted in any new attempt to tail – the Audi, perhaps.

(11) I would not tell Luke about the possibility. He would insist on trying to nail the driver. Too head-on, too wooden-top.

(12) I definitely would not, could not, tell him that I had wondered whether the driver was Chief Inspector Phaeton in a car from the pool, or even hired. What would that suggest about Phaeton, and especially the fact that he feared identification? It would mean, wouldn't it, that he had some sort of secret connection to the case and that he needed to be sure I only made those inquiries I had been told by him to make? Anything else might disturb a subtle, delicate network.

(13) What sort of secret connection? It could only be a dubious one, couldn't it? A corrupt one? Luke would

not be able to cope with such a terrible, destructive idea.

(14) Dear uncomplex footballing Luke. He was good for me, but not in work things.

(15) It might be significant that I didn't get to Luke until (11) – (14). A bad realization, but I couldn't avoid it.

At Terry Kale's petrol station garage, I saw pretty well instantly that any sort of illicit love link between Alice and the owner must be improbable. And maybe stronger than that. Cruel? Terry Kale would be a fair way into his sixties, very frail looking, big-nosed, big-chinned, watery-eyed, unkempt: not hideously unkempt but more than moderately, say multidimensionally unkempt. Much of the clothing looked Oxfam-reject. Of course, his appearance infuriated me. It meant that if, in fact, there were any sort of sexual motive in this case, Alice Huddart would more likely share it with Philip Otton. I felt another stupid, genuine rush of jealous resentment. Look: I fancied a possible murderer, for God's sake, and one I might have to bring in, along with his beautiful, smoking accomplice, Alice Huddart. Less than two hours ago I'd been groaning, convulsing, slavering with Luke, seeking a fire-burns-out-fire cancellation of Otton from dear, shag-the-arse-off-me-darling Luke. Dear Luke. Dear uncomplex, loving, cock-creditable Luke. Now, this grubby yearn for Otton.

Mayfield, you're a fucking slag. Yes, a fucking *slag.*

The place seemed very busy. Kale had some notable Chamber of Trade role. We talked alone in an upstairs office. 'I categorically do not take offence at your coming to interview me about the death of Mr Claude Huddart,' Kale said, 'in your capacity as a police officer.'

'That categorically *is* my capacity.'

'I'd be entitled to take offence, but I don't.'

'Thanks.'

He put those runny eyes on me, amiably enough. By this I mean I would not want any amiability from them that went beyond the present limited amiability, and certainly nothing *more* than amiability. But would Alice Huddart have felt the same? I'd thought any romantic aspect unlikely. There is never certainty in such things, though, is there? Petrol fumes can affect judgement, and especially when they come from an active forecourt with good profits. Kale had on a dark suit. This seemed to have done plenty of garage time, its sheen gone, the lapels as narrow as budgie wings, and around 2004 vintage. The waistcoat he wore open over a brown V-necked jumper and, showing beneath that, the top couple of inches of a pale blue thermal vest.

'Why might you have felt entitled to take offence at my visit about Claude Huddart and his death, although, as it happens, you don't, Mr Kale?'

'This is a measured response on my part.'

'Often they're the best.'

'I always aim for that, not just when talking to the police.'

'Do you talk to the police a lot?'

'Would you agree there are unspoken suggestions behind this kind of call on me today?' he said.

'Suggestions?'

'I suppose you'll say it's routine.'

'Routine,' I replied.

'A woman like Alice Huddart.'

'Well, yes.'

'We're all on first name terms here.'

'Many businesses are like that now, I gather.'

'Including myself – it's Terry to everyone, not Terence or Mr Kale.'

'Democracy. This can give a good, cooperative feel to a business. Like, We're all in this together, Alice, Terry, and many other first names.'

'What I'm getting at when I say "unspoken suggestions" is I'd call her Alice and she'd call me Terry, but this is general practice here, not special to her. You'd come out here looking for angles, I know. Or you'd come out here with the angles already in your mind, and you'll work hard to make them fit regardless.'

'What kind of angles are you thinking of?'

'No, what kind of angles are *you* thinking of?' He swung his big, sharp chin around to point at me, like a sentry with a Kalashnikov.

'That's not how a police inquiry works. We don't start from preformed notions. A blank page.'

'But you come out to see me. What's it about? What's the *notion* behind that? The unspoken suggestion?'

'Routine.'

'This is why I said I could have taken offence, but don't – on account of favouring a measured response. It's my nature.'

Nobody's going to suggest, spoken or unspoken, that you were banging Alice Huddart and wanted her partner out of the way as a step towards regularizing your relationship. Or, at least, nobody's going to suggest it, spoken or unspoken, now, having gazed at you and your kit and heard your big, croaky, self-obsessed, unctuous voice.

'Did you see much of Claude Huddart, as distinct from Alice?'

'What's that mean "as distinct from"? I've said I prefer a measured response, but I'll react to provocation. Don't toy with me.'

'As distinct from – well, obviously, you're going to see something of Alice because she worked here, but Claude – that might be different.'

'Alice, a very valued member of the staff, although only part-time,' he said. 'We all sympathize greatly with her now.'

'Did you see much of Claude?'

'I spoke just now about this call on me today, by you but you representing your masters.'

'I remember it.'

'Today. *Today.*'

'That's a fact.'

'It's hardly any time since he was found.'

'Yesterday morning.'

'And you're out here already.'

'An inquiry is naturally under way as a matter of absolute urgency.'

'And a visit to me, a priority, yes? I feature high, do I, in this absolute urgency?'

'There is a programme of interviews in such a case.'

'You see why I might have felt resentment, do you?'

'I'm glad you don't.'

'I'm married, you know. Are you married?'

'Partnered.'

'Shacked up. Like the Huddarts.'

'Like many these days.'

'Marriage means something. Partners? Well, I like a measured response. I don't do extremes, and partners are . . . well, partners, I suppose.'

'That kind of thing, yes. If you live with a partner it can be said that the two of you are partners. Most would see it like that.'

'Somebody running this investigation – I mean the top man – he says, "This is a situation of absolute urgency. Get there, Mayfield, and suck what you can out of Terry Kale."'

I tried not to shiver or gag at the wording.

'Rendale?' he said.

'Mr Rendale is in charge, yes. We don't do first names for people in the higher ranks.'

'How come I'm top of the list, or near it?' he said.

'Just how it happened.'

'There isn't any "just how it happened" with police. You'll notice I don't have a solicitor present for this meeting with you. That is my nature. Of an open, cooperative disposition. Tell me the process by which you received your orders to visit me.'

'In this kind of case, backgrounding essential.'

'Whose background?'

'The victim's and those close to the victim. We would assume that, although Alice Huddart's name is not really Huddart, being a partner only, not a wife, we assume a closeness between her and Claude.'

'I wouldn't deny it.'

'And you know them pretty well. Or at least Alice.'

'What does that mean?' he said.

'What?'

'"Or at least Alice."'

'She being the one you'd see most of.'

'In which sense?'

'Employee. When backgrounding, we discover that Alice Huddart had a part-time job here, and therefore this is an element in her background. And we decide to increase our knowledge of her background by talking to you, who features in her background, certain that you, with your Chamber of Trade link, will have a marked sense of civic responsibility and wish to help us chart this background.'

'What does it mean?'

'What?'

'"Backgrounding, background." So much of it.'

'It can be important.'

'What is it?'

'Background? Oh, her activities.'

'Activities? Which?'

'General.'

'Are you saying I'd know her activities?'

'*Certain* activities.'

'Which?'

'At least the work side.'

'What does that mean?'

'What?'

'At least.'

'We've discussed this. Work would be the obvious, basic relationship.'

'Whereas?'

'Whereas what?'

'What do you think was beyond the obvious, basic relationship?'

'*Was* there something beyond?'

'Who decides?' he replied.

'What?'

'That I should be interviewed relating to her activities?'

'This would be standard.'

'A business like mine – do I want police around the site? I'm referring to my reputation and the reputation of this business. What does this visit say to people outside about me and the company?'

'That you knew Alice Huddart, whose husband has been found dead, and that the police wish to build a picture of her life.'

'And *my* life?'

'Only in so far as it concerns *her* life.'

'What does that mean – concerns?'

'Is a factor in.'

'My life a factor in her life?'

'As her employer.'

'Is that how people generally are going to see this call?'

'How else?' Which could be interpreted as: *Get a look at your-self in the mirror, you ageing slob-scruff, and accept that nobody's going to think an attractive young piece such as boob-blessed Alice would enlist you as lover.*

'I expect you know how people are,' he said.

'Hardly any people will realize you've had a police call, unless you tell them. It's a plain clothes visit in an unmarked car.'

'Word travels. What I have to ask is, am I being linked to a woman who is suspected of involvement in a murder? Would you say that's a helpful development for me as a person or for me as owner of this business?'

'I wondered if while talking with Alice during, say, a quiet moment in the working day she might have mentioned something of significance about Claude,' I replied.

'Why would she?'

'Or that kind of thing. Did you see much of Claude?'

'Why would she speak to me about her . . . her partner?'

'In passing.'

'In passing from what to what?' he said.

The office was surprisingly spruce, taking into account what he looked like, and the filthy state of the plimsolls he wore with the rest of it. The room had two modern desk-work stations with computers and phones, three good tapestry up-holstered arm chairs, a water cooler and stack of plastic mugs, and three mahogany finish four-drawer filing cabinets. A framed painted cricket scene hung on the wall behind him, perhaps an original. He sat at a work station. I had an arm chair. He spoke on an intercom to order coffees. He waved at the other work station: 'Yes, Alice sat, sits, there. I can see you want to ask, but here's another of those unspokens. I've told her to forget about the job for as long as it takes to recover from this terrible shock.'

'Kind.'

'With pay.'

'Understanding.'

A middle-aged woman brought in the coffees and left. Kale said, 'Some people these days – I mean following all the police scandals, which we don't need to enumerate, oh, no, that would be too painful for you, I'm sure – some people, even people in decent commercial and professional positions, like, say, oneself, these people have come to regard the police as . . . well, yes, I have to say it, as enemies. This is almost trite now, the middle-class alienation. It's more than a matter of speed cameras. Whereas previously such folk would have been happy to aid the police – indeed, saw it as a natural feature of their lives to aid the police, a worthwhile social duty – oh, yes, that would have been the case, but now, something other, I fear.'

'Do you know Philip Otton?' I said.

'Why?'

'He has theories about today's policing, too.'

'Yet I, I feel most of this hostility to the police is hasty and wrong,' Kale said. 'Despite all the admittedly terrible failures, I think the obligation to help officers such as yourself is still powerful, still valid.'

'Thanks.'

'Or where is civilization as we know it?'

'Quite,' I said, though I felt I should reply in sentences as sweetly engineered as his.

'This is of a kind with what I mentioned earlier – my measured response.'

'I'd wondered about that.'

He touched his nose, a sort of inventorying movement. But, yes, it was still very much there. 'Is it fair to judge a whole organization of men and women by its weakest members? Hardly,' he said.

'Thanks.'

'Police – I certainly don't see them all as tainted.'

'Thanks.'

'I hope I know at least a modicum about civility.'

'I'm sure, Mr Kale. Oh, far, far more than a modicum.'

'Rudeness I abhor. No call for it. Rudeness diminishes not just the object of that rudeness but the deliverer of it. Who was it said, "Manners maketh man", which would probably include woman in this day and age?'

'What I'd visualize is a period of the day when you are both concentrating on business matters and then, maybe, a break from that – perhaps with coffee brought from elsewhere as just now – and a conversation about other things, ordinary, domestic things,' I replied. 'And possibly Claude would be mentioned. In, as I said, passing. Perhaps relating to his career, or where she and he had recently been together socializing, or, say, the cinema.'

'I've told you – I'm married.' He struck the desk a light, glancing knuckle blow, evidently meant to declare a change of subject. 'And then again, some people would detest a fellow like Alice's husband. So-called husband. Oh, I'm sorry – in view of *your* arrangement. A one-time snitch, as I believe it's termed.' He seemed suddenly to have discarded perfect syntax. 'You probably know his role. Or fink is another description. There are folk who cannot forgive this, and I don't mean only those criminals who felt betrayed by him. Finking – regarded as odious by even respectable, blameless figures.' He suddenly performed a volte-face. 'Such a narrow, illogical view, I think.'

'True.'

'How would detection work at all without informants?'

'Quite.'

'And, of course, there are all sorts of them. When an informant reveals bad secrets about a corrupt organization he knows from the inside, he is not reviled as a fink or snitch at all. He becomes noble – a whistle-blower, deemed to have the public's well-being as his motive. Far from being despised, he is beatified. Justifiably.'

'When Claude snitched, whom was he working for?'

'I also respect old-fashioned grammar,' Kale said. 'I hear people say that "whom" is defunct and so-called elitist. Let's have such elitism then, I reply.'

'Bravo!'

'Spying can be regarded as an odious trade, yet think of Alec Guinness in *Smiley's People* on DVD.'

'Did you actually know Claude Huddart yourself?' I replied.

'How do you mean?'

'What?'

'*Actually* know him.'

'Had you met him?' I said. 'Perhaps he'd come to the firm's Christmas party with her, or picked her up from work sometimes in the Citroën.'

'There'd be absolutely no need for him to watch over her at any office party or on excursions. I will not allow shabby behaviour of that description. Undue familiarity – I won't have it. This is why I am sensitive to the damage the firm's reputation might suffer from a police visit about a murder.'

'Perhaps a conversation with him about business matters?' I replied.

'Alice genuinely saw something in Claude, and that was enough for me, regardless. Many folk looked down on him, but nobody is loved by everyone. He was struggling towards something. I admired him for that, given his terrible drawbacks. Yes, admired, despite many of the methods he favoured.'

'Which?'

'Oh, yes, he had his own methods.'

'In which respect?'

'Very much his own.'

'Did you discuss these with Alice Huddart?'

'Tolerance should be a factor in everyone's life.'

'Certainly.'

'I regard tolerance as part of that measured response we spoke of.'

'Interesting.'

'One must realize that not everybody will favour the same methods as oneself, although one may believe in these methods absolutely.'

'Methods for what?'

'This is why I say tolerance.'

Vertical strip blinds on three large windows allowed a view through the gaps on to the petrol station forecourt and then the road. I watched for the Volvo – felt the driver to be talented enough or well-informed enough or bug-aided enough to locate me here. But it did not arrive. Kale had a strong, glib voice for such a ragbag physique and face. As garage owners went he must be up there among the hundred most rhetorical.

'What sort of thing does Mrs Huddart do for you?' I asked, but immediately regretted that wording. His phrase about sucking stuff out of Terry Kale floated for a moment in my mind.

'Do for me?' he said.

'Her work.'

'Alice has real ability with figures and admin generally. Alice knows as much about the innards of this business as I do myself.'

'Is that all right with you?'

'All right? Would I let it happen if it wasn't all right?' A true, crackling snarl. His eyes grew what could have been fierce if it were not for that great aged, drowning wetness. I had the feeling that part of him wanted to act old, so there'd be no question of a liaison with Alice Huddart, and part wanted to be thought only slightly post-prime, and still vigorous, tough, sexy, combative. 'I find the question objectionable,' he said.

Oh, good. In fact, bloody great! Let's get this measured-responding squawker off his bigmouth perch for a while. 'In which respect, Mr Kale,' I said.

'I think I mentioned that I strive to avoid resentment.'

'You aim always for a measured response, I believe. Incidentally, when you measure the response, how do you do it, how do you carry out the measurement? Which, as it were, method?'

'Nonetheless, I am bound to ask, forcefully ask, what lies behind that question about Alice's place in the business?' he replied. He struck the desk again, but a more powerful whack. Yes, he still possessed strength, as well as crummy words like 'nonetheless'. He could do damage. Probably he would occasionally frighten some employees with such sudden, violent anti-furniture behaviour.

I said, 'I was about to—'

'Shall I tell you what lies behind a question like that?'

Yes, most likely he bloody would. I said, 'Believe me, Mr Kale, it was just a—'

'What I find objectionable – to be specific – what I find objectionable is . . .' He wouldn't rush into rage. He required definition, exactness The sloppiness of his clothes didn't mirror a woolly, wrath-driven brain. His anger's topography must be correctly sketched. 'I've explained already that I am basically a supporter of the police even in the present climate, and yet you still come along with a question like that. What, I ask you, does it suggest, this question?'

'I love the way you, in fact, slaughter the question by asking another,' I said, with a small but admiring chuckle. 'This is resourceful, brilliantly defiant, hilariously evasive. Have you ever thought of standing for Parliament?'

'So, I'll tell you what it suggests,' he replied.

'It's good for me to see things from the point you see them from, Mr Kale. It gives a kind of roundness, a fresh perspective, however mad.'

'You hint that I'd come to fear the crafty power over my business Alice might have built for herself, using sly, subtle means, and perhaps in concert with her so-called husband. Or, more than perhaps – *naturally* in concert with her so-called husband. You have a so-called husband yourself, don't you? So you *will* assume that closeness we spoke of, even between unmarried, merely shacked-up couples. I take it there is a certain closeness between you and your . . . well . . . partner.'

'We try now and then.'

'I don't say it's not natural,' he said.

He did have a bit of a brain, then, this one. He was right. I *had* wondered while we talked, and I observed where Alice normally worked, whether her influence in the business had ballooned and scared/troubled him. Perhaps he feared she had given him some sexual come-on with a purpose. I, Samson, she, Delilah.

Kale said, 'And so you think that you see – you imagine that you see – an involvement in the death.'

'All sorts of possibilities will be under consideration at what you've already referred to as an early moment in the inquiries.'

'Is one implication that Alice could have passed on information about this business to her finking so-called husband, and that he retailed it to either business rivals or the likes of you, thus bringing about more hatred and his necessary removal?'

'I merely—'

'This is a damn slur.'

'A slur in which sense?'

'Yes, a slur.'

'Are there matters you would not want publicized about the business, then?' I replied.

'What does that mean?'

'Dodgy matters – regardless of what you've said about reputation and no bonking at office parties or on the excursion coach.'

'What kind of dodgy matters?

'Yes, dodgy.'

'Illegal?' he said.

'I'm not here to accuse you, Mr Kale.'

'Yet. But I'm in the frame.'

'Which frame?'

'You know which fucking frame, you cow. Not one with a Rembrandt picture in it.'

I felt delighted to have dragged the bastard into swearing, abuse and half-baked repartee. 'Mrs Huddart worked here. We would like background knowledge of her. I repeat – it's routine.'

'It's not *Mrs* Huddart who is dead. Why background on her?'

'Collateral. Yes, it might seem a bit oblique. I'm only a detective constable. It's the kind of off-centre assignment I get. Mrs Huddart is off-centre.'

'So far.'

'So far is where we are,' I said. *God!*

'Am I off-centre?'

'For most of her working days here, just Alice and you in this office together?' I replied.

'Many comings and goings – customers, staff. And I'd be out on various calls.'

'You could depend on her to run things in your absence?'

'Alice was chosen, in fact, for her total reliability and discretion.'

'Right.'

'Certainly one must be careful with confidential business matters,' he said. 'I expect you've heard of industrial espionage, have you? Almost any information can be twisted to make something else, can't it? But I don't think I need to tell a police officer that. The adjusted notebook. The "verbals" never verbalized by the accused, but which are quoted against him as word perfect and damning in evidence.'

Fuck off. 'Ah, I see. Did you feel Alice might have, say,

pillow-talked material about your business to Claude, her finking so-called husband, who sold it on? Where would he have sold it? What kind of insights?'

I watched to see whether he seemed hurt when I spoke of Alice and Claude close on adjoining pillows and also, consequently, close further down. We'd already had quite a discussion on closeness. Perhaps a tremor of jealousy in Kale now? I'm a world expert on that. He shifted in his chair, but apparently not as a twitch reaction to what I'd said. He leaned forward at his desk, to see more easily through the strip blinds.

'And, as to comings and goings, now here's someone on a visit who will no doubt set up even more poisonous notions in your police mind – though I stress again that I am in general one who regards the police with approval even affection, despite the kind of cow rudeness you treat me with.'

'Thanks.' I looked where he looked, and wondered if I would now see the Volvo on his forecourt, more of that motorized magic. No. This was one of the biggest silver Mercedes. It had parked away from the petrol pumps. I thought I recognized the bulky man who climbed out, perhaps from the media, possibly from dossier pictures. 'Gleeful?' I asked.

'These foolish, vulgar nicknames,' Kale said. 'He promised to look in. I'd rather refer to him as he should be referred to, Mr George Mittle.'

'Of course,' I said.

'What is the significance, for heaven's sake, of a trivializing, lightweight nickname like that for someone who is, by any reckoning, a truly successful businessman?'

'The Merc would say so.'

'The Merc and much else. A pillar.'

'Certainly.' Did Kale know the kind of business, the specifications of the Mittle pillar? More or less everyone knew, surely. The firm where Gleeful had his true and so far continuing success had entered into systemic, seismic merger talks with Philip Otton's outfit, to combat, perhaps extinguish, mighty Ian Linter in the drugs' game. That was, according to the Gospel of Ronald Blenny of the Mikado and roses. This might be a disputed gospel, admittedly. Several verses in it said Gleeful George Mittle, pillar and Merc owner, and Philip Otton, the blond, beautiful, prosy

Alice standby, possibly used Claude as marriage broker, fixer, middleman, facilitator extraordinary though very mortal. I'd already been required to switch direction abruptly on the journey to Kale because of that sticky Volvo, and I might also need a quick change in my inquiries now. 'Mr Mittle's here to call on you?' I asked.

'Why not?'

'Oh, unquestionably,' I replied.

'We are proud to look after his cars and so on.'

'Nice.' Which and so ons? But I did not ask this, not at once.

'Oh, I'm aware of the gossip,' Kale said.

'There's gossip?'

'Don't make out you haven't heard. A cop, yet you haven't picked up these slanders about the nature of his business? But they are only that, grubby slanders, the fruit of envy and malice. Any talented man of commerce must expect to attract them, unfortunately. It is a comment on our niggling, negative society.'

'And yet Gleeful remains gleeful.'

The desk intercom sounded and Kale answered, said to show Mr Mittle up.

'Would Alice Huddart have dealt with Mittle's account here, and so on?' I asked.

'What does that mean?'

'What?'

'*And so on.* There's an intolerable smear in those words. Another intolerable smear.'

'I'm sorry. I thought they were OK because you'd used them.'

'*And so on.* They pull a curtain over. As if some matters cannot be itemized.'

'Why not?'

'*I* don't know why not. They were *your* slimy words.'

'Would she have dealt with Mittle's account here, and so on?' I replied.

'I'm sure George Mittle won't be in the least put out to encounter you on these premises. Why should he be?' Kale replied.

'Yes, why? And I shan't be put out to encounter *him*. It might turn out to be an education.'

'In his work George meets all sorts, including, very possibly, high officers in your service.'

'Which?' I asked. *Did he, for instance, meet Edward Phaeton?*

'Very high,' he said. 'That's the calibre George is. In his own right. On an equal footing. Why I see him as a pillar.'

'A pillar propping what?'

The door opened. 'Well, here we are, here we are,' Kale replied with a delighted laugh and left his desk to greet Mittle.

Gleeful wore a very rural looking sports jacket and tan trousers. The pattern in the jacket had the slightly excessive vividness that could characterize real county quality or crap – reds and green, mainly, but also touches of yellow. I'd guess that Mittle's jacket was quality, grand quality, virtually squirearchical. An obese squire. His hair did not get to the top of the scalp any longer but bunched reddish and thick just over his ears. He and Kale went through a really thorough handshake in the middle of the room, something suggesting a huge, futile effort by each to trust the other. I found this inspiring to watch in its unstinting, doomed way. I'd seen chief constables greet each other like that.

'We have a detective with us, George.'

Gleeful glanced at me. His podge neck swung the heavy, wide head easily around, like moving a regularly used lock gate. 'I thought cop right away. The clothes. The garden shears hair-do.'

'Whereas yours?' I said.

'What?' Gleeful said.

'Hair-do. Some pissed maniac with a blowtorch?'

'You haven't got to stay, have you, kid? So, on your way.' His voice was light, belligerent, full of true loathing. 'You've had a going-over, Terry, on account of that Huddart dame?'

'Fortunately, our only connection is through the business, of course,' Kale said.

'You've had contact with Alice, Mr Mittle?' I asked.

'Contact? What's contact?'

'Whatever you like,' I said.

'I don't like the word "contact",' Gleeful said.

'Pick your own then,' I said.

'I've told her, George, you would not feel affronted at her presence – that like me you are tolerant of police, even with all we know about them in this tragically soiled twenty-first century.'

Gleeful changed the glance at me into a stare. 'So, it's re what? Alice Huddart and . . .?'

'Claude,' Kale said.

Mittle became sort of solemn. 'What happened to Claude – definitely right out of order.'

'Absolutely,' Kale said.

'Shall I tell you one thing you'll never hear me say?' Gleeful remarked.

'This opens quite a vista, owing to your habitual tact and reticence, George,' Kale said.

'You won't never hear me say that crud, Claude, had it coming, the fucking scheming, pestilential microbe,' Gleeful replied. 'He deserved to be squashed, yes, but am I likely to glory in it?'

'Hardly. Like myself, George,' Kale said. 'I've mentioned to Detective Constable Mayfield that I believe in a measured response. I think you, also, are inclined that way – averse to extremism in any form. Before your arrival, George, we were discussing background, and that measured response in both you and myself comes inevitably from our respective backgrounds, not identical, yet with much in common.'

Gleeful still had the gaze on me. 'I never seen you before, did I? You the squad? I'd remember someone with a hairdo like that.'

'Do you know people in the squad?' I said.

'George knows all sorts.'

'This is a murder, Mr Mittle,' I said.

'That right?' Gleeful said. 'Well, well, well, is that right?'

Kale, in response, had a small, measured, laugh.

'So, you trying to put it on to Ter?' Gleeful asked me. 'The Claude thing.'

'Some routine background inquiries,' I said.

'Look, you titted sleuth, do you think someone placed so nice and tidy such as Ter would ever get himself dirtied by a slaughter and by face surgery on some nothing man like Claude? What would be in it for Ter?'

'Thank you, George,' Kale said.

'We're doing a lot of visits,' I said.

'So, you trying to put it on to Terry? In my view, a work relationship only between him and Alice Huddart.'

'I've made that point,' Kale said.

'Did you know Claude well, Mr Mittle?' I replied.

'I never seen you before,' Gleeful said. He sat down at Alice Huddart's work station. 'What right you got to ask questions, kid, just coming out with them the way you do? I'll grant you that.'

'What?' I said.

'You comes out with them questions just the way you want to,' he said.

'I noticed that, too,' Kale said.

'I think it's best like that,' I said. 'I reason it this fashion: if you're going to ask a question, the most useful way to do it is to ask it. There's a simplicity to that.'

'You got any notion in the least how things work?' Gleeful said.

'I've mentioned this to her,' Kale said.

'What?' Gleeful said.

'The intricacies. The connections,' Kale said.

'How which things work?' I said.

Mittle's voice boomed for a little while, and he put on magnanimity. 'All right, you're a kid, and I don't want to browbeat, nothing like that. There's a place for people like you.'

'It would be *so* unlike you, George, to browbeat,' Kale said. 'Reasonableness – that, above all, is the quality you're famed for.'

'Maybe it's not fair for me to expect her to know how things work,' Mittle said, 'in the sense of *really* knowing.'

'Which things?' I replied.

'Generally,' Mittle said.

'Generally, but at a certain level,' Kale said.

'Let me ask you this,' Gleeful said. 'Are you asking questions alone, off your own impulse, like? Do your chiefs realize you're out by yourself, intervening?'

'Intervening in what?' I said.

'That's the point, isn't it?' Gleeful said.

'What?' I said.

'If you knew what you was intervening in you wouldn't be intervening like this, because you'd see that what you're doing is intervening.'

'I told Mr Kale that it might be an education to meet you,' I said.

'Your chiefs – they could be put out by that kind of operating,' Gleeful said.

'Which kind?' I said.

'Yours,' Gleeful said.

'It's very useful – lucky – to have bumped into you here,' I replied.

'Useful? Lucky? In which way?' Gleeful said.

'Taking things forward,' I said.

'Which things?' he said.

'We echo each other,' I said.

He frowned for a spell and seemed to mutter 'Useful. Lucky' a couple of times. The benevolence left his voice. He spoke like a revelation, breathless, contemptuous, his huge, flabby chest bucking. 'You trying to put it on me? You trying to put the Claude Huddart job on *me*?'

'We're doing a lot of visits. We're talking to everyone who was in touch with him in a business sense or otherwise.'

'In touch?'

'Close.'

'Close?' Gleeful said.

'In a business way or any other,' I said.

'Which business way or any other?' Gleeful said.

'That's what we're trying to find out,' I said.

'You know how they are, George.'

'Would I do business with some little twerp like Claude?' Gleeful said. 'You seen his car?'

'Well, yes. He was dead in it,' I said.

'That's the sort of car he *would* be dead in,' Gleeful said.

'*Would* you do business with him?' I said.

'Ah,' he replied.

'What, George?' Kale asked.

'I see it,' Gleeful said.

'Not much can defeat *you*, George,' Kale said.

'She's swallowed the rubbish talk that's around the place,' Gleeful said.

'Plenty of that,' Kale said.

'You know what I mean, Ter?' Gleeful said.

'As I remarked, so much of it,' Kale said. 'Which do you have in mind, George?'

'I'm sure she'd like to tell us,' Gleeful said.

'What exactly did Claude's twerpishness consist of?' I replied.

'I hope I would never speak harshly of the dead,' Gleeful said, 'old Citroën or not.'

'You're not like that, George,' Kale said.

'This is someone who had his face sliced, so you got to sympathize with the little twerp,' Gleeful said.

'Why would Claude's twerpishness stop you doing business with him?' I said. 'There must be quite a few twerps on the business scene. Maybe you'd *need* a twerp now and then.'

'You can see where this is going, can you, Ter?' Gleeful replied.

'There's a definite direction to it,' Kale said.

'It's about Claude Huddart trying to con me,' Gleeful said.

'That really would make him a twerp!' Kale said. 'A foolish, presumptuous twerp.'

'And maybe con Otton as well,' Gleeful said.

'In which respect, George?'

'Isn't that right, detective constable? The talk around says me and Phil Otton wanted to join and wipe out Sociable Ian. Claude to do the preparatories. He gets up someone's nose, or more than one, during all this, and so gets a knife up *his* nose etcetera. That's the chatter.'

'It's rubbish, is it?' I said.

'Would I join with Otton, for God's sake?'

'Would George join with Otton, for God's sake?'

'Would you, Mr Mittle?'

'*Would* he, for God's sake?' Kale said. 'Where've you been all your life, detective constable?'

'Sociable's firm is well out ahead.' I said. 'Enviable? A target?'

'Are you here to stir, just to stir?' Mittle said. 'What she here for, Ter?'

'General inquiries,' I said.

'Alice?' Gleeful would be thirty-six or seven, between fat and gross, white, unnimble, his heavy hands well-jewelled. 'You think Alice would do her own man in his own car on his own drive?'

'We're not certain he was actually killed there,' I replied.

'What *are* you actually certain about, kid?' His voice minced, making fun of what I'd said. Somehow the thinness of the tone seemed just right for his bulk, like a big kettle whistling on the boil.

'I don't understand the relationship between you and Mr Kale,' I replied. 'Yes, I'm struggling.'

'Relationship?' Gleeful asked.

'The business connection. I see the heart-to-heart greeting when you arrive. This is supreme bollocks, of course, but you obviously consider it worthwhile doing the big chums act.'

'I got cars, haven't I?' Gleeful said. 'Terry's a garage.'

'We're proud to look after the Mittle fleet,' Kale said. 'The staff enjoy working on such vehicles. They feel fulfilled.'

'It's like a network,' I replied.

'What network?' Mittle said.

'You, Mr Kale, Alice, Claude,' I said.

Gleeful thought some more. And then there was what looked like the biggest change yet. He put a real gaze on Kale. 'Did you call her up, Terry – get her here to fucking talk to me like this?'

'Call her up, George?'

'Arrange this. She says it's lucky she met me here. But *was* it lucky? You fixed it, Ter.?'

'I didn't know she was coming, believe me, George.'

'Well I'm not sure about that,' Gleeful said.

'What?' Kale asked.

'I'm often lucky about being in the right place,' I said.

Some concentrated leg and arm effort came from Gleeful and he stood, his superb jacket done up around the blob frame on all three buttons, as if for a bet, or like a corset. None popped, despite the threshing. Kale was still at his desk. Gleeful waddled over there with quite a bit of stunted majesty and sat on a spare straight-backed chair in front of him, packets of his behind hanging in nicely equal lumps to each side. 'What don't I feel sure about? What I don't feel sure about is if I believe you. You trying to push something off of you on to me, Terry? The old drill? She got you all tied up as relative to Alice, yes, so you're thinking fast. Stick it on to George instead.'

'George, I swear—'

'You and Terry fixing this one between you, kid? Trying to

fix this one between you. Don't you know how things work here?'

'You've asked me that,' I replied. 'You sound like a sodding parrot.'

'Don't you know how things work here?'

'Where?'

'Don't come the fucking dumbo with me, you fucking dumbo,' Gleeful replied. 'You think you can cook a plot with someone like Terry, and between you see off George Mittle? George Mittle personal. That's mad. That's an insult.'

'Of course it is, George,' Kale said. 'Would be, if it were so.'

'Kid, I could pick up a phone and you'd be nowhere.'

'Calling whom?' I replied.

'Calling never mind who,' he said.

'Good, George,' Kale said. 'Don't kowtow to her, the cow bully, and her grammar. A college kid.'

'So, just be careful, Terry,' Gleeful replied.

Lovely, this sudden gap between them: Gleeful's paranoia and jumpiness. I said, 'Was Mr Kale doing something with Alice Huddart – something deep and creative, not just account books?'

But these two had begun a private battle. 'George, please, please, you mistake things,' Kale said.

'You're turning into a real disappointment, Ter.'

'An accident she was here,' Kale cried. 'Absolutely no intention to put you on a plate for her. Who puts George Mittle on a plate? Oh, detective, tell him this or—'

I said, 'Was Mr Kale doing something with Alice Huddart – something deep and creative, not just account books?'

'You sound like a sodding parrot,' Gleeful replied.

'A special intimacy – through the company books, and possibly the usual, despite what you said, Mr Mittle. What is this garage? What is it a cover for? But whatever it is, you're involved, aren't you, Gleeful? You're not going to tell me.'

'I've asked her not to call you that, George,' Kale said. 'So impertinent and mannerless. The tactics, as always with police, to diminish, to humiliate. She's a novice, but she's learned that much already.'

'As I see it, this was to be an emergency session between you two,' I said. 'I strayed in. Sorry. Oh, so very sorry! Maybe Terry

– Terry, this high-flying Chamber of Commerce man – maybe
Terry's supposed to advise you, Gleeful, on how the join-up with
Philip Otton should be managed, now Claude's delicate skills
are no longer on offer. Or maybe how to get out of it. Possibly
you've done your firm real harm by killing Claudey, Gleeful, no
matter how badly he might have been betraying you. That's if
you did kill him, obviously.'

'Kid, you want me to tell you what I notice?' Gleeful replied.

'About what?' I asked.

'About you.'

'I shouldn't think it's favourable,' I said.

'What I notice is the way you say his name.'

'Whose?' I said. 'Claude?'

'No. You say it full of sex,' Gleeful answered. 'This is pussy-
speak.'

'I thought that, too,' Kale said.

'Whose name?' I asked, sure of the answer, naturally.

'It's happening all the damn time,' Gleeful said. 'You've met
him, have you? You're not the first, kid. Them suits. The
blondness. The sick slimness. That way he talks – the slim slim-
iness. The women really go for him. Even cop women. Maybe
especially cop women.'

'Oh, I'd definitely think so, George,' Kale said. His eyes
seemed to grow more clouded, as if he were quietly weeping
about a loss.

'You gets a knee tremble every time you thinks of him, don't
you, detective?' Gleeful asked. 'Your clothes and that haircut –
but you still pray he will notice you, don't you?'

'Who?' I said.

'Philip, of course,' Kale replied.

'Philip Otton?' I said, with the widest laugh I could lay on.
'Oh, really!' *Did* I get a knee-tremble every time? No. Only now
and then.

'Which is why you come and try to put it on me, instead,'
Gleeful said. 'Get the heat off of dear, darling Philip Otton. Or
you'll put it on Terry. You'd love to frame me. Or Terry. One or
other – as long as it's not the marvellous, adorable Phil. How
police operate. Women police.'

'You move about, don't you?' I replied. 'First you say I'm

trying to stick Claude's death on to Mr Kale, then you accuse
Mr Kale of joining with me to frame you, and now you're telling
me Philip Otton did Claude.'

'There it is,' Gleeful said. 'Again.'

'What?' I said.

'The way you say him, killer or not,' Gleeful replied. 'So
loving, so full of . . . well, of dirty detective passion and protection. You're taking care of him, seeing he's safe and untouched,
aren't you?'

'I picked that up, too,' Kale said. 'She's looking for fall-guys,
so her glossy favourite gets no aggro. You and I, we're mere
victims, George.'

Gleeful's huge face gleamed with big anger. 'I won't take it,'
he shouted. 'I got friends.'

'What kind of friends?' I asked. 'Where?'

He waved down towards the Mercedes. 'I got position, I got
wealth.'

'Good for you, George,' Kale replied.

'Who the hell gave you the name Gleeful?' I said.

He said, 'Women – they see a bit of extra weight here and
there in someone like me, and think they can treat me like shit.
All the time it's happening. I show them the Mercedes or the
BMW, and even my properties in various desirable locations, but
I know they're still looking at my very minor body thickening
here and there, and making their selfish, inhuman decisions. Why,
oh why, won't my money talk to them?'

'Inhuman indeed, George,' Kale remarked. 'Dismayingly short-
sighted of them.'

'Yes, both, both,' Gleeful said. 'So inhuman. So short-sighted.'
He sobbed twice. His head fell forward, like someone waiting
for the axe. It would have to be a big axe and a first-class cleave.
'They turn away to someone like Otton. Alice the same.'

'She's his?' I asked.

'Is this what life is about, then – looks, suits, rotten glamour?'
Gleeful said. 'I got to say I think there's more than that to it.'

'Like what?' I asked. 'Like building a mighty drugs cartel?
How are you going to work with Otton if you hate his looks and
his suits?'

'But *you* don't hate them, do you?' Gleeful replied.

'Is the hate because you decided Terry and Claude were trying to rip you off some way, Gleeful?' I said. 'The merger's dead – as dead as Claude? This conference with Terry was to bury it officially?'

'Haven't I protested about your calling him Gleeful?' Kale replied. 'Intolerably insolent.'

NINE

A nd then, of course, of bloody course, the Volvo was behind me again when I drove away from my meeting with those two bonny charmers, Kale and Gleeful – behind me as it had been behind me earlier, two vehicles back, almost unnoticeable but not unnoticeable if you had been trained to look out for such things. And especially when you'd already spotted the Volvo on its previous appearance and expected/dreaded a reincarnation. The driver I could still not make out properly but I found myself muttering to myself, 'Phaeton, Phaeton, Phaeton. Why, why Phaeton?' The idea scared me. It scared me far more than if I'd been able to decide definitely the tail was that middle-aged mystery lad at the Dince street pick-up. To be tailed by a possible villain might be chilling, but easily understandable. We, the police, are at war with villains and possible villains. Hostile behaviour from them is natural. Tailing would usually be regarded as hostile. But, to be followed and observed by a senior colleague suggested something shady, maybe rotten, in the system we lived by and in. It could signal the approach of breakdown, even chaos. Boyfriend Luke constantly feared this kind of collapse, and looked for early symptoms of it. He'd see them in the Volvo, if it contained Phaeton. Yes, Luke would diagnose a systemic fault, and forecast danger for anyone touched by it. And I'd more or less agree. I liked a little private enterprise, but I also liked good systems. I liked reliable, properly managed systems: one of my reasons for joining the police. And, especially, uncorrupted systems.

Although I wished to, I could not decide whether Volvo man equalled older Audi man. I struggled for glimpses of him in the mirror during those moments when the snoop car became a bit more visible. And I concluded that the driver's upper body was, in fact, not the upper body of someone short and bulky, but of someone tall and well-built, someone more like Phaeton. Blobby people had their own blobby, bulbous way of sitting behind a wheel, like Mr Toad. And this time I also settled in my mind – or more than half settled it, anyway – that the driver must certainly be younger than middle-aged, more like in his thirties, Phaeton's decade. I couldn't be sure how I diagnosed this given all the difficulties, but I felt it like a fact.

Question: if it was Phaeton, should I be trying to get rid of him, and get rid of him in a pretty obvious, rudimentary way – a dash to the side streets? Would he assume I needed secrecy? And he'd wonder for what, and why? Let him wonder. After all, for what and why did I merit surveillance? Yes, I could wonder, too. And, wondering, I went back to the basic query: why should a colleague dog a colleague? I didn't like having the attendant, wanted to be rid of it. Difficult. But I'd been trained in another anti-surveillance dodge, which I hadn't tried yet. I'd seen no chance for it. The objective is to turn the situation inside out. That is, instead of being tailed oneself, get on to the tail of the tail. One way to upend matters, to reverse matters, and bliss-fully become the stalker not the stalked requires a decent-sized roundabout. There'd been nothing suitable on the route to Kale's garage after I first noticed the Volvo, but I would find one now. A small roundabout or a token flat one won't do. You need manoeuvring space for this act of magic.

Here's the drill:

(1) You enter the roundabout as though meaning to take one of the exits on offer.
(2) Instead, you accelerate right the way around, come full circle and, if you have the luck, find yourself nicely behind the shadow vehicle.

My mind seemed not totally clear, and my grip on local road geography consequently uncertain, but I reckoned I could lead the Volvo to a spot where this stratagem might work. True, it amounted to another of those tricks known to any police-trained driver, and I couldn't be sure Phaeton would be fooled – if Volvo equalled Phaeton. I longed to believe I had it wrong. To repeat the question, why would a police officer, a mate, tail another police officer, a mate, unless:

(1) The tail believed the target officer corrupt and should be watched.
(2) Or, the tail had his own corrupt and secret connections.
(3) Or felt anxious in case someone disturbed them?
(4) He might want to check I went only where I'd been deputed to go.
(5) He might somehow have heard of my other, private discoveries on this case, or what I *thought* private, and real, discoveries.

Rumour – and more than rumour – haunted this case, and a successful cop like Phaeton would have his established, discreet ways of tuning in. The scenario terrified me, not just because I could be in danger the way Claude had been in danger. It had grown wider than that – weightier than that: at the least philosophical and almost religious. Big, big ideas? Maybe. But they could be true, all the same. If Phaeton were corrupt it meant that even the most gifted people in the service could be spoiled and soiled by temptation. The whole law and order structure became imperilled. Money – dirty money – could win. Disintegration. To confirm: systemic, seismic. Luke for ever feared such apocalypse. I began to share this massive qualm.

I drove out towards Barracks Yard roundabout, off my true route, but necessary and, as I remembered it, suitable. The Volvo stayed. Obviously, no question now, I had a tail. And, yes, nice one Sharon, here comes the roundabout, bush-rich, mounded, extensive. A flapping bed sheet fixed to a couple of saplings had 'HAPPY SIXTIETH MAURICE YOU CODGER' written on it in fluorescent silver paint. I signalled I would be taking the second left exit so he would know where to go off the roundabout. And so that, as long as he behaved to plan – *my* plan – I would know where to follow when I'd done my circle and needed to take a place behind him fast, with one or two vehicles between us, maximum, and before more traffic engulfed him. I let the signal light blink its momentarily false message until automatically cancelled and then belted around to the right all the way. Angry horns blared, though probably not the Volvo's. Perhaps some drivers thought I wanted a second look at Maurice's birthday linen – might imagine I knew good old Maurice, the codger, and was doing a sort of motorized celebration. I kept going, touched fifty and got some wheel squeal on the turns, then came off where I'd indicated I intended coming off originally. The signal had been absolutely correct, but early.

And it worked. It worked? The Volvo lay ahead, its driver presumably baffled because he no longer had me in sight through the windscreen. And he might be uncertain whether the Ford in his mirror at third back and part hidden was mine. Vehicles coming towards us on the other side of the road prevented him from bringing his car around to get back on to the roundabout and search. I'd taken exactly the sort of position he had kept earlier, those two cars between him and me, not that I needed to shield myself as he had. He knew my identity. He'd be aware soon enough that I'd conned him by maverick driving. What did I make of the back of his head, then, in the intermittent sightings I had of it now? I was not an expert on Phaeton from this angle, but I still thought it could be him, was more likely to be him than that other main contender on my shortlist. God, I could be wrong altogether and it might be neither of them. The idea produced more worries. Who else would want to follow me?

The neck undoubtedly looked more like the neck of a six-foot heavyweight than of a middle-height tub, didn't it? Didn't it? Necks – their structure – I lacked expertise in this area. I knew my assessment might be crude. I had to go by it, though. I considered that the back of a fat neck would look all lateral, fibrous and splurged. The other type of neck back always appears strong and has some width, but the chief impression is of upward thrust towards the head and brain, and beyond this towards fine realms of high achievement. Naturally, the most powerful argument against the Phaeton choice was that he would never let me get into his wake by such a famous, elementary, old ruse, would he? Would he? Lead the chief inspector into a roundabout and he'd expect tactics. He'd know that the Ford's swift circumnavigation did not relate in any way to Maurice's sixtieth, the codger. I imagined I'd been clever, but could it be only that: imagination? I knew it was a weakness of mine sometimes, to think myself smarter than the opposition, any opposition. It's called competitiveness by some – the kinder folk. But, yes, there's a helping of arrogance, too. Useful arrogance? Essential arrogance?

A girl needs at least a cupful of that, especially a police girl. Luke used to warn me about it, in his very intelligent, documented, well-meaning, down-to-earth fashion. Thanks, Luke.

Perhaps Phaeton felt content to have me in this position so he could lead to somewhere he regarded as suitable for . . .? As suitable. No denying, I felt anxious. Just the same, I kept with the Volvo, sweat on my paws and elsewhere, a pain across my chest though probably not an absolute heart attack, yet. Nothing in the training covered the subtleties of gum shoeing a boss. He led towards the edge of the city. We passed headquarters. For a moment I wondered if he'd pull in there and expect me to do the same. Then, with the authority of the building near, he would tell me it had all been harmless, a test of my alertness and skills. But he kept going at a nice comfortable pace. He didn't want to shake me off. Once we left the centre the traffic thinned, and after another few miles I had nothing between him and me. I lay far back but not far enough to lose him, and so not far enough for him to have doubts that I was a tail. He did not seem to check the mirror very much. It was as though he felt sure I would continue.

This apparent casualness brought my doubts back. Was it really Phaeton after all? He would have been taught to get the maximum from his mirror. In any case, how could he be so confident? On the other hand, that middle-aged stranger from the Audi might feel very sure I would not let him go, because he might take me to Dince. Or take me somewhere and tell me what had happened to Dince. He possibly knew this would interest me – had probably seen me urgently following Dince on foot in Cinder Street, including a run.

The burbs faded and we were on a flat coastal road running between a mixture of fields and a developing industrial estate with its bright-coloured, repulsively angular, metal-framed, grant-aided, economic-miracle, new factories. Horses and sheep grazed. Fly-tipped builder's waste blocked a few field gates. A burned-out caravan stood on its nose in one of the stagnant, weed-covered, narrow canals. After a few more miles the Volvo turned off on to a single-track, poorly made-up road that must lead right down to the sea. It was remote here, no housing or factories. I traipsed after. He would know I'd traipse after, although I had a couple of moments when I considered abandoning, if I could find somewhere wide enough for a three-point turn. But, no, I went on.

In a while, I saw the silver car parked at the end of this road. Edward Phaeton, in civilian clothes, had left the vehicle and climbed the earthwork sea wall. He watched my car draw in and beckoned me. I went to join him. The tide was down. Nearby stood a small, brick, windowless building with one locked door. I guessed it must be a sewage control point for the outfall pipe that stretched across black-brown mudflats.

'Some spot,' I said.

'It's not Cannes. Best like that.'

'Best how?'

We stood between the little building and the mud flats, so we would not be outlined on the sea wall. The cars below lay hidden unless anyone came right down the side road. It was like a lovers' meeting, and not at all like.

'I wanted to be sure you stayed safe,' he said.

'That's why you followed me?'

'It's important you keep to what you're ordered to do, only that.'

'I did,' I said. 'Visit Kale.'

'I know. I needed to be sure. I feel you might be into other aspects of the case.'

'You feel?' I said. 'That's not a police word.'

'Yes, I feel you might be. It's dangerous. I mean dangerous if you leave the set path.'

'Why?'

'I can't really explain now.'

'Why? Why, sir?' I asked.

He seemed to think about that, maybe wavered. 'No, I can't,' he said eventually.

'Aren't I entitled?'

'And then I let you get behind me so we could come out here and talk,' he replied. 'It's not something to discuss at headquarters.'

'I'm being warned off?'

'You're being asked to remain within certain defined limits.'

'That seems a normal sort of instruction for a superior to give a subordinate. It couldn't be said at headquarters? Did we need this rigmarole?'

'Will you stay within the specified limits?' he replied.

'Absolutely.'

'For instance, I saw you leave the Huddart house for some reason on the day the body was found,' he replied. 'When you returned I heard of no explanation.'

He waited but I did not respond. He hadn't asked a question.

'Was a character called Dince there? Sometimes called Dince,' he said.

'You know him?' I asked.

'And then contact with that old stirrer and junkie piss-artist, Ron Blenny. Flowers and so on.'

He waited but I stayed silent.

'These are possibly not good areas for you to drift into.'

'I haven't drifted into any areas. Sir.'

'You'd like to. You'd try to.'

'Are you referring to some confidential police operation that I might barge into and spoil?'

'People talk to you, I imagine,' he replied.

'Some people do.'

'It's an asset in a detective.'

'What?'

'The ability to win their confidence.'

'Whose?'

'People like Dince and Ron Blenny. I imagine they've talked to you.'

'I seem to bump into all sorts,' I said.

'That, again, is a plus. If we take a lad like Dince – I suppose you went after him because he'd said something, without actually saying much at all. You went after him for clarification, I expect. You seemed to regard this as important. You ran part of the way, I understand.'

'When you say "a lad like Dince", what do you mean? What kind of a lad is he?'

'Changeable. And not just his names.'

'Changeable from what to what?'

'I take it he approached you, rather than the other way about?' he said.

'I didn't know him. I couldn't have approached him.'

'But you interviewed people around the Citroën. Naturally. Basic. You could have come upon him like that – another accident, as it were. Whereas, if *he* contacted *you,* that's not at all an accident. He knew you, and possibly quite a bit about you.'

Yes, quite a bit.

'This could be worrying,' he said.

Yes, I worried. 'In what sense?' I said.

'He *did* make the first move, then, did he? What kind of information did he have on you? Work place? Home address? I can see why you'd be troubled and want to get after him down Cinder Street. You treated this as private between him and you. That was possibly not the way to handle it. Similarly Blenny. The floral tribute. What prompted him to that? Had you given him some insider stuff? He's a great collector of unconsidered trifles.'

'He'd tried a grope. He felt ashamed.'

'He was willing to wait more than half an hour in the vestibule.'

'He'd bought the flowers. They had to be delivered in person.'

'Couldn't he have left them, with a note?'

'He might not want to write down what it was about. Cornelius, on Reception, would have read it. That could have been embarrassing for me. Blenny already felt guilty. He wouldn't want to give me more trouble.'

'In the Mikado, was it – where the familiarity took place?'

'Attempted familiarity.'

'Do you do much of that?'

'What?'

'Go to nightclubs alone. I don't think Luke was with you, was he?'

'I'd had a crawl – visited a few places.'

'Why?'

'Luke was working.'

'A search? Still on the Dince trail? And then, next day, over to the coffee shop with Blenny the Fingers. Apparently a serious conversation.'

'My feeling is you have to listen to people. A lot of what they say will be rubbish and lies, but, also, there might be something worthwhile.'

'Was there?'

'He theorizes, doesn't he?'

'Not to me, ever,' Phaeton said.

'There are a lot of people like that, sounding off when they've taken a bucketful, or been snorting.'

'We're talking coffee shop, though.'

'It's his way.'

'I'll be interested to see your notes on Kale,' he replied.

Phaeton was round-faced, blue-eyed, boyish, frank-looking, somehow priestly in appearance, and not at all frank or boyish or priestly. He would never have made his rank at this age otherwise. Was I being told to stay out of private arrangements he and perhaps others had somewhere? I thought of Gleeful's threat to get on the phone to a friend if I created real trouble. *Tried* to create real trouble. Perhaps Gleeful hadn't needed to get on the phone. Maybe the friend could act unprompted and get me into this delectable conference venue by playing about with surveillance procedures. Or, by letting *me* play about with surveillance procedures – the same thing.

'Gleeful George was at the garage,' I said.

'Yes.'

'You knew he'd be there?'

'I saw him arrive in the second-string Merc.'

'You did turn up at the garage then, eventually?'

'As I said, I wanted to be sure you stayed safe.'

'How could you do that if you disappeared?'

'I didn't disappear. I went out of your view for a time. That's different. I saw you go in to meet Kale. You didn't spot me then, that's all.'

'Where were you?'

'Yes, I watched you go in.'

'But I was looking out for you.'

'Of course. You failed to see me.'

'I don't believe it.'

'I admire that,' he replied.

'What?'

'The aggressiveness. The scepticism. Not afraid to express them. These are good starting points.'

'I'm not just starting. I've got four years in. You make me sound backward.'

'You have a lot of the tailing skills, Sharon. Not the lot.' Phaeton began to descend the earthwork wall towards his car. 'So, stay within the limits. I'll tell you exactly what you can look at. Don't stray. I can't be around non-stop to guard you.'

'From?

'I'd like to. Impossible.'

'I don't want that.' *God, he was patronizing.*

'Of course you don't.'

'You know the Mercedes, and the grade of Mercedes. Do you know Gleeful?' I had to yell the questions. He'd reached his car.

Phaeton waved – a single, brisk movement. He shouted back, 'I'm keen to see your notes on Mittle, too.' He climbed into the Volvo, manoeuvred around and left up the side road.

TEN

S ex: complicated. Relationships: super-complicated. We're in bed, Luke and I, and he says, 'I saw Warren Dell at a soccer team practice today. We had a drink afterwards.'

Men don't usually talk about other men immediately post coital. They want their uniqueness appreciated. I was ready to appreciate Luke's, so it pissed me off to hear his mind had switched so fast to footie. Think of those lines from Byron's *Don Juan*:

Man's love is of man's life a thing apart,
'Tis woman's whole existence.

Not totally true, but near. 'Ah, how's the Drug Squad?' I said.

'Strange. That is, I don't know about the squad, but Warren was strange. He obviously wanted to talk.'

'About the gorgeous art of throwing in from touch or roughing up referees?'

'About work.'

'Which?'

'Drug Squad business.'

'What business?'

'It sounded like some of his own inquiries.'

'He opened up? Warren did? Warren! Yes, that would be strange.' I tried to stay as relaxed and comfortably enmeshed in Luke's body as I had been before, but knew I tensed. That's the way of bodies, isn't it? They can be impressionable and a give-away.

Luke said, 'More than strange. Weird.'

I detested such a word. It melodramatized. It revealed nothing. It clouded.

Luke said, 'He told me things I sensed he wanted passed on to you.'

'He *what?*'

'Yes, I know . . . but . . . yes!'

I thought back to our hotpot lunch meeting in the pub with Warren, and to his customary, trained uptightness and lack of communication behind the dozy-looking face. There'd been a shift? Something seismic? The term was around. As a matter of fact, at the lunch I did occasionally feel – half feel – that Warren would like an information swap. Had the latest talk between him and Luke been a sequel to this? I would have preferred to sit up in the bed now, make sure I gave full concentration, and ask Luke, What things did Warren want passed on, what, what, what – and why, why, why? Since when did Drug Squad people dish out secrets, dish out secrets even to eternally beloved soccer confrères?

I wished I could have been head-on, face-on, to Luke when I flung these queries, if I ever did fling them. But, instead, I stayed put and spoke to the patch of skin on Luke's back between his shoulders, where my mouth happened to be, spoke sleepily, casually, as if sated. This is what I meant about the complexities of sex, and the super-complexities of relationships: I'd felt aggrieved because Luke wanted to spout male talk immediately after love-making, but now I longed to hear what it was Warren had told him.

Before all this business chatter, I'd sensed a special brilliant joy about Luke tonight; about *him*, and therefore about me, though I'd graciously and gratefully admit he started it. That old black magic, reciprocity, had me in its spell. Let's get mutual, OK? OK. Well, of course, there should always be a special brilliant joy about sex. There isn't, though, is there? Or there hadn't always been between Luke and me, lately, at any rate. Joy's an elusive item, and not always easy to hook and bring aboard. Joy's bigger than, say, only pleasure or delight. Sex: that body melange, that nicely violent interlocking, can unfortunately emphasize all the other disharmonies, spiritual/mental, I mean.

Would I fantasize and emote about some elegant derelict like Philip Otton if things between Luke and me had been all right? But, listen – I mean this as a rhetorical question. That is, one not needing an answer, because the answer is built-in and obvious. Say nowt in reply, thank you. And the built-in and obvious answer is no, to my question: Would I fantasize and emote about some

elegant derelict like Philip Otton if things between Luke and me
had been all right? No. No. No. That *is* the built-in, obvious
answer, isn't it? Isn't it?

Tonight, it was as though Luke and I were closer than we had
ever been, even closer than at the beginning months ago: closer
in all ways, not just the sex ways, though these turned out very
right, too. Complete merger. I could have said I felt happy, but
I never risked such a boast: an invitation to all the circling, flying,
stalking, creeping, ganging snags to move in and fuck up. Fuck
up a fuck in this case. My parents had a very majestic cat called
Hubris. It was succeeded by one called Nemesis, because Hubris,
on one of his strutting explorations, got accidentally locked in
a neighbour's garage and starved to death while they holidayed
in Mexico. As a result, I grew up knowing what both words
meant, and their connection. Later, I came to understand them
even better. They made me wary of contentment.

'You think Warren talked stuff he'd like passed on to me?' I
said. 'Which? Crumbs from the know-all man's table?'

'I don't think he knows all and he knows he doesn't know
all.'

'All detectives know they don't know all, but they know how
to make a show of knowing all so they can bluff the punter into
talking and, by listening, get closer to knowing all.'

So, then, this bizarre – weird? – mix of love and love talk
and job talk. We lay folded around each other and our minds
meshed pretty well, too. I thought I could see what had happened,
what had transformed things. It was marvellous. It would last,
I knew. Yes, I knew it, didn't I? Didn't I? I could tell Luke
suddenly understood me better and more deeply. He realized it.
He knew he had somehow nipped past most of those blocks and
barriers that my sort of work planted around me. Until now,
they'd excluded him from sections of my life, important sections.
These were not just the normal confidentialities of the job –
those routine bits of secrecy which anyone in all sorts of careers
might observe. Though, actually, of course, most people spill the
confidentialities to their spouse/partner, because such items are
often the most interesting in their domestic conversation, and
domestic conversation always needs a lift.

I'm talking wider than that, here. Wider, again, yes: the waffle element will probably become a danger, but I'll watch for it, attempt to squash it. Here goes then: after a while, detective work begins to impose a new personality, an amended self, on almost all those in the game. If it doesn't, the likelihood is you could still do the job, but it would be *only* a job, not what it ought to be, an obsession, a holy apostleship to that seriously fractured concept, law and order. And if it does instil those changes in your psyche, you might begin to find relationships outside the confines of the snoops' snoopish trade guild very difficult. It's why I said Byron in the *Don Juan* quote had it only part right. How could I claim love was my whole existence when I've just been blathering on about the mighty compulsions of the detective's life, man detective or woman?

Let's get back to that waffle warning: am I trying to elevate one branch of copdom into a mystique? Am I saying much more than that some people get too caught up in their jobs – and not just police jobs, but many people in many sorts of jobs? Detectives did tend to think of themselves as exceptional. Exceptionally exceptional. That's why they'd – we'd – refer to uniformed officers as 'wooden-tops'. Only detectives had brains? I had a brain and Luke didn't? Obviously, that was idiotic.

But perhaps detectives had a particular kind of brain, a purpose-designed brain relevant to detection. I don't necessarily mean the super-logic of Sherlock Holmes. But a brain shaped to nobble villains by whatever methods, to defeat QCs' cross-examination and judges' footling scrupulousness, and get their catch sent down for plenty. This could be seen as a flair, definitely, but painfully narrow, utilitarian and isolating? At any rate, maybe some kind of ring fence established itself now and then between Luke and me because of our work. Well, it was no maybe, I knew it did. Crazy, crazy – both cops, and yet this awful barrier occasionally, or oftener. Yes, oftener.

All at once, Luke seemed to have found the way to deal with such nonsense. Thank God he still wanted to. For this I loved Luke. He had patience and constancy. Did that sound patronizing? OK: I rather fancied being a patron. I don't mean just the information offerings he brought me now, though they turned out breathtaking and magnificent. No, what touched me was the thrill, pride and satisfaction he obviously felt in presenting these.

He wanted things to be good for the two of us, knew they would be now. He revelled in that. And I revelled, too. Undoubtedly, joy – the real article! Perhaps I did also glimpse an element of farce in these developments. Possibly, too, Luke felt horrified as well as thrilled, proud and satisfied by what he had to say. It did not matter. It worked.

Luke said, 'Yes, Warren seemed very aware he's only found out bits. It's why he's looking for your help, I think. Forced to it. But what he *does* know obviously scares him.'

'*Scares?*' Another odd word – one that struck me . . . struck me as, yes, all right, all right, struck me as weird when applied to Warren. Could anyone look dozy and scared at the same time? To me, he'd always seemed insulated against fright, or any other extremes, by inborn nonchalance upgraded to a deliberately languid display of semi-stupor – at least off the football field.

'Yes, scares. And, God, it scares me as well, appals me, Sharon,' Luke said. 'If I believe it. Not sure.'

What the hell was this, then? What would scare and appal Luke? I tried to formulate it in that bureaucratic way of mine:

(1) The kind of changes to scare and appal Luke would almost certainly result from some big breakdown and mess-up in the way society kept itself safe and intact.

(2) He believed the police provided what used to be called 'the thin blue line' – to keep society, as in (1), safe and intact.

(3) If the line broke, on account of its thinness, or from any other cause, chaos would come trundling and whooping in. Myself, I didn't go for the, (2), thin blue line idea. I thought of policing as tinted not blue but grey, so as to operate as unnoticed as could be in grey areas, meaning all areas, except where the tinting went darker still.

It was Luke who sat up now. He, obviously, could not play at being at ease any longer. The blissful sex seemed in a different era. I saw he'd developed a combination of excitement, fright, gravity. I lay there, pretending composure for a little while longer. 'Why scared?' I asked, and found a convenient yawn.

Warren wasn't the only one who could do languid. 'And appalled? Really?'

'Yes, scared. *And* appalled. Remember Warren asked you about the man with the aliases?'

'Jeremy Naunton Dince?'

'Dince and—'

'Also known as Charlton and Marshall-Cape, according to Warren,' I said. Did this smart and comprehensive memory flash betray that I might not be so sleepy/languid after all?

'Of course, he phoned you early one day. I took the call.'

'I never found out how he got the number.'

'Before that call, you'd seen him disappear, hadn't you?' Luke asked.

I sat up. 'Who says so?'

'Warren. Did you?'

'See him disappear?' I replied.

'It's a buzz he's picked up since we met at Bertie's. Buzz. That's his word.'

'Oh, a buzz. A buzz is a quarter of a quarter of a tenth of a rumour.'

'Did you see him disappear, Sharon? Warren thinks it's terrific if you did – shows you were ahead. He believes you know more than anyone. I said, of course you did, that's the way you are, always in front.'

He turned and kissed me on the side of my neck. Sweet. This is what I meant just now – Luke seemed to want to understand my kind of work, suddenly could appreciate it. Empathy, by God. I kissed him back, on an eyelid. Yes, something slightly farcical about all this: we'd been brought back together by sleuthing and footie, probably much more effective than Relate counselling might have been. But it all counted.

'What buzz?' I asked.

'Bits of it more than buzz.'

'Which?'

'Some kids in Cinder Street saw Dince get into an Audi, I gather. Two men with him, plus the driver, though they didn't get a look at the driver. A little later the kids spoke to you. Or possibly didn't, although you tried to interview them. You, gasping a little. You'd been running? One of the girls lives near

Warren. Talks to him now and then – for money, I suppose. Do
you remember the kids? Off for half-term. Pole-fencing.'

Insolent, blank, malevolent little twerps. Or blank to me, at
least. They had wanted money for talky-talkies, had they? 'These
kids knew Dince, recognized him?'

'He's a minor pusher, isn't he?' Luke replied. 'School gates?
Junior raves? I expect a lot of kids know him.'

'Where is he?' I asked. 'Is he all right? He was going to talk
to me.'

'You did see him disappear, then?'

I could have grown ratty at the plug-away, interrogation-room
questioning, but it was not that sort of night, was it? We had
consideration and sympathy for each other. We still had – or I
certainly still had – matey wetness. Anyway, Luke clearly thought
it showed how sharp I was if I'd been in Cinder Street at the
time. Ahead, as he and Warren apparently called it. They'd seen
me as the owner of amazing, accurate instincts. I don't know
why I'd acted dumb, opaque, with Luke about the Audi. Dismal,
automatic, detectiving habit?

'Is he all right?' I said.

'One man in his twenties, the other older, an imperial beard,
well-dressed, with the Audi,' Luke replied.

'I saw them.'

'You knew the men with him?' Luke asked.

I hated admitting ignorance, especially to Luke, but it remained
a special night. 'No. And I'm not sure they were "with" him.
They intercepted him. It looked planned. Why I'm bothered.'

'Warren had names.' He left the bed and went naked to his
uniform which hung on the wardrobe door. I hated that – the damn
silver buttons gleaming in the electric light like self-righteousness.
He produced a piece of paper from his tunic pocket and read,
'Aston Jandor, Ray Mondal. Jandor the older one. Not note-booked,
you'll notice. I'm learning your ways, Sharon. I'll destroy this in
a minute.' He rejoined me in bed. 'They're pushers, too. Warren
knows them all. So did the kids.'

I saw now why the children wouldn't speak. If they knew
Dince and the other pair there must be a chance that those three
knew the kids, and where they lived. Grassing could be dangerous,
as it almost always *was* dangerous, and a conversation with me

might have been regarded as grassing, perhaps definitely would have been. Grassing is in the eye of the beholder. The kids had learned this. Some kids did get street savvy fast They might talk to Warren, but that would be done off Broadway in some discreet, unobserved spot, not on Cinder Street during a day of exceptional police busyness after the discovery of Claude in the Citroën. I took the paper, memorized the two names, then gave it back to him. He tore it up.

'Where's Dince?' I said. 'What did they do to him? Is that where Warren's knowledge stops? He thinks I can find him? Is that why Warren's become chummy? He needs Dince as part of a squad inquiry? Does he think I'm secretly in touch with him still? Listen, Luke, Dince could be in an amateur grave somewhere, or sinkered in the sea. Those two—'

'Ah, you thought an abduction, did you?' Luke asked. 'Natural, maybe.'

'What's natural?'

'To imagine he was grabbed and taken away.'

'Imagine?' That really riled me – Luke offering a correction, putting me and my imagination right, the cheeky prat.

'But no,' he said. 'They're all pals. Warren seemed to assume you'd know that.'

'So, I wasn't ahead.'

Luke said, 'Yes, I think he believed you could still reach Jeremy Dince.'

'How?'

'He didn't know how, but seemed sure you'd have a link.'

'A link to where?'

'Well, that's the point, isn't it, Sharon?'

'Is it?'

'The three of them plus the driver got out of town. Stayed out of town, according to him. They took fright because of what happened to Claude Huddart. Perhaps they worked like him – between the firms. No fixed loyalty base. Dicey in the present situation. I believe he thinks you advised them.'

'To do what?'

'Scarper, for the present.'

'Do I advise crooks?'

'For some special purpose. He had the idea that, if you told them to clear out for a while until things settled, you'd naturally keep tabs on where they went.'

'How does Warren know they've gone? More buzz?'

Luke laughed. He obviously didn't want to be shoved into ill temper tonight, either. How controlled we were! 'Some buzz, some deduction, I think. The three dropped out of sight. They were missed around the usual trading sites. Warren noticed, asked here and there. It became obvious they'd slipped away. They certainly worked sometimes for Sociable Ian, apparently. I expect you're clued up on that.'

'No.'

'Big upheavals beginning among the firms. Realignments. *Attempted* realignments. Perhaps already begun. You're probably up to date on that, too.'

I'd heard about the last bit, although only as . . . as a buzz from my odd Mikado friend, Ronald Blenny. 'Yes,' I replied.

'They thought they'd get caught in the middle. Not a happy place to be. Like Huddart.'

Dince's Cinder Street confrontation with the Audi and those two men from it was friendly, then. I'd wondered at the time. The pavement talk had looked tense to me, and probably was. But tense because they had finalized at that encounter the plans to escape, not because they had snatched Dince.

'Caught in the middle of what, Luke?'

'The negotiations, the deals. The power adjustments.'

'Which?'

'Exactly. That's what makes the scene so tricky.'

'What does?'

'Warren's got a scenario,' Luke replied.

'Of what?'

'He says that anybody hearing about a couple of the firms getting together to see off the third would probably expect an alliance between the two smaller ones. They'd feel stronger against the giant with a treaty binding them. But Warren believes it might not be like that. Perhaps the biggie – Ian Linter – and one of the others might join together. They're all always chasing monopoly, aren't they? It's in their commercial blood. Maybe Sociable thinks that by absorbing one competitor and squashing the second he'll have it – a monopoly. They never feel secure, these people, even those who look the strongest, Warren reckons. They eternally want to be moving forward, and moving forward can mean using their weight to push someone smaller out of the way and under.'

'Which firm are we talking about as a possible Linter ally, Otton's or Gleeful's?'

'Warren hasn't got that. Not yet.'

'Why he wants Dince? Guidance?'

Of course, I saw a complication. If Warren and Luke were right and those three stayed in hiding out of town, Ronald Blenny had possibly invented the trio who arrived at the Mikado and supposedly told him about me. Perhaps Blenny wanted to conceal from me how he knew my name and where I worked – conceal that he'd been researching me for his own hidden purpose. He'd told me he got these leads from them. Or, possibly they were three different men. Ronald Blenny had said only that they looked as if they worked for Sociable Ian. Did that mean anything? He hadn't done much of a description. Guesswork by a piss-artist snorter? He could be all wrong and they might have arrived from anywhere. From anyone. That struck me as disturbing. Conceivably Edward Phaeton had it right and I did need protection, if the threats came from all over.

'But Dince was going to talk to me,' I said.

'Warren knew that. Why he's interested. Yes, I'm sure he thinks you can locate Dince and put the questions to him.'

'How does Warren know Dince promised to talk to me?'

'He's a detective. He hears. He's got contacts.'

'Is *he* in touch with Dince now?'

Luke raised his hands to indicate ignorance or assumption. 'Well, I thought not, obviously. He wouldn't be making the approach to you then, would he?'

'Or it could all be more buzz.'

'Something like that. But Warren would be careful. He doesn't swallow rubbish.'

Luke had said the same to Warren about me in Bertie's. Luke liked to believe the best of people. 'Who says?' I replied.

'I know him.'

'You know a footballer, Luke. The detective might be different. Detectives have their own way of thinking.'

'I know that. I live with one. I admire the way you think. I've *come* to admire it.'

'Occasionally, we're dealing with such hazy stuff we'll snatch at what we hope is something solid and good and it turns out . . . well, yes, rubbish.'

'OK, so we hope this is not one of those occasions.'

'And would Warren's contacts have an idea of what Dince wanted to talk about?'

Luke paused, rubbed a hand across his mouth, almost as though wanting to stop the next bit for a moment. 'That's the central question,' he replied.

'I'm at the centre? Wow!'

'Dince had apparently been sent by Sociable Ian Linter.'

'Sent to me?'

'His order, to contact you and brief you. Contact and brief *only* you, DC Sharon Mayfield.'

'Does Linter know me?'

'Linter knows all he needs to know, apparently.'

'What's that mean?' I asked.

Again Luke paused. He rushed the next words. 'This was to brief you about a supposed bought cop, someone at the top, who works for one of the rival drugs firms – Gleeful or the other crew you mentioned.'

I made out I had to do some thinking to recall the name. 'Philip Otton's outfit?'

'Right. Linter wanted it exposed that there was a high-place crooked officer, because obviously it could hurt his business if one of the other syndicates had a tame cop aboard, and a tame cop with rank and clout. And especially if this tame cop is in the outfit Sociable and his ally want to destroy. That's the nub, isn't it? Linter might feel he can wipe out a rival firm, with or without the help of another company. But he'd probably be wary of trying to see off a fellow travelling-high officer.'

'So, he sends someone to talk to a very low-placed officer – a detective constable? How does that help him? Oh, come on, Luke.'

He looked hurt, as if slighted. 'You're simplifying, Sharon. You're editing out.'

'Editing out, what?

'He sends someone to talk to a detective who lives with a uniformed cop famous for his simple-minded integrity and all those other corny, considerable virtues.'

'They want to involve *you* as well as me? I don't see it.'

'Linter reckoned you'd tell me and I would be sure to whistle blow. People do talk to their mates, don't they? He calculated that I wouldn't be able to prevent myself doing an exposure. I'd have to apply my famous purity and wholesomeness. And he could be right. If I did, there might be such a stink that it wouldn't be necessary for Ian and his chosen pal to eliminate the opposition. Linter would like to avoid the perils of war. This way, it would all be done for them. Charges and jail all round – the bribed tame officer and the bribing baron.'

'My God,' I said.

'It might have come off. Dince had begun working on it for him. Well, obviously – he turned up on the Huddart drive. He'd identified you and said he'd be in contact, hadn't he? That's what Warren assumes. All fixed. Or almost. But Jeremy Naunton Dince's pals apparently panicked after Huddart's death, thought nothing safe at present and persuaded him to get out with them. That's what you saw happening on Cinder Street, persuasion, not compulsion, and in his own interests. They'd grown afraid – terrified – that they might also be on someone's list for what they knew. '

It was possible. Dince had looked at one point as if he'd turn around and come back towards me. I'd assumed he wanted escape from the Audi pair. But perhaps they'd already said something to him through the car window on the first encounter that convinced Dince he should disappear with them – or at least get into the Audi and think about it. He might have considered coming to meet me and say he meant to put things on hold, possibly even tell me to forget the lot. He'd ditched that notion, but gave the message later in his early-morning phone call answered first by Luke. I'd made another wrong deduction then: that his 'captors' forced him to ring up, and listened in.

'And the bought cop?' I said. 'We believe this?'

'I don't know. Warren believes it. Maybe he lives in that kind of climate. Detectives do, don't they?'

'Some.' I remembered Warren's words in Bertie's about the

inadequacy of the police pension. Had he been hinting at the need to build a store while there was the chance and the time? Did he suspect someone of building a retirement store, someone with rank?

'But, me, I don't know,' Luke repeated.

He would not want to believe it, of course. Luke needed to have faith in his leaders or he felt abandoned and adrift. I waited and then said with all the offhandedness I could, 'Warren named Phaeton, did he? I admit, I'd wondered myself. He's been spying. Gave a tale about needing to look after me, and said he would limit my scope. What did he mean? To keep his own secrets secret?'

Luke shook his head. I thought at first it came from Luke-type despair and sadness that someone like Phaeton could slide so far. But then I saw he meant I had things wrong. Again. Luke was telling me I'd misread the pointers. Again.

'No,' he replied, 'Warren doesn't think Dince would have said Phaeton.' His voice almost faded out. 'Worse.' For a second it seemed as if he really could not speak what had to come next. Then he muttered, 'It goes higher.'

I found I'd started whispering myself now, almost as shaken as Luke. 'We're talking about Stuart Rendale, are we?'

'It's chaos, Sharon.'

'This is based on yet more buzz? Only that?'

'Warren says almost certainly Rendale.'

'Almost.'

'A strong almost.'

'But evidence?'

'That's the point, isn't it?

'What?'

'He thinks you might have it or could get it,' Luke said. 'The conclusive material. Perhaps Dince, perhaps some of your other sources.'

'Which other fucking sources?'

'I don't know. It's not the kind of thing you'd tell me. And, of course, Warren doesn't know, either.'

'No, I haven't got it. How could I? I don't even believe it.'

'But you could get it, couldn't you, Sharon? Of course you could.' He put another of those understanding kisses on my neck, understanding and confident – confident in me. He sounded idolatrous, acting like my acolyte.

I didn't mind some idolatry. 'Perhaps I *could* get it, but I won't.' Of course I could. Of course I'd try and try. Of course. Of course. 'It's rot,' I told Luke, 'not even buzz standard.'

He folded further down into the bed, ready for sleep. I had seven more questions/observations but didn't speak them, reserved them:

(1) If Dince had been sent as a messenger from Ian Eric Linter how did he know I would be on the Huddart drive that morning, my call there being absolutely unplanned, no matter what people thought?

(2) Why hadn't he given the message while we spoke then? He should have recognized its urgency, surely. People did not dawdle when they had orders from Ian Linter.

(3) But perhaps he thought there were too many people about, including too many eavesdropping police? Couldn't we have moved to a more secluded spot?

(4) Why doesn't someone – Warren – go and ask Linter about the supposed bribed superintendent? If one form of message sending had failed, try for the information in some other fashion.

(5) But, Linter was a crook. His word wouldn't count in any official inquiry. He'd know that, which was why he might have chosen the devious way to publicizing Rendale's treachery with himself kept out of it: Linter would tell Dince, who'd tell me, who'd tell impeccable Luke.

(6) In any case, neither Linter nor any other head of a firm talked to police, not even when it seemed in their interests. The vow of silence went too deep.

(7) Wasn't it . . . wasn't it . . . *weird* for Luke to keep all this startling information/speculation in his head until after we'd made love, then bring it out as close-of-day pillow chat? Maybe Byron in *Don Juan* had it wrong and some men did give love precedence, or, at least, fucking. Perhaps I shouldn't have felt offended because, sex over for the moment, he had eventually seemed on

the point of gabbing footie, especially as he had *not* gabbed footie, but *had* gabbed what might turn out to be a crucial, alarming, account of something wholly different.

ELEVEN

(1) Provenance.
(2) Status.
(3) Motivation.

I see these as three key terms when testing information – information that might one day turn itself into evidence, or better than that, get transformed by me into evidence. To explain:

(1) Provenance. Or, where exactly does this info come from? Very exactly. It's an art/antique world term meaning, what's the history of this picture or piece, so we can establish, or not, its authenticity and value: true find or fake? Same, for us, with whispers.

(2) Status. This overlaps with (1) Provenance. What is the credibility, authority, situation of the person/persons giving the information? Is/are he/she/they in a position/positions to know what he/she/they is/are talking about?

(3) Motivation. If the person/persons giving the insider material has/have, on the face of it, suitable status, a further tricky, core question then presents itself. Why is the person/are these persons, coughing this stuff? In other words, has/have he/she/they a personal interest to advance by doing the blab? Is the disclosure, therefore, biased, slanted, edited, unreliable, despite the approved status; or even *because* of that status: the person/persons offering confidentialities may talk only so as to hang on to his/her/their good position

Actually, I didn't make up the three checks myself. They came in the training. We learned that solid status communications (2) from a known provenance (1) would give useful results, if the

motives (3) were not suspect. When I apply these requirements
to what I have at present on the Claude Huddart case, things do
not appear too rosy. In fact, what I have looks poor, or less. If
I'm going to get anywhere, I'll have to do some more on-the-
spot, street-level, very private and possibly dangerous work. Let's
just tot up under those three headings – Provenance, Status,
Motivation – what I hold:

(1) Provenance. The immediate provenance of my most
recent information is Luke, in bed between sessions of hearty
love-making. He did not, in fact, go to sleep when he seemed
set to and we resumed our multi-positional, uninhibited,
sweetly imaginative, interdependent search for joy. If joy was
out there somewhere waiting to be had it seemed wasteful
not to search for it, snare it, cage it for a while, though
without in any way taming it. Hell, no. This bed context did
not of itself downgrade the information. Fucks either side of
it were, in a sense, not relevant. That is, not relevant to the
quality of the info as info, not to their own quality – that is,
the fucks' quality – which rated as more than satisfactory in
both instances.

But Luke did not originate the information, of course. Where
did it originate? What was its *initial* provenance? Tough to define.
Warren Dell told Luke some of it. Right. And how did Warren
obtain it? (a) From those bolshie kids. (b) From an unnamed
'contact' or 'contacts'. So, (a) Could children of that age be
trusted to get things right and/or to tell the truth? And, (b) Who
were these contacts? This takes us on to:

(2) Status. (a) The children's status was . . . was shaky,
because that's the way of it with children: the word – 'status'–
might, in fact, seem quaint applied to them. Their description
of what they'd seen, whispered to Warren, then passed to Luke,
then delivered to me, tallied with my own memory of events
in Cinder Street, so they might not be entirely unreliable. Just
the same, I didn't like depending too much on the interpretations of kids. (b) The status of Warren's contact/contacts
could not be judged, because neither I nor Luke knew who
he/she/they were. There had to be secrecy to protect a detective's sources: I understood this, and practised that secrecy
myself. Occasionally, though, a detective hid the identity of

a contact from colleagues because the contact's status was low and liable to weaken the detective's case. Occasionally, too, the contact/contacts didn't exist at all and were invented and quoted to authenticate a bit of professional fantasizing. (c) The status of the information from my own contacts remained dubious, especially anything provided by Ronald Desmond Blenny. Likewise his personal status. I hadn't heard much praise of him.

(3) Motivation. (a) What was Blenny's? Did he simply like intrigue and gossip, as a means to brighten his autumnal days, and nights? (b) What were Phaeton's real reasons for tailing me – not that Phaeton had provided any information. He had the status, and the provenance would probably have been OK, if there were any information to *have* a provenance. Did he really believe he needed to guard me, keep me 'safe'? From? No reply.

This review of the shadowed areas depressed me. I saw nothing *but* shadowed areas. How could I get a shaft of light on to matters? According to the tale told by his contact/contacts to Warren, and purveyed to Luke, and retailed to me, a top police officer trousered money for cooperation from one of the drug firms. That's a very fruity accusation. From more than one of the firms? Unclear. Either way, there should be signs of extra cash somewhere.

Of course, methods exist for secretly getting a look at somebody's bank account. But they are official, strictly regulated ways, unless one is a brilliant hacker and can penetrate the computer. At the time of the 2007 big financial scandal involving the Revenue and Audit Office, television news agencies ran alarming clips to show how easy it was to break into even coded material on disc. But I'm not a hacker. Nor would I ever get authorization for an official search. You could imagine the conversation with the assistant chief (Operations):

'I want to do a check on deposits of funds into a National Westminster and a Lloyd's account, sir.'

'That would seem a perfectly routine request, Sharon. And whose accounts would they be?'

'Superintendent Rendale's, Chief Inspector Phaeton's, sir.' Despite Luke, despite Warren, I had not ditched my worries about Edward Phaeton.

'Of course,' the ACC would say, wouldn't he? 'And what would be the reasons for this intrusion?'

'Come, sir, I can't disclose sources.'

'Certainly not. Please forgive my attempted, entirely unprofessional intrusion.'

'Let's just say that one or other of them, or even both, might be drawing vast backhanders from a drug's operation, or operations. I can't be wholly sure which officer it is, or whether it is only one. I get hints about each. The bank accounts might clinch things.'

'A clever move, Sharon. That will be fine then. Do proceed. Let me know if you wish to look at the chief constable's account, too, or, naturally, my own.'

I did dream it like this one night, but even in the dream I thought, This is at least a little unlikely, could probably never be. If I wanted to unearth any rough truths about Phaeton and/or Stuart Rendale I would have to do it alone and by my own means. Informal means. Go to bed with the bank managers? It would take too long, even if I skipped the shag etiquette that said not on the first date. You could hardly ask *après* tussle, 'By the way, Vernon, would you happen to have copies of Edward Phaeton's last half dozen statements about your sexy person?' In any case, many bank managers are women these days and I don't know whether I could switch to that track, even in the revered cause of detection.

Instead, I wondered about a session of surveillance of one or other of them. Tailing, probably. I would most likely try Rendale as opener. Hadn't I done enough of that type of thing with Phaeton, for the time being, anyway? And then there was Warren's information from the deeply unfamous contact/contacts, if you could call it that. I *had* to call it that since I possessed nothing else, but I remained aware all the time that it qualified as information only in a limited, best-of-a-very-bad-job sense. Perhaps the whole notion started from idiocy. What did I really have against either boss? I had buzz, and buzz is nothing but buzz. Some of it reached me as only third-hand hearsay buzz. Now and then my instincts screamed out at me that neither of them could be involved, and told me to think of Dince as the killer, or Ronald Blenny, or glamorous Philip Otton – in which case,

Alice Huddart might also be part of it: a combined sex and trade plot?

My so-called instincts had become a bit of a jumble. More than a bit – jumble all the way through. My thoughts on Dince? An utter mess: sometimes I worried for his safety, and sometimes I blamed him for a foul killing. Was he little-boy-lost or a hit man, a hit-and-cut man? Ronald I wondered about because . . . well, possibly only because I still scarcely knew him, could not explain his role and his knowledge and therefore assumed, in best police style that he must be at least dodgy and perhaps evil. And yet, secret information hardly ever came from punters who looked like and behaved like ordinary, respectable citizens. Ordinary, respectable citizens tended not to know very much about the kinds of extraordinary, unrespectable life that interested the police, and made police necessary. It took shady people to offer shady insights.

Philip I felt wowed by off and on in that silly, dangerous, hormonal way, but I could also see why it might be part of his business plan – and his love plan? – to do Claude, if Claude had been playing dirty. And everything I heard about Claude said he might. His whole career involved playing dirty. Alice Huddart I wanted to believe innocent and devastated with sorrow, but I couldn't *altogether* believe it, and my view of her was darkened, anyway, because she might be having Philip Otton, and might have been having him pre-Claude's death. God, I felt so vainly jealous: vainly in two senses – uselessly, arrogantly. Terry Kale? Gleeful George Mittle? Possibles. But I found they sat only on the edge of my suspicions, though I could not have explained properly why. Instinct again? More like guess. Normally, I'm someone who trusts my unconscious promptings, possibly non-logical, possibly anti-logical, promptings. I consider mine are pretty good. But on this case I had so many, each contradicting all the others, that I couldn't sort out which should get priority. However, I must. As part of this process I shelved the instructions to do a survey for possible sex or other motives among Claude's neighbours and relatives. After all, who gave those instructions? Answer: the officers I now thought should really get some scrutiny. Didn't that make the orders questionable?

And so back to Rendale, or Edward Phaeton. More trailing/tailing, by car and on foot? More risk of being rumbled by people who knew a basketful more about trailing/tailing than I did, so far? Yes, daunting. But I don't let myself get daunted, do I? Maybe I'm like the cat called Hubris, with Nemesis waiting to take over. Anyway, I decided to have a go at it and drove out to Rendale's house in the evening. If Warren had known about the top spot I gave Rendale I hoped he would feel flattered: he burbles gossip, I alchemize it into evidence: try to. Warren hints at what Luke called 'chaos' in the law and order system, and I'm the one nominated to nip out and determine that, yes, this is truly how things are. My job, to conclude that we are all about to break up. Luke is always on the qui vive for chaos. He thinks it's man's natural state. Like me, Luke did a degree before joining the police. He came to admire a philosopher called Hobbes who apparently thought human beings would unceasingly fight and kill one another, unless kept in check by powerful leadership. From this, Luke deduced that, when one or more of the leaders grew flaky, carnage must follow, because carnage happened to be man's natural state, only kept in abeyance by a honcho's resolve and talented ruthlessness. Luke would argue: 'See what happened to Yugoslavia when Tito went, or the Conservatives after Thatcher, or Labour after Blair.'

I decided that, should Rendale emerge from his home, I'd get behind him, if I could. I thought that picking him up from his house and at night was more likely to work than following him from headquarters. It might be daylight then and more difficult. And perhaps he wanted darkness himself, if I had it right about the kind of furtive excursion he would make to off-colour people: that is, if Warren Dell had it right, and Warren's mysterious tipster/tipsters. Rendale might spot me. That would be disaster for ever. Disaster to this project, and disaster to my career. You did not gumshoe a detective superintendent. At least, not as detective constable. Hubris.

I knew Rendale was divorced and at present lived alone in a slice of high-grade suburbia on the western rim of the city. I found, eventually, he had a big, detached place, perhaps five bedrooms, gardens on two sides and an Edwardian style conservatory. His ex-wife and the two children were with somebody else. Canteen talk said he hadn't tried to sell the house yet, though plainly too big for him on his own, because he hoped she and the children would come back. The talk said the house signalled that he'd still welcome her. Maybe. Very maybe. But such a lovely tale. I did as I'd done at the Huddart house and left my car out of sight, though not so far this time in case I needed to get to it fast if Rendale drove out, and fix myself to his back bumper. Preposterous, this idea? It wouldn't take someone of Stuart Rendale's experience long to spot a tail. Then, if he *were* on his way to a sensitive rendezvous, he'd abandon that destination for now. He'd probably drive to somewhere neutral and meaningless, and perhaps confront me – more or less a rerun of the Phaeton episode. But I couldn't see how else to put my almost amateur, unsupported surveillance on to him. And that was necessary, wasn't it? Wasn't it?

The drive wound around to his house through tall bushes and some trees like the approaches to a country mansion and I could not see from the road whether Rendale's Peugeot lay parked up nearer the property. Ironwork gates to the street stood open, so if he did come out by car he could be away very swiftly. A metal plaque on one of the gates gave the name Esposende. Someone had been on holiday to Portugal. Honeymoon? Perhaps that was another reason he hung on to the house, sentimentalizing it. Through the foliage on my walk past I saw lights on in at least one room downstairs, none above. Although the gossip said he lived by himself, how up to date was the gossip?

I walked on. I would not be able to patrol too often. There'd be few people on foot at night in this kind of area. I might become noticeable. Homeowners here would feel jumpy about a stranger persistently eyeing up the neighbourhood, possibly doing a shortlist for burglaries: a moll given the task as less suspicious. Neighbourhood Watch might be doing what it specialized in – watching the neighbourhood. Then there'd be some phoning around to arrange a meeting: me and several of them. It was a leafy spot and not very well lit. Although I tried to keep in close to the hedges like a hunting fox where

I could, on some stretches of ground I'd be very visible. My behaviour would look strange. For instance, now I turned and started back. I mustn't leave Rendale's house unwatched for very long. He could stroll into the road and disappear without my knowing he had gone. If he drove I would at least hear the car and try to reach mine before he went out of sight.

And, approaching Esposende, *re*-approaching Esposende, I thought for a second that, in fact, Rendale *had* come from the house, had turned left and was now walking away from me. I corrected the impression at once. This was a shorter, slighter man than Rendale. Like me, he seemed to stay hard against the hedges when possible, wanted to merge with them, get some minimal cover from them. He wore a long, dark overcoat and an Afghan-style, tiered, close-fitting woollen hat, also dark, pulled down half over his ears. Had he come from Rendale's house? I needed to identify this figure and fast in case he had a vehicle close. I should try to gain on him. But he might hear my footsteps, turn and see me.

I reached the junction with a side road of similar big houses and grandiose privet and estimated that if I took this and then the first to the right I would have circled a block and might meet him coming towards me. That should seem more natural. As in Cinder Street, I ran. I would really draw attention now if anyone glanced from a window. And, of course, I gambled: Rendale's house would be out of sight while I did my circuit and he could leave without my knowledge. How had my urgencies moved like this? Why had Long Overcoat suddenly become so crucial? I remained convinced he was not Rendale.

When I finished my dash I saw I'd guessed well. I would meet the man head-on. I still did not know why I'd made him important. Even less so now. 'Ronald?' I said. 'Ronald Desmond Blenny? Yet another chic outfit?'

'Ah,' he replied, 'the girl detective. Ill-met by gloom-light. My dear, I *thought* I might see you here.'

'Why?'

He seemed to think the gross precision of words could never give me an answer. He shrugged. Nothing more. Overcoat eloquence: the garment moved sweetly up and down with his shoulders and all the time kept beautifully curved contact around the nape of his neck. This was some item: a triumph of material, cut, and indistinct when set against a plump hedge at night.

'You're still interested in Mr Rendale?' I asked.

'And now *you're* interested, too.'

'He's my chief.'

'Deservedly?'

'You doubt it?

'And you visit your chief alone at home at night, Sharon?'

'You're watching him?' I said. 'It's not all instinct and antennae, then. You trawl, do you?'

'The two don't exclude each other – instinct and industry.'

'Have you called in on him?'

'I was passing by, that's all. I don't know him. Would I be likely to call in?'

'Would you?'

'And you? Will *you* call on him? Or is this just another of your lurks, like at the Mik?'

'Why?'

'Why what?'

'Your interest.'

'I wonder about him,' he said. 'Connections.'

'With what, with whom? How does it concern you? *Does* it concern you?' *What's your motivation, mate? Leave aside provenance and status for the time being.*

'Quite,' he replied

'So would you follow him if he appeared?'

'Would *you*?'

'Tell me, Ronald, was it just a spontaneous lech-grope in the club, or did you plan it, so you could get in contact with me?'

'Contact with you is what I disgracefully tried for at the Mik, my dear. I hope you recognize my shame and regrets.'

'Not sexual contact. Business. And did three men really arrive at the club and give you my details? Or had you discovered them already?'

'It's a hub, the Mikado.'

'You've got some role?' *Tell me your status.*

'Role?'

'In all this.'

'Which?'

'The developments after Huddart.'

'There've been developments?'

'Did you follow me out here? Do you work for someone?' *Tell me your status.*

'And in a way you're right, Sharon,' he said.

'You do work for someone? For Philip? Gleeful?'

'Yes, you're right to say I can't do it all just on what's in the air, by what you call my antennae – just by thinking about things and making a bright guess at where they're going. I do need to step close to the actuality now and then.'

Provenance?

'I need to watch people in the clubs. I need to come out here and see Mr Rendale's home, breathe the comfortable bourgeois scents he breathes in his off-duty times, perhaps sneak a glimpse of him driving up, or in the garden or even at a window. This kind of experience can touch off all those other minor flairs I seem to have, give them a shape, a concreteness, a certainty. It's my little, old-man's hobby – to be in touch, to know what's called "the scene", I think. It's harmless. It's an understandable yen.'

'And total shit, isn't it?' I said.

'I'll push along now, leave you the field, as it were.'

'You told me you just happened to be passing. Now you say you felt a need to get close to Rendale's house – and possibly more than near, I wouldn't wonder.'

'Anyone could tell you're a detective. An ace at spotting discrepancies. And the way you sprinted around the block to get ahead of me, so everything looks normal. Bravo! Like Cinder Street.'

'Have you been in the house tonight?'

'Architecturally not too awful, as modern places go. I don't mind a Doric pillar or two.'

'Look, where do *you* live?' I said. 'I ought to know how to reach you.'

'*I* can always reach *you*.'

'Dince said something like that.'

'Ah, Jeremy Naunton.'

'I must be able to get in touch.'

'You'd have your methods, I'm sure. It's good that we meet once more,' he said. 'I see it as a sign that we share a wave-length, don't you? Not just a matter of Mikado chance. But I feel incomplete without a bouquet of flowers for you.' He raised a nicely gloved hand, turned away and began to walk quickly out of Rendale's road, hugging the line of the front hedges still, now and then seeming to be swallowed by the shadows, then appearing again a long way ahead, a shadow himself, that thin, blurred, vigorous figure briefly under one of the street lights before fading out again, like an illusion or Ronald Desmond Blenny. Where was his car? Why had he parked far away? Did he need to breathe so much of the district's bourgeois scents just for the sake of general interest – a hobby?

It worried me, the clever, dark appropriateness of his clothes and his crafty approach to the house; he had obviously decided not to have his vehicle associated with this road by residents if inquiries came later. But what inquiries? What had happened? Had anything happened, or was he merely doing what he said, collecting atmospheric information to give backbone to his voyeuristic, old fart's fascination with low life? Did contact with the underworld get his heart pumping hard and for a little while keep him out of the Underworld?

I suddenly felt like a voyeur myself, not an old fart voyeur, just a hopeless voyeur. What was I doing skulking around the edges of this situation and this property, sneaking back and forth in front of the house, picking up useless, fragmented glimpses of it through the greenery and altogether putting in a lot of time to discover nothing? I must get nearer. True, the house had not been my objective when I first arrived here. That would have seemed outrageous, mad. I'd intended following Rendale, if Rendale appeared. He had not appeared and it did not seem he would. The only encounter I'd managed was with Ron Blenny, and he had changed my aims. I could not escape the thought that he might have been into Esposende – perhaps only the gardens, perhaps the house itself – possibly to see Rendale, possibly only because he wanted a good look at the place for his own woolly purposes. Either way, he had done better than myself, and this irritated me, the old fart. He'd seen the Doric pillars.

Next time I walked past I looked for gaps in the hedge. I did not want to go in by the open gates. It was too light there, too obvious to neighbours opposite, and in full view if Rendale did suddenly come out from the house. I found what seemed a thinning in the growth and forced myself through it, no subtlety or gradualness, just maximum speed, a crouched, battering-ram push. I had on jeans and a black leather jacket which did their bit to protect me, but I took a couple of digs in the face from short, spiky branches and tore the lobe of my left ear. Thank God my hair was cut close or it might have entangled me. I emerged to the side of the conservatory, about twenty metres from the house and shielded by hydrangea bushes. I paused and dabbed with a handkerchief at the blood on my ear which was now running down my neck. This was policing. This was policing?

I took my first proper view of the front and one side of the house. The room immediately opposite me might be a kitchen. The window was uncurtained and I could see dark wooden wall cupboards up to the ceiling. Light from the room reached into the garden. I would be caught by it as soon as I moved out from the bushes. I became very aware of my situation – could visualize myself cowering among these shrubs, invading the garden of a gifted senior policeman's home, and contemplating a break-in at the gifted senior policeman's home. Such a run-of-the-mill caper for a detective constable, yes?

The compulsion to get in here off the road suddenly seemed lunatic. What did I expect to do? The question hammered at my mind because I had to think what I would say if Rendale or anyone else discovered me. Really, there would be nothing I *could* say. I'd come in case Rendale had sold out to some firm – to Sociable Ian or Philip or Gleeful – and hoped to find something that would tell me one way or the other. Yes, one way or the other. Which did I want: Rendale's implication in the killing or not? I'd never shared Luke's belief that chaos always stood ready on call just around the corner and we, the police, must head it off because nobody else could. Luke would pray that Rendale and the system were OK. If

I'd prayed, it would be to ask for help in discovering what was what with Rendale. I had no real preference as to the outcome. I did not think I would be telling Rendale in detail my motive for being here, though, should he notice me and come asking. And I couldn't have said, 'It's not my fault, Mr Rendale, it's all because of footie Warren and his anon contacts.'

Now, I did consider picking my way back through the hedge to the street and letting this impossible, stupid project die. The investigation had become too big for me, hadn't it? Somehow, the passably sensible plan to tail Rendale had been distorted and inflated, had turned into foolhardiness. It would suck me into a vast muck-up. And I knew what that somehow was – or who it was: Ronald Blenny. I had elevated him into a competitor, and if there were competitors I always had to compete, no matter how crackpot the contest. Very crackpot. So, abort. Abort at once, while I still could.

And I had begun reversing slowly towards the hedge, tense, crouched, my handkerchief still held to my ear to stop the blood flow, when I saw very briefly upstairs a slim beam of light shine on one of the bedroom windows, then dart hurriedly away before being switched off. The curtains were open. To me it seemed that someone now wanted to correct a mistake. The ray should not have hit the window. The gleam didn't come from house lights, more likely from hand-held equipment, perhaps a torch. Possibly it had been swung carelessly. I remained still, between the hydrangeas and the hedge, watching. After three or four minutes the light might have come on again. I could not be sure. If it did, it was this time a long way from the window and possibly shaded in some way, faint and maybe deliberately directed down to the floor to limit spread.

And so, another change of purpose. Lead kindly, cryptic, upstairs light. I forgot about retreating through the hedge and moved forward again, this time not even pausing with the hydrangeas as cover. I skirted as well as I could the patch of glare from the kitchen window and moved along the side of the house. Then, crouched over again, I began to edge my way towards the front door. I had no idea what I would do when I reached it, if I did, but kept going slowly, watching where I put my feet, to cut noise. The front door was heavy, mock-chateau-real-timber, and looked intact, formidable. A white Doric pillar stood on either side. Now, I could also make out some light from behind closed curtains in two downstairs rooms. I did not even try the front door but kept on around the house towards the other side, and possibly the rear and the conservatory. I was still learning very little, but the gleam in that bedroom kept me enthralled. I could hear nothing from the house, no voices, no television or radio.

A narrower door at the far side of Esposende led out to what might be a herb garden. I couldn't tell in the darkness. As I grew closer I saw that this door did not seem to be shut properly and, when I gave a slight push, it opened fully. Did Blenny know how to get a sliver of plastic to persuade a lock, then? The house did not seem to have alarms. Some police thought them an advertisement that the property contained things worth pinching. And nobody took much notice when they went off, anyway. I could see no damage to the door or frame. But maybe Blenny was on such excellent terms with Rendale that he had been given a key. Or the door might have been left unlocked for him. Crumble-brain, Mayfield: you can't even be sure that Blenny had entered this house. If he had, he might simply have gone to the fine front door and rung the bell, especially if he were expected. Why then, though, had he not come all the way in his car?

Again crumble-brain, Mayfield: you don't know as a certainty that he came by car at all. Taxi? Bus? I had to ask, did Blenny really break into houses, or this house, at least? Why? It would be quite a step for someone allegedly wanting only to imbibe the flavour of a place to aid his telepathy. And, if Blenny *had* charmed the lock, who was upstairs in the house now minimally flashing a torch? It could hardly be Rendale. Would he be so jumpy about showing a light in his own home? I could have done with a torch myself, or with anything that might do as a weapon.

I had another of my contemptible, treacherous sessions of hesitation then, and actually considered ringing up Luke. Could I ask him to get over here and come with me into the house?

He would be appalled and snotty. Of course, he'd be appalled and snotty. Anyone sensible would be. I'd be proposing we went together into a house where we had no right to be, where the owner might be present, a rising, distinguished police officer. OK, I'd explain that because of:

(1) what Warren, salt of the earth and soccer team, told him;

(2) Blenny in the street here tonight;

(3) the open door;

(4) the momentary show of light upstairs, yes, because of these four indicators, I felt there must be something badly wrong in the house. Would this convince Luke – or anyone sane? I doubted it. Did they convince me? Say about thirty-five per cent. But my hesitation definitely did not stem from being a woman and weak, did it? Did it? No. It was a matter of being alone and going into a predicament with unknown hazards – the nature of them and the quantity. Our training – Luke's and mine – stressed that if possible you did not act solo when the risks remained unclear. It applied to both sexes equally, no special, protective terms for women. That phrase 'if possible' left room for argument, obviously. People would interpret a situation differently. For instance, did I consider there was no option here – I had to go in? Yes, and I wouldn't call for male help, even when the help would be Luke, supposing he'd agree: a very big supposing. Or perhaps *especially* when the male help would be Luke. I mustn't cave in to him and his constant dreary frets about my methods. I shouldn't be so damn dependent, so half-baked, should I? This investigation belonged to me. ME. It could not be more personal, more maverick, more outright subversive: I was on the point of slinking in illegally to the home of the chief of detectives, and my master. At least, I hoped it would be a slink, and an efficient slink – unseen, unheard, unsuspected, unresisted. Returning to prayers, 'Oh, Lord, let it certainly be that, unresisted.' I assured myself that one person could move

more quietly than two. Slinking was for one. And maybe a woman alone could slink better. Men were too often clumsy, they looked for crude face-to-face incident. And, if Luke did consent to come, it would take him a while to reach here. By then, there might have been changes. Perhaps Rendale would emerge from Esposende and go out by car or on foot. I'd want to leech him. I might not have time to tell Luke by mobile that the plan had altered. It wouldn't be fair on him. No.

Just me, then. Solo, whatever the training said. I slipped slowly into the house, leaving the garden door open behind me. The training also said, always prepare an exit, and this was one bit of instruction I did not care or dare to dump. It had probably been learned from burglars, so would be wise, practical, well tried. I glanced about. Some sort of utility room. Its other door, leading to the rest of the house, stood part open and a little light entered from one of the main downstairs rooms. I saw some gardening tools and a pair of big-footed wellington boots; a couple of full plastic sacks closed with cord at the top, perhaps waiting for the refuse collection; a long, low freezer, its red 'on' indicator bright in the half dark; a blue, iron, rusted stepladder. Seed boxes containing soil, lay higgledy-piggledy across the floor. I went gingerly around them, tried to visualize Ronald doing the same very recently, the long overcoat almost sweeping that possibly potential plant life. Would there be any in winter? I felt, as I'd expected to feel, and was probably right to feel, that I radiated highly efficient silence, more totally than Ronald would have, or Luke, if he'd come.

In a corner of the utility room near the inner door stood a tall, slim, rectangular cheval mirror, perhaps meant to stand in a bedroom one day and give a top-to-toe scrutiny of one's get-up. I was reflected in it now and thought I did not look too bad at all. No, not too bad. My mouth was clamped hard shut through stress and my eyes had almost disappeared because of the frown of focus, but I could not trace actual full-out terror in my face. I did *feel* actual full-out terror, very

actual, very full-out, no question, but it must be good it failed
to show, surely. Terror? Did that put it too violently? I might
be alone in his house with a senior police officer. Blenny had
asked about that. It could be embarrassing and awkward if I
were discovered. But terror? Cool it, Mayfield. Perhaps I'd
have to account for myself to someone in this house, and it
would help if I seemed composed, in charge – in charge of
at least me. I decided not to hang about in front of the mirror
in case I did spot some signs of terror and indecision. Maybe
I was entitled to both, but best not to catch them on display.
They could be disheartening.

I felt aware, or nearly aware, of some other, very vague unease
which badgered me while I stood before the glass. Thank heaven,
it remained hopelessly, elusively imprecise. Ignore that, Sharon,
dear. Strangle that, Sharon, dear. Escape that, Sharon, dear.
Concentrate on this house where something might be gravely
amiss. Or where nothing at all might be amiss, except a door
carelessly left unlocked. In either case, you could be due some
suffering.

The utility room opened into a short carpeted passage. What
looked like framed certificates hung on the walls but I did not
bother to examine them. If Ronald had been here, looking
only for background, he might have scrutinized these, perhaps,
to establish whether Rendale boasted commendations, or a
degree, or a runner-up award in the Whitsun Treat Sack Race,
1977. They would offer the sort of things that made a rounded
portrait and Ronald could be into rounded portraits. But these
were ludicrous thoughts. No matter how much background
Ronald Blenny might have been seeking, it didn't explain why
he would break into the house. And maybe he didn't. Ronny,
a card, a wild card.

Me, I wanted to get on, quickly look through the rest of the
place. For a while, I kept still and quiet near the certificates
while trying to pick up any sounds elsewhere. From where I
stood I could see the foot of the stairs now, broad, heavy banis-
ters, rich-red carpet, in keeping with the minor, would-be
Chatsworth, magnificence of the house. I tried to concentrate
my listening there, waiting for movements by the torch bearer
in one of the first-floor rooms. As much as possible I must keep

the stairs in sight or I could be surprised by someone coming down. Someone? It had to be Rendale, hadn't it? But why would Rendale use a torch in his own home and not the bedroom light? Why would he seem so edgy about the beam being spotted from outside? It had to be Rendale, but how could it be Rendale? I had a flair for intelligent questions. *Too* bloody intelligent. They fucking floored me.

I reached a sitting room, its door wide open. A couple of table lamps burned there. The curtains had been drawn. I gave the room a very quick survey without entering. The stairs had reminded me of what I should never have forgotten – that the real problem and any possible discovery would almost certainly be on the first floor. Every indication said nobody was downstairs. The sitting room looked comfortable and clean. Rendale probably employed domestic help since his marriage ended. How had he been able to hold on to the house in the break-up? Did that suggest he settled his wife's share of the assets with cash? Half the value of Esposende and its contents would be at least £350,000. Property prices had slipped lately. At the time of the divorce the house and furnishings might have been worth nearly a million. Rendale had had enough capital to buy her out? Where would that sort of money come from? The most expensive houses had seen some of the biggest drops in value. Did Rendale find himself stuck with what accountants called 'negative equity' – the worth of the house fallen below the amount borrowed by mortgage and going lower, led by the US market? Ah, yes, I'd have loved to get a squint at his bank statements.

The room was respectably furnished with fairly modern stuff, no particular style that I identified, but all the pieces solid-seeming and not tatty. Free-standing, real mahogany shelves on the far wall contained a mixture of books, hard- and paperback. They looked as if they'd been given some use, and were not there just to fill space. Some people would be surprised to hear of a reading policeman. A lot of the downstairs remained for me to cover but abruptly I thought, Leave it, leave it, dozy, jittery kiddo, and get up to the bedrooms. I suspected I postponed the obvious and the urgent through fear. You're never more exposed than on a staircase. You can be done from above or below: especially from above, here, and not necessarily with boiling oil. To get up there was necessary, though, and overdue. I turned around in the doorway and almost took that first step towards the stairs, but my mind gave another sudden lurch – perhaps still trying to keep me from the upper floor. All at once I realized what had unsettled me so much about the utility room. It was, in fact, the oblong cheval glass, which had worried me at the time. But my mind clamped itself now on to something other than my own image in the cheval. The glint of the mirror, the bevelled edges, its changing pictures as I moved about, galloped bright and upsetting into my memory. I'd restricted my contact with it to a swift glance, in case what I saw should ruin my morale. I'd been afraid of looking in the looking-glass and . . . Afraid of looking and, when looking, seeing that I looked . . . afraid. Another version of *The Looking Glass War.*

And, as I pointed myself towards the first stair now, I realized what it was about the reflection that had threatened to disable me: not just the uptight picture of myself, but something behind me appearing there. At the time, I had managed to ignore it, shove it down into my deep, messy subconscious, so virtually harmless. Yes, virtually. I found I couldn't force myself to ignore it any longer, though. In the cheval I had naturally been able to see a part of the utility room, and the part included the freezer, the long, low freezer. In that distant, shut-off pit of the subconscious a word had stirred as I stared briefly at the glass, a word which I had been able to suppress and obscure then, before it could properly spell itself out. I had moved on fast, rejected the looking glass and all it wanted to reveal – all it wanted to reveal about myself and about the utility room. The word which I so deftly sidestepped, so firmly prohibited? 'Coffin' naturally. The long, low freezer was white, of course, but, this apart, in its length, width and closure resembled a farewell casket – though admittedly wreathless – whether viewed in the mirror or head-on.

I forgot the stairs now. My legs seemed shaky and I doubted I'd be able to climb. That was not why I stopped, though. I felt ashamed – ashamed of whatever had prevented me from recognizing in the utility room a few minutes ago that I must

open the freezer and check inside. Fright had a strength and
range that I'd stupidly underestimated. It had made me neglectful,
sloppy, evasive. Luke, darling, you should be with me after all.
Please, Luke. But too late for that. In a moment, I compelled
myself to move and go back to the utility room, but this time,
because I dreaded entering it, I did loiter for a second and read
the framed certificates. I discovered that Stuart Rendale attained
Grade Six in his piano lessons as a boy and Intermediate with
Distinction on the flute. A mad, flippant thought came. Perhaps
I needed it. God, I muttered, what a loss to music if he's corpsed
and finger-stiff in the freezer, never able to hit a note again. It
was long enough to accommodate Rendale with only a little
folding of his long, cop legs, which would be possibly pre-rigor
or post.

He was not in the freezer. It contained a couple of ready-made
Mediterranean style meals, lying there like a self-catering
conspiracy, nothing else. As I looked at the colourfully illus-
trated boxes – prawn-pink, tomato-red, hake-white – it seemed
contemptible, abject that I should have slipped into such an
alarmist fit, should have allowed the mere shape of the freezer
to commandeer my wits and imagination. Sharon, dear, you're
a laugh, you're a fantasizing child, not much past the horror
comic stage and Peter Pan. You need special tutoring on the
difference between a freezer and a coffin. However,
Superintendent Stuart Rendale *was* dead in the other main downstairs room, this room with a markedly Victorian or Edwardian
motif, except, of course, for the television, DVD and video
machinery and CD system. He had been shot in the back of the
head, probably from a small calibre pistol. Not much mess.
Nothing like the interior of that car in *Pulp Fiction*. I bled more
myself from the torn ear. I'd given up dabbing at it with the
handkerchief and must be leaving a trail through the house, right
up to the body.

Rendale occupied a tall-backed, handsome armchair in front
of the television, though the set was off. The chair had an
Edwardian frame recovered in some excellent modern blue,
speckled material. He sat sideways on to me, so that I could
see his eyes were open and unmoving, and could also see where
the bullet had entered his skull. I observed a little scorching,

which suggested the muzzle of the gun had been very close: this could mean someone not confident with firearms, unsure of hitting from a distance. But how would the killer get so near? Had the television been on at the time, noise from a programme drowning the sound of the executioner's approach? And the executioner had switched off, to conserve energy? Rendale wore excellent black lace-up shoes, suit trousers and a white shirt, the sleeves of the shirt shortened by metal armbands worn just above the elbow. Somehow, the brilliant whiteness of the shirt made him appear especially vulnerable and pathetic, like a prisoner smocked for execution in some US jail. And the armbands ate at his dignity, seeming fussy and crude, as if he couldn't pick clothes to fit him properly. Someone in clothes too big always appeared sad. The armbands had a manacle look.

As soon as I saw Rendale I knew he was dead. Or is this hind-sight? I've always been excellent at that, when it's in my favour. In fact, from my spot a half step into the room I spoke, 'Excuse me, sir. I'm sorry to have entered your home uninvited, but it's well-meant,' I remarked, and waited a while. God, after all the boldness that brought me here, was I still really only a girlie peasant, sure to tumble back into curtsy subservience as soon as I met crisis? 'It's Sharon Mayfield,' I explained to the shirt, armbands and lace-ups. 'I'd just looked in to see you were all right following certain worrying rumours and tip-offs . . . but . . .'

But you're blatantly very *not* all right. I left this last bit unsaid. It did not need saying. None of it had needed saying. Nobody listened. I've always thought it symbolized everything about the modern robotic human condition when you saw someone sitting mesmerized in front of a television screen. Occasionally, I'd even seen someone sitting mesmerized in front of a dead television screen: obviously worse. But what about someone dead sitting in front of a dead television screen – not mesmerized, because the dead can't be mesmerized, but dead? The set was probably digital: all those channels ready to be tapped into, yet Rendale not able to tap into them, and not able to be tapped into himself, either. This must be the acme of non-communication, mustn't it, that appalling, continuing, modern day malaise?

Oh, God, *prêchi-prêcha*. It can strike anywhere. I turned
away from Stuart Rendale and at once began to climb the
stairs. This time I kept going, with quite a bit of speed, but
also still with remarkable and expert quietness, I thought. I
approached what seemed like almost complete darkness on
the first floor: only a little of the downstairs lights reached
the landing and gave a bit of visibility. I kept my head up,
staring towards the bedrooms and bathrooms, looking for any
momentary fleck of that other light, the torch beam. But no.
Conceivably, someone had come down the stairs and perhaps
left the house while I loitered in the utility room on my dim
set-to with the freezer, or gazing in at Rendale and doing my
inane, crawler's post-mortem monologue. *Am I hogging this
conversation, sir?* Alternatively, it would be an easy escape
for anyone experienced to drop from a bedroom window into
the garden.

I would have to be cagey when I told the tale of discovering
the body, eventually – if I ever did tell it. I might have to edit
out the torch or there would be questions from senior people
about why I did not immediately call for aid. If the sight of that
beam was enough to take me into the house why hadn't it also
been enough to convince me I should contact the Control Room?
Even if I edited out the torch, they would want to know how I
came to enter the house without back-up. They would be especially enraged if it appeared we'd had a suspect for the killing
on the premises who had been allowed to leave. Why hadn't I
whistled up the firearms people, when a firearm had been used
and might still be in play?

I had another option, too. Would I leave the body un-
reported? If I did not, I would have to explain how I had come
to be in the property at all. This would mean describing my
secret and solo inquiries, starting from the first day on the
Huddart drive, and Dince. Powerful people at headquarters
would be very ratty. If I did stay silent, the body was sure to
be found by someone else, when Rendale's disappearance
became noticed at work. Could they identify me then from
the trail of blood? Most likely not. Police did not do DNA
tests on police. But they would start looking for someone with
my blood group as the probable killer of Rendale, unless I

could come up with the actual killer. Charming. I had better get this ear healed before the official hunt began. I thought that perhaps the bleeding had stopped now. I wiped myself clean, I hoped. I stepped on to the landing and did another of my pauses there. Underfoot, the carpeting felt thick and expensive. Yes, a year or so ago this Doric-pillared package could have easily sold for a Big One.

I could make out nine doors. That would probably mean five bedrooms, a couple of bathrooms, a lavatory and perhaps an airing cupboard. Four doors stood wide open, three to bedrooms, one to a bathroom. Two others were only part open and I could not see enough to know what lay beyond them. The rest, shut. I tried to work out which room would be the one where the torch beam had flitted undisciplined over the window pane. This meant imagining myself back in the garden and mixing what I made of the shape of the house then with what I saw from inside now. I'm not too good on visuals and perspectives. Eventually, though, I fixed on a part-open door and stepped towards it, but not the whole distance straight away. What you do not do when entering a problem area of this sort is to go in direct, framing yourself like a free gift, especially if the only illumination is behind you, so generously outlining the target. A loaded pistol was around in the house, or had been until recently, and someone who knew how to use it, at least from very close up. Very close up is how things could be in this room. Small calibre the gun might be, but it still did the job. Stuart Rendale R.I.P. I stood with my back to the landing wall for a few seconds alongside the gap left by the open door and listened again. And then I bent low and moved very fast around the frame pillar of the door and flattened myself against the bedroom wall on the other side.

I had it right: this was the room. Oh, hell and torment, I had it right and this *was* the room. There had been absolute darkness here, but at once now the torch came on from over near the window and held my face in the beam, its light not so very strong, but strong enough. Perhaps the batteries had begun to fade after whatever duties they'd been doing. But, even though the ray had weakened, I could not see past the glow to who directed it. I was still bent over in an attempt to minimize myself, wanted to straighten yet found it impossible: for a while power had gone absent from my body. I'd noticed that at least once before this tonight. I felt aware above all of what I'd been aware of on the landing: that there might be a gun in here. I presented as much a target in this half passed-out yellow beam as if I'd stood and posed in the doorway. I stayed hunched because I thought that if I straightened, if I moved at all, it could look like resistance, even an attack, and the shooting would start.

A woman said, 'Who's with you?'

It took only a second to recognize the voice. 'Alice? Mrs Huddart?'

'Of course. Who else is here? There was talking downstairs.'

She had heard my respectful chit-chat to the dead. 'Other officers,' I said. 'We're going right through the house, as you'd expect. It takes a battalion. I'm allocated upstairs.'

'Police like sending in battalions.'

'You've been sitting in the dark?'

'I heard the sounds from below and hoped you'd all go away if I stayed unnoticed. Naturally, I knew you wouldn't.'

'Hardly,' I said. My mind was doing a lot. Mostly, though, it concerned itself with the gun. 'You know shooting?'

'Claude's pistol.'

'He'd go armed sometimes?'

'I had it hidden when you people arrived on the death day.'

'Hidden where?'

'Hidden. I know where the trigger of a gun is and how to squeeze it. Enough expertise. I'm not going to try for the Olympics. Rendale had gone to sleep in front of the TV.'

'You switched it off?'

'It seemed grotesque.'

'What?'

'Those busy pictures on the screen, and only a corpse watching. And before that, someone blotto. I didn't need to be a markswoman, you see.'

'But are you?'

She was not. Some strength had returned and I began to straighten from my stooped posture against the wall. I couldn't tell at once whether that did scare Alice Huddart, made her think I'd try to rush her, as I'd imagined. Or it could have been simply an accident, as in *Pulp Fiction*. At any rate, the gun went off. She'd spoken no warning. I heard the bullet crack into the wall a few centimetres from me. Yes, the gun and the bullet sounded small, though like a real gun and a genuine bullet, just the same: a genuine bullet, but an acceptable distance from me. *Thanks, Alice. Let's not try to do better, OK?* Instead of straightening I went fast to the floor and lay there. This came from training for a gun situation, though not the present kind of gun situation, where the weapon was so near and the person firing it could approach to make sure there'd been a hit, and try another pop, if necessary. Getting to ground express like that, I bumped my ear and felt the blood start to course again.

The ray of the torch swung as Mrs Huddart stood up and I heard her walk swiftly from the other side of the room and come to look down on me under her flickering light. 'I'm obviously a better shot than I knew,' she said. 'A natural. I go instinctively for the head. Yours, Rendale's. More blood from you, though.'

So, not an accident.

'You'll die,' she said. 'Like Rendale. Your colleagues will come now and collar me, but you'll die. Can you hear me, understand me, or are you already on the way out?' It did not sound triumphant or sorry, just a statement. A résumé. *Hard luck, kiddo, you're dead.* She wouldn't blazon feelings. Rather cliché Brit. No, blazoning was not up her street – and she'd hardly have any feelings about me, anyway: a cop nuisance. 'You shouldn't have come here,' she said.

I did what I reckoned might sound like an impending death groan, something without too much power and resigned and final. Maybe it also said that duty demanded I *should* come here, regardless of risk, and that, as a serving police officer, I naturally accepted my fate. From across the room, and with only a weak torch beam, she must have failed to spot my ear wound. The injury had been dormant then, anyway, and spruced up.

'Colleagues?' she said. 'Where are they, this battalion? Why haven't they come running to help you? They ignore a gunshot?' She looked back towards the door. In a while she said, 'Do you know what I think? You're here alone.' She paused and listened. '*Are* you here alone? How could that be? You people always go mob-handed.'

Her voice rose a little, but still nothing extreme. I tried to guess how she'd think. If she guessed there were no other police in the house, Alice might calculate she could get out and disappear. Would she do that second shot to make totally sure I really did die like Rendale, and could not talk her into jail? This would be her kind of killing situation: fine proximity, no chance of mistakes. In a moment, she'd possibly come to realize I had an insignificant ear scratch, not a fatal round in the brain. She did peer down at me now.

And before she could make out properly whether I was badly hurt and helpless – whether I was about to croak – I let her know I, in fact, wasn't. I swung my legs around hard at hers and got full, destructive contact just above the ankles. She yelped. The torch beam once more yawed out of control and I heard what I took to be the pistol hit the carpet a moment before she crashed down herself. I turned fast on to all fours and stretched out an arm, moving my right hand in wide, frantic, scrabbling arcs, feeling for the weapon. It didn't work. The torch, only just alight, glowed nearby and I grabbed at that instead. She still had hold of it, but I tugged with the ripe power of a top class panic and tore it from her. Then I used this feeble ray to make the sweeps I'd tried with my hands and almost at once found the pistol, closer to me than I'd expected and missed by my gropes. It looked like a 6.35 mm Baby Browning automatic. She could see the gun herself then and reached for it, but I sensed a weariness, a slowness about the movement, almost a hopelessness. Perhaps she'd been dazed by the fall. It had sounded a heavy, uncontrolled collapse when I knocked her legs away. Or perhaps she did not much care any longer. A fraction of her mind might believe the house stuffed with coppers, despite her comments just now. What would a detective constable be doing alone in someone else's home? Worse than that – lawlessly invading a bossman's property? She must doubt she could escape, and had possibly lost the will to try.

I stood with the gun in one hand and the torch in the other.

I stepped to near the door, found the switch and turned on the bedroom lights. I switched off the torch and put it on a roll-top desk. Going to Mrs Huddart, I held out my other hand to help her up. Then I put her to sit on the side of the bed. 'Are you all right?' I asked, and gave her the full, formal, arrest caution. There were still no curtains shut in this room. I held the Browning behind me briefly and went to pull the drapes across. In this kind of neighbourhood, it would have looked barbarous for a woman to be at a bedroom window with a piece on view in her fist, even a baby model.

'Do you understand?' she replied, but seemed to assume I did not and would dislike admitting it. Correct.

'Understand what?'

'The whole carry-on,' she said.

'Most of it.'

She switched. 'The bullet in your brain. You'd better get help, I suppose. How come you're so . . . so, well, OK? Seemingly.'

'It merely winged me,' I answered. I'd been going to give her a Walter Mitty answer: 'It's only taken three quarters of my head away, so I'm fine.' But I did not want her to think of me as the sort of blunderer who got shot, nor did I want her to feel stupid, useless with a gun. She had enough trouble and humiliation coming. Her pallor was even more intense than when I saw her last, those large eyes brimming with defeat. She wore jeans and a denim jacket over a brilliant amber T-shirt, but there were times when an attempt at casualness failed, made people look as if they had given up seeking a mode for themselves, and, instead, turned limply to recent fashion history: how she seemed now.

The room contained a double, unmade bed. Two walls of the room housed built-in wardrobes. A small, pretty Edwardian dressing table stood in the window bay and the large, old-fashioned roll-top desk against the left wall. It was open and the writing surface covered with papers. Had she been going through that material with the torch, afraid to put the bedroom lights on and become visible from outside, but also afraid to be seen drawing the curtains? A tall, straight-backed antique chair stood near the desk and I thought this must be where Mrs Huddart had been seated with the flashlight and automatic ready when I entered the room.

'No, as you say, I don't *really* understand,' I replied. Now and then you had to admit failures.

'Who could? Why are you here – in the house?'

'I don't even understand that properly,' I replied. I could do diffidence occasionally. It helped make people talk, worked especially well as a soother, if you'd already scared them with the caution.

'I made an error – the torch. You saw it, did you? Sharp.' She gave a small sigh. I thought it would be as much as she'd allow herself as an expression of mood. But then she said, 'I can't stand the sound of blood dripping from your head like that.'

'It's ruining the carpet. Who'll get this place and the fittings now, I wonder.' My handkerchief was sodden and could do no good. I opened a wardrobe, took a folded white shirt from one of the shelves and held it against my ear. 'You think Stuart Rendale killed Claude? You've done Rendale as revenge?'

She paused, maybe on a mental audit. '*Mainly* as revenge.' She gave a grunt, as if offended, insulted. 'A business aspect, too. Revenge is – well, revenge on its own is a bit naff, isn't it? Even when there was disfigurement. I know he killed Claude. Know. That deserved a response.' She gave a tiny wave with her left hand – not much more than a flick – as if to banish explanation as pointless. 'But you're never going to cotton. You don't know the trade, do you? Claude was more or less totally debased, you see.'

'You stayed with him, killed for him.'

'I said *more or less* totally. Only that. It leaves some room for affection. Some room for love. If every woman left every man who was more or less totally debased there'd be no couples left. These fine points become crucial in a relationship, don't they? The pluses are rare and must be made much of.'

'Well, yes. Marriages of inconvenience.'

'Claude schemed and struggled to give us a life. There's something moving about that, something loveable. All right, the scheming and struggling didn't always get us anywhere. But he'd try. Now and then he'd turn pompous and prattish – usually after a failure. He had to boost himself. I could forgive it, put up with it.'

'He was a grass?'

'Of course, originally. This would be before me, or so I thought. I'd draw the line at shacking up with a grass. Probably. Yes, probably.' She looked towards the door again. 'So, you *are* alone. You'll win a coconut for this, won't you?'

'I need a distinguished victory or two. My boyfriend and I both missed out on graduate fast promotion.'

'Most likely you're too cheeky for them.'

'And after his time as a grass?' I replied.

'As a grass he used to whisper to Rendale. He even had a key to Esposende. Claude never said how he got it. But he mentioned, as a sort of black joke, it was for the tradesman's entrance. That kind of insult might mean Rendale actually gave it to him and described which door. Police despise grasses, don't they, even when they're dependent on them? Perhaps *especially* then. It would make sense for Rendale to choose that fairly obscure entrance, not the front, so Claude could sneak in with his tips. Or, Claude might have managed somehow to copy a key. He could be very clever. And wily. So, we keep the old sepulchral Citroën. A new car could have told people we had money, and they'd wonder how. Anyway – the key. He had one. How I got in. I found it with Claude's stuff at home. I hid that, too. I left the garden door here unlocked, in case I needed a quick exit.'

'I left it open. Ditto.'

'But I failed to take it – the quick exit,' she said.

'Yes, I did suppose Claude informed to Rendale,' I said. I walked over to the desk and glanced at some of the papers. They seemed to be only household bills and insurance documents.

Mrs Huddart said, 'I made a search for evidence that Rendale took payola from Otton or Gleeful, a sort of justification for what I'd done. Crazy of me? Would he write down stuff like that, or keep anything incriminating written by someone else?'

'But if the backhanders came from Otton . . .?'

'He'd have told me? No. It's not that kind of arrangement between us.'

'No?'

'No – absolutely.'

'What kind of arrangement *is* it?' I asked.

'You sound very interested.'

'My job to be interested.'

'As interested as that?' she replied. 'He *is* gorgeous, isn't he, dear, glossy Phil? But somehow it doesn't reach me. We're pals. Claude could reach me. So, what's wrong with us?'

'Who?'

'Women. Our taste.'

'*Is* Otton gorgeous? I don't think I'd noticed.'

'Not much,' she said. 'I watched you go breathless and intemperate when you met him at my house. I've seen plenty of other girls hit in the same way.'

'Which other girls?'

'Yes, he's gorgeous,' she replied. 'He's also cagey and secretive on business things. He'd tell me only a fraction, even if it concerned Claude. But I guessed. Claude had managed to draw Rendale into the business. Claude could be creative. He felt *so* proud of recruiting Rendale. Like a football manager signing a new genius player. A coup.'

'Are you interested in soccer, then?'

'Enlisting someone like the superintendent – it's the kind of thing that can develop from a grassing arrangement.'

'Is it?'

'Oh, all that grey area realm. So easy.'

'I don't know the realm.'

'Yes you do. Cops are ending up in the dock all the time because of it – the vague but defining line between running a grass and being run by a grass. Judges and juries hate such blurring. It scares them. They smell shambles.'

'And Claude was—'

'Claude had to get super-clever and super-devious, didn't he, because that's how Claude was – what I mean, more or less debased, ultimately? Greedy. It doesn't matter now. I can speak. Anyway, I expect you've heard.'

'Claude had climbed from grassing and was go-between for an alliance between Philip and Gleeful,' I said.

'There you are! I knew you couldn't be as dumb as you pretend.'

'I have my contacts, naturally.' Thank God for Ronald and his busy intuitions. Perhaps that's all they were – good and fairly accurate, but not proving any involvement. His pastime – keeping well-informed about villainy, yet no part of it. A leisure activity, instead of golf or radio-controlled toy yachts.

Alice Huddart said, 'Claude was supposed to fix this teaming of Philip and George Mittle, but, of course, Claude being Claude, he fed the details of the negotiations to Sociable, so he'd know how to smash the alliance. "Debased" the word? What else? Claude thought he saw a bigger, richer future with Ian than with those other two. He regarded them as light-weights, I expect. Perhaps he had it right. But he also had it wrong. There'd be no rich future for him.' She paused, seemed about to weep, as she had seemed that morning alongside the Citroën. Again she avoided that, though, or reserved it for a moment alone. She'd have quite a few moments alone. 'Ian Linter's a thinker,' she said. 'When rough-housing can be avoided he avoids it. His original scheme? But you may have been briefed on that.'

'To do with me and Luke? Yes.'

'Get the dirt about Rendale to you, and then you'd almost inevitably tell your boyfriend. He's rather impeccable, I gather?'

'Rather.'

'Ian's a believer in dossiers. He'd have one on you two, and likes to use what he knows. The tactics – indirect and maybe too elaborate. How he is, though. This time it turns out to be unduly slow because Rendale gets active himself and does Claude, or has him done. Dince's mission is suddenly obsolete, and contact with any firm looks hazardous. Vamoose, then, and take his mates with him. I heard they joined up in Cinder Street. while you watched from far off. You'd gone around a corner, so I couldn't see all this from the house.'

'Heard where?'

'They used an Audi. Green? Some info still comes my way.'

'From?'

'But not much,' she replied.

'Rendale had found out Claude was two-timing?'

'Rendale found out and Claude found out that he'd found out. Claude always told me everything. Everything? A lot, at any rate. I think – well, I know, Claude threatened Rendale that if he fingered him to Philip and Gleeful he, that's Claude, would tell the world about Rendale's second job with whoever it was – Gleeful, I think. Maybe Philip. Doesn't matter. So Rendale made him quiet, dead quiet, you see.'

'And carved him?'

'Can't believe it, can you?'

'Hard to.'

'Because he was an eminence?' she said.

'Like that, yes.'

'Well, you could be right. The carving might be an extra from someone else – an added touch to make it seem a fink termination. Maybe Rendale had some help. It would be difficult working solitary to get Claude into the car on the drive. The eminence wouldn't do the defacement himself, not because he was a rather decent fellow – give or take a murder. No, because, with his experience, he'd know the post-mortem would show the cuts happened after death and didn't fit the torture scenario. Who tortures a cadaver?'

'Help from?'

'Some full-time artisan thug.'

'I wondered about Phaeton.'

'Phaeton? Why do you say that? Oh, no. From someone in a firm. A run-of-the-mill heavy.'

'Which?'

She did a major pout. 'Don't know. Don't care now.'

'Phaeton's straight? At the beginning you certainly didn't think so.'

'I had the idea Rendale might have pulled or pushed or pressured him into the dirty work, as aide and accomplice. Wrong. There *was* a closeness between them, but not that sort. I discovered Phaeton suspected Rendale had gone over and stalked him, aimed to nail him if he got the evidence. So, Phaeton needed the proximity.'

'Discovered it how?'

'Oh, yes,' she replied. 'Phaeton's not just pure but a would-be purifier. To date. He believes in the system. To date.'

'Maybe I should have picked that up from things he said to me.'

'In any case Phaeton would know as well as Rendale what the autopsy must say about the mutilation.'

'I've blundered about.'

'With help or not, it was Rendale who actually did Claude – killed him – no question.'

I more or less believed her. Although Rendale had moved up so fast, perhaps he judged it not fast enough and felt himself worth more money. You could meet people like that in all jobs. He might have looked at the future, as Warren Dell looked at the future that day, and found the pension prospects unthrilling. Even a detective as bright and seemingly wholesome as Rendale could get grossly compromised. And, if that happened, his apparent brightness and wholesomeness might make him more ruthless, because he had a superb image to look after. Consider Lucifer. I thought I saw now how Rendale could afford to buy out his wife in their divorce.

It might even be that the divorce began from Rendale's corruption. Some wives could not tolerate this, if they discovered it – the way other wives/partners could not tolerate grassing, like Alice. Or things might have gone the opposite way, and Rendale went looking for additional money when menaced by the divorce and possible loss of his house. Perhaps Jeremy Naunton Dince had known some of this, even *all* of this, and would have told me, had we met – re-met. Then, though, he and his friends did a runner and he grew scared and telephoned to say I should quit. They must have feared ripples caused by my future inquiries would find them, even in their hideaway. He was only a fetch-and-carry messenger boy, probably never far from panic: a little like me. Somehow, though, I felt vastly comforted that he had no part in the killing – the reverse.

'Why was it so important to see Rendale's papers, for heaven's sake?' I asked Alice Huddart. 'I mean – with the risk of staying in the house.'

'I've already told you, I wanted to find it spelled out, the link with Phil Otton. Or Gleeful. To see it actually in words. Or money figures. You asked me once about accounts, didn't you? They would sort of make it official.'

Yes, she'd already told me, but I didn't believe it. So, I'd had another go. I wondered if in fact she had planned to continue Claude's slippery, gainful work, however debased she seemed to think the ex grassing, if it *had* been ex. Seemed, yes. She had a fat quota of ambivalence, this lady. She might have been in search of something official here, as she called it – information to convey to Sociable Ian Linter and help him in the eternal crusade for monopoly. She knew Claude's career activities in such detail that she must have been well into the business herself. But would she do that to Philip Otton if the connection with him entailed more than business? Perhaps it really didn't, as she had said. I found I longed to believe that, yearned to believe it. Still. Cow-fool, Sharon. Nothing would ever come of this for me, would it? Would it? Hadn't I just seen one cop finished by disgusting closeness to the wrong folk, and now here I was lusting for a big sip at the dregs myself? Sometimes, I thought that perhaps I went in for all that neat tabulating and listing and placing things in order to correct the potential in me to go ungovernable.

'We ought to leave,' I said.

'You're the one with the gun. Anyway, yes, before you bleed to death.' She stood up, supporting herself for a moment against the bed with the back of her legs. Then she moved away, seemed reasonably stable.

'I wondered if you knew someone called Ronald Blenny,' I said.

'Who? Your contact? Who is he?'

'Well, I wasn't sure. But apparently just what he claimed to be, an inspired onlooker, someone who needed a bit of gutter to keep life meaningful.'

'They're always a nuisance. These folk – obsessed by slumming. They long to be "in the know" as they call it. Or, "*au fait avec le milieu*". Yes, they can do it in French, *aussi. We* are the *milieu* – you, me, Rendale, Claude, Phaeton, Philip, Gleeful, all of us. Not really very pleasant as *milieus* go.'

We began the small hike to my car. 'Dince,' I said. 'How did he know he'd find me on your drive that morning?'

'Mobile phone? Someone from Ian Linter's firm might live near us. It's that kind of area, isn't it? How else would we be there? Respectable looking, comfy. Not someone I'd know about. He, she, hears from a neighbour what's happened at the Huddart place and goes to join the crowd, then calls in to Ian. He, she, tells Linter the police are already there: Mayfield. You announced your name on arrival, didn't you? Dince is told to move his arse over to our drive. Typically opportunistic by Ian. But – also typically – he'd prepared properly. He'd pre-selected DC Mayfield, and, for instance, could supply Dince with your phone number and so on from the dossier on you and your partner. We know the rest of the tale, don't we?'

'Why didn't Dince blurt the Linter message there, on the drive, or somewhere less peopled but close?'

'It looks as if he'd already decided to quit, doesn't it? Hence the Audi meeting. He wouldn't want to hang about in longer discussion with you. He'd done the basic thing – made contact. That was presumably to keep Linter happy. Dince would be scared to ignore instructions. He'd play along with Linter until an exit and disappearance had been fixed. An exit, disappearance and safety.'

I took Alice Huddart to headquarters and said what needed to be said, but not a crumb more. Phaeton sent a party and an ambulance to Rendale's house. 'I can't see how you came to be there in the first place, Sharon,' he said.

'You're never going to get that out of her,' Alice Huddart said.

'I made sure you weren't tailing me tonight,' I told Phaeton.

'You're learning fast all the time,' he said.

'You bet I am. That's S. Mayfield.'

They took Alice Huddart away. 'It's more than half done then, if we believe her,' Phaeton said.

'I do believe her,' I said.

'She can't *know* Rendale did Claude. I mean, know it as in saw it.'

'I believe her on that, anyway.'

'But without any evidence able to stand up in a trial.'

'There can't be a trial on this, can there? He's dead. Alice Huddart is the sort who gets things right and acts.'

'Yes, I suppose we do know that much. She told you. Congrats, Sharon.'

'Which much?'

'That she killed him. Now, among the living, we need to find who helped Stuart Rendale, assuming Mrs Huddart *is* right. Who did the art work? I'd say probably Otton or one of his people.'

'Would you? Why, sir?'

'Was there some talk of him doing a turn with Alice Huddart?'

'Was there?'

'So he'd be very keen to make it seem like a grass execution, in case we decided a sex motive.'

Hell, did I fancy, to a sickening, knee-knocking degree, someone who chivved deads and who was too dull to realize the medics would say the wounds had been added after death and couldn't be torture, only a drab gesture? Outright stupidity I despised. And I didn't think much of poisonous, overstrained guesswork. How could Phaeton decide it must be Philip Otton, not Gleeful, involved in the Claude killing? Why should Phaeton unjustifiably believe in a love interest between Alice Huddart and Philip Otton? Hadn't she denied it? Male police – they see the power of cunt everywhere, ahead, even, of the power of money.

I rang that noble, uncompromising boyfriend of mine at work in the Pomeroy Crossfield nick. He'd heard about Rendale and that I'd found him, and seemed to have a basically accurate version of *how* I'd found him. Grapevine, and fast grapevine, for something of that rosiness. I feared Luke would feel shattered, permanently wrecked by the revelations about Rendale. 'He can be replaced, Luke,' I said. 'The system survives. It's not a collapse of order.'

'Isn't it?' He sounded shattered and permanently wrecked.

'I thought I did a really good thin-blue-line job discovering what had happened to somebody who used to be part of that thin blue line.'

'*You* would think so.'

Oh, sod off. But now and then it was best to look for something neutral, harmless and beside the point to say to Luke, something that couldn't angst him, dear lad. 'Did you know Rendale played the flute?' I replied.